To Eva and Jack and
Annie Maria and Percy

VICTORY ON TEN BELLS STREET

Mary Collins

PIATKUS

PIATKUS

First published in Great Britain in 2020 by Piatkus

1 3 5 7 9 10 8 6 4 2

A CIP catalogue record for this book
is available from the British Library.

ISBN 978-0-349-41620-5

Typeset in Palatino by M Rules
Printed and bound in Great Britain by
Clays Ltd, Elcograf S.p.A.

Papers used by Piatkus are from well-managed forests
and other responsible sources.

Piatkus
An imprint of
Little, Brown Book Group
Carmelite House
50 Victoria Embankment
London EC4Y 0DZ

An Hachette UK Company
www.hachette.co.uk

www.littlebrown.co.uk

Chapter 1

June 1950

Looking out across the narrow river as the sun set was something of which Moritz Shapiro never tired. Birds flocked to the tranquil waters of the Crouch – he didn't know which species they were but that didn't matter. Just the pleasure of seeing so many creatures wild and free was enough for him. And, of course, the silence. Sometimes back home in Spitalfields he imagined that the Blitz was still going on. Tortured by the sounds of bombing in his imagination, he would get up and walk around his huge dark house, quietly lest he wake his daughter Rebekah, until the panic passed. But here it never happened.

He heard footsteps and looked up. A young woman with long black hair sat down beside him and said, 'Do you want a cuppa, Uncle?'

Moritz put one gnarled hand on her shoulder and said, 'Don't worry about that now, enjoy the sunset with me.'

Rose Lynch smiled at him. With her six-year-old son tucked up in bed, she too was free to enjoy the gathering darkness that surrounded the little candle-lit cottage on the southern shore of the River Crouch. Born and bred in London, Rose had never imagined herself wanting to spend time in the country, but this place, a distant Essex backwater, was bewitching.

After watching a flock of seagulls fly off in the direction of the river's mouth, Rose said, 'Why'd you never come here in the war, Uncle Moritz? You could've got away from the bombing down here.'

He shook his head. 'Rebekah was working at the London Hospital, I couldn't leave her.'

'No.'

'And this place was just a piece of bare land then. What should I have done? Lived in a tree?'

Rose laughed.

Although not generally one to take a leap into the unknown, widower Moritz Shapiro had bought two adjacent plots in a place called Hullbridge in Essex back in 1930. He'd learned that land, albeit of poor quality, was going up for sale from a customer. Mr Smith – not his real name – was a businessman with interests, it was said, in 'entertainment' in Soho. Moritz, as his tailor, never pried. To be honest, the two of them rarely spoke during or after fittings. But then one day Mr Smith said, 'I know you Jews like a bargain. How d'you fancy some land out in the country? Dirt cheap. Maybe you can put a nice house for yourself on it one day. Get out of this dark old pile.'

Rose got to her feet. She said, 'I'd better light the fire, Dermot'll be hungry when he gets home.'

The house – some would call it a shack – where the young couple lived had been built by Dermot Lynch, Rose's husband, using bits of old boats, logs and the remnants of an ancient railway carriage. Moritz was only too happy for the young couple and their little boy to make their home on his land. It also meant that he and his daughter could occasionally spend weekends with them in the country.

Rose went to the shed where they stored wood and built a fire in the pit in front of the veranda that they used for cooking. What they had chosen to call Ten Bells Cottage didn't have any gas, electricity or mains water and drainage. Like a lot of properties in the area it was a 'Plotlands' cottage – a home that had been hand-built from scrap materials. Just as Moritz had, many people from the East End of London had bought land in Essex in the 1920s and '30s and cobbled together low-cost houses on it. Originally intended to be holiday homes, some families, like the Lynches, had moved into their makeshift properties permanently.

A quick trip inside the cottage saw Rose return with three large potatoes that she placed carefully at the bottom of the fire on its glowing heart.

'Baked spuds tonight,' she said to Moritz, who smiled fondly at her.

It felt strange going home to an empty house. Most of the time her papa was waiting for her with a cooked dinner when Becky got home from work. But then, he deserved a few days down in Essex with Rose and her family. He'd had more work this year, so far, than he'd had for a long time. Now that the '40s, that decade scarred by total war, were over, people were starting to invest in things like suits once again, especially since clothes rationing was over at last. And although she didn't pay much attention to fashion, Becky was aware that women's clothes were becoming more opulent. After years of skimpy, unflattering Utility styles, women's skirts and dresses had become longer, fuller and more flattering.

Becky set her handbag down on the kitchen table and put the kettle on for a well-deserved cup of tea. Due to staff shortages at the hospital where she worked, the London in Whitechapel, she'd just finished a double shift and was shattered. Although all the surviving men who had fought in the war were now back home, many others had died and London in particular had lost a lot of people in the Blitz. Places like hospitals struggled to get enough staff and there were rumours that soon more folk from the Caribbean would be asked to come over to Britain, to make up the shortfall. Rebekah Shapiro for one couldn't wait. Recently promoted to the position of Ward Sister on the Marie Celeste Maternity Ward, Becky knew her department had neither enough nurses nor midwives. Thank God for it, but the coming of the free National Health Service, back in 1948, had only increased demand for medical services. Lots more women now wanted to have their babies in hospital rather than at home, which meant that some medical centres were struggling to cope.

She'd just sat down when the front doorbell rang. Wearily, Becky got to her feet and went to answer it. The person on her doorstep, a man clutching his flat cap between his hands as if in supplication, was familiar to her.

'I'm sorry to bother you, nurse,' Solly Adler said, 'but it's our Natalie. She's bad with her chest again.'

The Adler family, Solomon, his mother, wife, and daughter Natalie, lived on nearby Commercial Street. Once a prominent member of the Communist Party, Solly had been tipped for great things until he lost a leg in the Spanish Civil War. Now he worked as a cutter in a garment factory belonging to his wife's family. His daughter Natalie was asthmatic.

Becky said, 'If Dr Klein's surgery's still open you can take her there. You know you don't have to pay anymore, don't you, Mr Adler?'

'Yeah, but Dr Klein's gone home,' he said. 'I don't know what to do.'

'Take her to hospital. They'll look after her there, Mr Adler.'

'Yeah, but . . .' He looked at the ground.

'What?'

When she'd been a teenager, Becky had been wildly in love with Solly Adler. But he was married now, with a child, and she . . . well, Becky had her work.

'I don't like taking her down there,' he said. 'Couldn't you just come and have a look at her?'

Becky had done just that about six months before when little Natalie had been bad. What the child really needed was to be out of London away from the awful smog that choked the streets even in the summertime. But what was to be done? She said, 'I'll get my coat. But if I think that Natalie needs to go to hospital then that's where I'll take her.'

Solly Abrahams nodded his head. 'If you think that's best, nurse.'

Kitty Lynch saw the two of them go from the bottom of her area steps. It was rumoured that Solly Abrahams was unhappy with his missus, Sharon, and she wondered whether he was now looking for comfort at the door of Rebekah Shapiro. It was rumoured Rebekah had had a crush on him as a youngster and Kitty's own daughter Bernie had been bowled over by him too. Back in the 1930s all the local girls had been smitten by Commie boys like Solly. They'd been so passionate, so committed to a new, fairer world order. Just like Kitty's late husband, Pat.

But all of that had fallen apart in the war and now, although things had changed for the better with the coming of the National Health Service and the Welfare State, Britain was still a long way from being an equal society. Kitty for one worked like a dog just to make ends meet. She went back inside the flat and closed the front door behind her.

Two of her six children still lived at home: twenty-four-year-old Aggie worked as a seamstress in a local clothing factory and twenty-eight-year-old Marie drove ambulances for the London Hospital – something she'd started doing during the war. To Kitty's annoyance, neither of the girls seemed interested in marriage and Marie at least seemed permanently dissatisfied with her lot, maybe even depressed.

When Kitty sat down to drink the cup of tea she'd made for herself earlier, Marie said, 'Mammy, I want to do the Knowledge.'

Kitty sat up straight. 'You what?'

'I've thought about it and I want to become a black cab driver,' Marie said. 'I can't carry on at the hospital forever.'

'Why not?'

Kitty saw Aggie look at her sister uneasily. Both girls tried hard not to provoke their mother into losing her temper since an angry Kitty was a fearsome sight.

'Because it ain't going nowhere and the money's rotten,' Marie said. 'We just get used, Mammy.'

'Everyone does. That's life, my girl.'

'That's not what Daddy would have said,' Marie snapped. And she was right. Patrick Lynch would have applauded his daughter's desire to better herself.

''Sides, doing the Knowledge costs,' Kitty said. 'Learning all them routes across the city. Every bloody street! Takes years to get a licence to drive black cabs.'

'I can do it in me spare time,' Marie said. 'I'll pay for it meself.'

Kitty shook her head. With her eldest daughter Bernadette out of the country, Aggie seemingly dreaming her life away and Marie set on being a cabbie, for God's sake, it seemed that Kitty would never get to see even one of her daughters wed any time soon. It was something she'd dreamed of for years. Having a daughter celebrate a proper white wedding in church was something she'd always wanted.

'Don't you want to go out and have fun instead?' Kitty asked.

Marie rolled her eyes. She knew all her mother's code terms for meeting men.

'I don't want to get married, Mammy,' she said. 'I've told you.'

'You say that now but you're nearly . . .'

'Thirty, yes,' Marie said. 'Which means I should be getting on with me life. I don't want to be stuck in a bloody ambulance when I'm fifty . . .'

'Then . . .'

'Nor do I want to be surrounded by loads of screaming kids!' She lit a cigarette for herself. 'I'll still pay me keep, Mammy. It won't affect you at all.'

Kitty shut up. It would affect her. She worked full-time at Tate & Lyle's sugar factory in Silvertown and if only the two girls would move on maybe she could have some sort of life for herself. Tate's was the sort of place where something social was always in the offing. But with the flat to take care of plus two daughters to cook for and clean up after, there was no way Kitty could join in. Pat would have told her to leave the girls to their own devices but Kitty wasn't like that. What she wanted most in the world was to get those girls settled into good marriages. God knew she'd failed with her eldest daughter, Bernie, so she wasn't going to give up on this pair.

Eventually she said, 'Well, provided you go out sometimes, Marie ...'

'I'll meet other people training to be cabbies, I expect.'

Who'll all be men, Kitty thought. Whoever heard of a female cab driver? The blokes'd think she was some sort of freak!

'Yes, but you won't meet no one ...'

'Mammy, I've told you, I don't want to get married!' Marie said. Then with a shake of her head she got up and went outside into the yard.

Kitty looked at Aggie who avoided her eyes.

After a moment's silence, Kitty said, 'So what you want to do with yourself then, Ag? Work down the mines?'

Rose spooned fresh, soft butter onto their potatoes from the jug she kept in the cold larder underneath the veranda. It was made by a woman who kept a couple of cows on a plot of land down by the road that led to the ferry crossing.

'Thanks, love,' her husband said as he tucked into his evening meal. 'That's handsome.'

Moritz Shapiro smiled. 'One can always taste when food is fresh,' he said.

'Right.'

Dermot Lynch, Rose's husband, was a slim, dark-haired man in his early thirties. A docker by trade, when he'd come back from overseas after the war, he'd taken the opportunity to move his wife and son out of London by taking a farm labouring job in Essex. Unhappy in the docks, it had been one of the best things he had ever done – apart from taking on Rose and young Maurice who was not his biological child. But that was the couple's secret – as far as Dermot knew.

'I wish Mum'd come down here sometimes,' Rose said as she mashed butter into her own potato. 'She was born in the country, I think she'd like it.'

Moritz Shapiro nodded. 'Her people come from Essex, don't they?'

'Epping Forest,' Rose said. 'Not round here.'

Rose's mother Nelly Larkin was a Romany gypsy who had come to Spitalfields and taken a flat in the same street as the Lynches and the Shapiros not long after Rose had been born. And although she now knew that her father was another Romany called Nelson, he and Nell had never been married. Her mother had been excluded from her own family ever since she had disgraced herself.

Dermot put a hand on his wife's knee. 'You know she don't like going far these days, love.'

Rose didn't reply. But Moritz could see the sadness in her face by the light of the fire. Nell Larkin wasn't an easy woman. An alcoholic who could neither read nor write, she'd cried herself hoarse when her daughter and her family moved to the country. When Rose was a child her mother had lived with a number of men who had prostituted her on the streets, but now that she was older Nell made a meagre living as a maid to a working girl who lived in Stepney. She rarely got any time off but when she did, rather than go and see Rose and her family, she spent it down the pub at the end of her road, the Ten Bells.

As if reading her mind, Dermot said, 'You even named this place after your mum's local to encourage her to come down, didn't you, love?'

'Maybe she thinks she might meet some of her family out here,' Rose said. 'When I told her I met me dad back in 1946, she said she didn't want to know about him. He was going to give her some money then from selling his horse up Appleby but she wouldn't have nothing to do with him.'

Moritz nodded. 'Some of the wounds people bear are too deep to be easily healed,' he said.

A German had recently moved into a flat in Fournier Street, three doors down from the Shapiros' house. He was a young man, a doctor apparently, but because of his nationality, Moritz felt unable to speak to him. In Germany and Occupied Europe, Hitler and the Nazis had killed six million Jews, people just like Moritz and his daughter Rebekah, in the most organised act of mass genocide the world had ever seen.

'But me dad was going to give her money ...'

'Sometimes that's not enough,' the old man said.

It was dark now and there was a nip in the air. Soon they would all have to go inside and prepare for bed. Little Maurice had been asleep for three hours already. As was his custom, he'd be up with the sun in the morning and raring to go.

Rose got to her feet and took the empty plates away from the men, to go and wash them at the pump. 'You know, on summer nights like this,' she said, 'I always think of Bernie and what she might be doing now.'

'You and Becky and my sister always were the best of friends,' Dermot said.

Rose suddenly felt her eyes fill with tears. 'I really miss them both,' she said.

'Bernadette has gone to the Promised Land of Israel, she'll be fine there,' Moritz Shapiro said. 'I should go myself one day, God willing.'

Chapter 2

July 1950
Jerusalem, Israel

Would she ever get used to the heat of this country? Bernie Lynch wiped the back of her neck with a handkerchief and then sprayed cologne on her wrists. Outside in the street she heard a sherbet seller plying his thirst-quenching wares. She leaned over her desk towards the young, moustachioed man sitting opposite her and said, 'Here, Gibrail, how many *prutah* do you want to go and get me a sherbet? I'm a European blonde, if I go out in this heat I'll shrivel.'

The young man looked up and said, 'From you, Miss Bernadette, nothing.' He got to his feet. 'What flavour do you want?'

'Rose.'

He ran through the small office and out into the street. Other people sitting at their desks smiled to see his eagerness.

An older man with greying hair walked over to Bernadette

and said, 'You know he's only in love with you because you're the only other Christian on the staff?'

She laughed. 'He's an Arab,' she said. 'His family'll have a nice girl already chosen for him. And he's way too young for me.'

The grey-haired man slid his arms around her shoulders and lovingly kissed her cheek.

Bernadette Lynch had been a photographer with the *London Evening News* until 1949 when she'd decided to join her lover, Heinrich Simpson, in the newly formed State of Israel. He'd got her a job with him as a photographer on the English language *Jerusalem Post* where they'd both been ever since. Together, Heinrich and Bernie had reported on the tail end and aftermath of the Arab-Israeli War that had followed on from the establishing of the new Jewish state. Heinrich's wife, back in England, had refused him a divorce years before, but the couple had made a good life for themselves in the ancient city of Jerusalem, albeit one that was not always approved of by everyone.

Bernie pointed to the broadsheet newspaper on her desk and said, 'I've been reading *The Times* piece about this rising military star in Egypt.'

Heinrich sat down beside her. 'Which one?'

'Colonel Gamal Abdel Nasser,' she said. 'There's a photograph and, I have to say, he's a bit of a dish.'

Heinrich looked at a small black-and-white newsprint photo. 'Ah, yes,' he said, 'one of the Free Officers. There are some who reckon he and his comrades may bring down the King.'

'What, fat Farouk?'

Heinrich smiled. 'That's no way to talk about the King of Egypt.'

'But he is fat ...'

'True. But more to the point, he's squandering his nation's wealth on his own pleasure,' Heinrich said. 'And since we pushed back the Arab advance, Farouk is on shaky ground. The Egyptian people, quite rightly, want to know what he's going to do about the success of our Jewish forces.'

The young man, Gibrail, ran back in and placed a cup of cold, white liquid on Bernie's desk.

'Rose, as you requested,' he said.

'Thank you!'

Bernie dug inside her handbag for her purse. But Gibrail shook his head. 'No,' he said, 'is my present to you, miss.'

'Well, I'll buy you your next sherbet,' Bernie said just before she drank deeply from the cup. 'That is glorious! So lovely and cold!'

The young man glanced at the copy of *The Times* on Bernie's desk.

'Oh,' he said. 'You read about Colonel Nasser?'

'Seems to be a rising star in the Arab world,' Heinrich said.

There was an awkward pause until Gibrail said, 'The British don't like him. They support the King.'

Heinrich shrugged. 'The British may nevertheless have to deal with Colonel Nasser or someone very like him one day,' he said. 'It's not just this country that is breaking away from the old colonial powers.'

And he was right. Although technically a kingdom in its own right, Egypt was still largely controlled by the British but there were rumblings of dissent among the Egyptians about that while nearby Syria had broken away from its French masters four years before. The Middle East was a region that was only just beginning to find its feet and, so far, its early steps onto the world stage had been faltering and bloody. Those who knew about such things, Heinrich's contacts in the Israeli Government, were full of grim predictions about further conflict to come in the region, particularly in Egypt.

'You wanna go down the hospital with that.'

Nell Larkin looked up at the young woman standing on the steps in front of her, smoking a cigarette, and said, 'You don't pay me enough for me to do that.'

The woman, who was tall, statuesque and black, said, 'Oh, Nelly, don't be silly! Nobody has to pay for medical treatment now! We have the National Health Service.'

Still clutching her painful abdomen, Nell waved the suggestion away with the other. hand 'You need a number or something. Something I ain't got.'

'So get one. Go to the hospital and ask.' The woman lowered herself down on her haunches so that her head was level with Nell's. 'Lovey, you know I care about you,' she said. 'And if it takes money then I'll give you money. But I know it don't. Go now. Get a taxi and go down the London.'

Nell took the woman's hand. 'You're a good girl, Blessed, but you know I can't leave you alone. That's why you pay me.'

Ever since she had arrived in Britain back in 1948, Blessed Latimer had worked. Her first position, as a nanny to a family in Berkeley Square, a job for which she had trained back in Jamaica, had ended when her employer had dismissed her in 1949. This was not because she was bad at her job, but because he, having forced her into his bed, got her pregnant. It was while Blessed, desperate and alone, was getting an illegal abortion that she learned of ways she could make money without proper references. She'd been in her flat on Albert Gardens in Stepney for almost a year, during which time she'd built up a considerable list of clients.

'I've got Mr James at one and then nothing until this evening,' she said. 'I'll take you to hospital myself once he's gone.'

Nell smiled at her. 'Alright.'

Nell Larkin had been on the game herself most of her life before she had come to work as a maid for Blessed Latimer. Even after her daughter Rose had got married and had a baby, Nell had still plied her old trade on the East End streets. However, by the time she met Blessed back in 1949, she'd had enough. Although being a tart's 'maid' – a combination of receptionist, cleaner, nurse and guardian – didn't pay all that much, it at least meant that Nell could keep her flat in Fournier Street and feed her addiction to booze.

She'd been having pains in her abdomen, roughly in the area of her stomach, for about four months. It was, she said, like being punched in the guts. Of course, the one thing it hadn't stopped her doing was drinking because, she told Blessed, that actually soothed the pain. But it clearly wasn't a cure.

'How about I make you a cuppa and then go and change the bedsheets myself?' Blessed asked.

'Oh, you can't . . . '

'Yes, I can.' Blessed stood up and turned towards the house. 'It's only Mr James and so the sheets are purely for show.'

In spite of the pain, Nell smiled. Mr James was a very old man who only ever wanted to talk to Blessed and, maybe, touch her hair once or twice. Probably past being able to have sex, he turned up once a month for a chat with a lovely woman, which he said 'sets me up for the rest of the month'.

As the pain began to subside, Nell found herself thinking about how fortunate she'd been to meet Blessed too. It wasn't often in recent years that she'd had cause to visit Mrs Swan, the abortionist, down by the Royal Docks in Canning Town.

Since the war it was like a wasteland of bomb craters and rubble down there. But, back in '49, Nell had found herself there with a young working girl called Rita whom she knew needed 'help'.

When Nell had first come to London, Mrs Swan had 'helped' her a couple of times; she'd also performed an abortion on Nell's daughter Rose, which had gone badly. But when Rita had asked Nell where she might go to get rid of her baby, she could only think of Mrs Swan. So they'd arrived in Canning Town together, and somewhat to Nell's surprise the old woman's place had still been standing. A flat above a shop, it was the only building left upright for about a quarter of a mile. Still assisted by the woman who was rumoured to be her lover, Mrs Swan had let Nell and Rita in just as another client was leaving.

This client, a frightened-looking black woman, had been Blessed. And while Rita had her abortion at the hands of Mrs Swan and her accomplice, Nell got to know the other girl as they sat on the steps together outside. Nell was one of those who'd suggested that Blessed go on the game and so it was Nell Larkin that the other girl thought of when she was able to consider getting herself a maid. It had all worked out well for Nell ... if only she could get rid of this blasted pain in her stomach.

'You know, maybe you need some rest,' she heard Blessed call out to her from the bedroom. 'Why don't you go and stay with your daughter in the country for a few days? You know Mr Dobbs the butcher?'

'Yes.'

'He wants to take me to Brighton for a weekend soon,' Blessed said. 'Why don't you go and see your Rose when I go down to the seaside with him? Do you good.'

It was a thought, although it wasn't without its problems. Going out to Essex meant being near to where her family lived – and Nelson. When Rose had told Nell that she'd met her father on VE Day, she'd nearly gone mad. What did he want, coming back into their lives like this? And offering her money from the sale of a horse at Appleby Fair ... the nerve of it! She'd avoided him ever since and had no intention of changing that now. Not that this Hullbridge place, according to Rose, was anywhere near her folks' old routes in Epping Forest. And it would at least mean she'd be able to spend some time with her grandson ...

A lovely hot June had turned into a wet July and, with little Maurice off school now, Rose was finding the cottage and its inadequacies difficult to cope with. Their old flat back in Spitalfields hadn't had running water or electricity either but it had been on the gas, which at least meant that she didn't have to cook outdoors. As she watched the rain form into puddles outside, Rose wondered how her neighbours were coping.

Even though they'd been in Essex for over a year, she still hadn't really got to know anybody here. When she took Morry to his little school on Ferry Road, she saw other mums and their children standing at the gates but they always seemed to be deep in conversation with each other. Lacking the confidence to introduce herself, she usually just dropped Morry off and then left.

There were shops in the village, but not like back home in London. The ones in Hullbridge consisted of people selling things out of shacks. And there were stories that Dermot came home with that she found frightening. At the bottom of Ferry Road, just before the river, there was a row of cottages people called the 'Plague Houses' apparently, built to house people fleeing the bubonic plague in London in the sixteenth century. Ever since she'd learned their name, whenever Rose saw them, she shuddered. And then there were stories about witches ... there were lots of those.

When the sun shone and the days were warm, life in Hullbridge was good, but when it rained, and during the winter, she often pined for London. Increasingly these days she thought about her two best friends, Becky Shapiro and Bernie Lynch – one a busy nurse at the London Hospital, the other a photographer in the new State of Israel. But then, they'd both always been clever, not like her. Just like her mother Nell, Rose could neither read nor write. Dermot had tried to teach her, but she just couldn't seem to get it. What she was good at was cleaning. Even though the cottage was ramshackle and leaky, it was always clean and that was something Rose felt proud of. But soon she'd have to think about helping Dermot bring more money home so that they could improve the place. Working as a farm labourer didn't bring in anything like what he'd earned in the docks.

She put her hand in the pocket of her skirt and took out the letter that had come for her over a week ago. Of course, she could have got Dermot to read it to her, but she hated it when that happened and so she'd just secreted it away. Eventually she'd chuck it on the fire like she'd done with some of the other letters she'd had over the years. Looking at it now, she still couldn't make head nor tail of it. Who could it be from? That it wasn't from her mum was the only thing she really knew for sure, unless that girl she was working for had somehow taught her to write? Or written for her maybe? Rose put the letter back in her pocket and walked out into the rain and down the lane to the road. Although it was wet, it was warm out and she needed some air. Just as she was about to go back inside, a very battered-looking car pulled up beside her.

Becky saw the child first: Natalie Adler, all dark-eyed and fighting to breathe outside the chest clinic. If the little girl was on her own here, that wasn't right! But then Becky saw the child's mother. Still heavily made up but thin and lined these days, the woman who had once been the man-eater Sharon Begleiter sat by the little girl's side, smoking a fag.

Warily, on Becky's part at least, the two women looked at each other. Back before the war, Sharon had got Becky's friend Bernie sacked from her job at Sassoon's factory – mainly because Bernie had kissed the man Sharon had wanted for herself, Solly Adler. Then, when she'd finally 'got' Solly, Sharon had, it was said, given herself to other blokes who weren't crippled like her husband was. Becky knew Sharon didn't like her even though she'd been trying to help little Natalie for years. Every other woman in the world was viewed as a threat by someone like Sharon.

But Becky retained her dignity. 'Good afternoon, Mrs Adler, Natalie,' she said. 'Are you going to see Mr Roberts?'

Alisdair Roberts was a specialist in diseases of the chest and Becky knew that he would do his best for Natalie. It was encouraging to see the little girl here at all given her mother's hospital phobia. Not that Sharon Adler was alone in that. There were still millions of people who, despite the coming of the National Health Service, saw hospitals as places that made them poor.

'If he's the chest bloke, then yes,' Sharon said.

'He's very good,' Becky replied. 'I do hope he manages to get something sorted out for Natalie.'

'Yeah, well . . .'

Sharon looked away. Clearly the conversation was over as was Becky's shift and so she said, 'Hope you feel better soon, Natalie.'

The little girl smiled and Becky walked away.

If Sharon was still in love with Solly and saw Becky as a rival then she could understand this attitude. But not only did Sharon treat her husband with contempt, Becky had absolutely no designs on him. That was all well and truly in the past now. Only her work mattered to her these days, making sure that pregnant women in the East End got the care they needed and deserved. And anyway, she was happy living with her papa. He loved her and, for the time being, that was enough for her.

'Tilly!'

Rose flung herself into the open arms of a man dressed in the most amazing suit she had ever seen. High-waisted and baggy, it had a kind of a sheen to it that made it look as if it was made of satin. But then that was quite possible given that Herbert Lewis, aka drag queen Tilly de Mer, was wearing it.

'Oh, Tilly, it's been such a long time!' Rose said. 'And you've got a car!'

'Told you all about it in me letter,' Tilly said.

'Oh, yeah, 'course ...'

Tilly removed her Trilby hat and lit a fag. 'Blimey, it's a bit carrot-cruncher-land round here, ain't it?' she said.

'Carrot-cruncher?'

'Countryside.' Tilly hugged her. 'Mind you, you do look well, girl!'

Rose, whose time at the infamous Windmill Theatre in London had taught her that 'well' had a double meaning, said, 'What? Fat?'

'No, you daft moo!' Tilly said. 'Well. Blooming. You know.'

20

Having left the car in the lane leading down to Rose's place, the pair walked arm in arm through trees and bushes that Tilly seemed to look upon as things alien to her and not a little dirty. As she gingerly pulled a sprig of hawthorn out of the way, she said, 'Not up the duff, are you, girl?'

'No.' Rose smiled.

'You being blooming and that.'

'No. So what you ...'

'Doing here?' Tilly stopped and spat out an insect that had somehow insinuated itself into her mouth. Bloody countryside! She stared accusingly at her companion.

'What are you looking at?' Rose said.

'You, lady,' Tilly replied. 'Not getting your fella to read your post for you, are you?'

Rose looked away.

Tilly shook her head. 'Blimey,' she said. 'So you can't read and write! So what? You either do something about it or you don't. But if you won't then you've got to get people to do it for you.'

'I've tried. But I just can't seem to ...'

Tilly threw her hands in the air. 'Oh, well, I'm here now and can stay until Saturday if that's alright?'

''Course it is!'

Three whole days! It would be so wonderful to have someone to talk to – and especially someone like Tilly. They'd first met back in 1938 when Rose had run away from her home in Spitalfields after stealing money from old Mrs Rabinowicz, the local Jewish matchmaker. Although Rose had only stolen in order to pay her mother's rent, she'd felt unable to return to the area until Christmas 1941. In the event, Becky's father had repaid the matchmaker and all had long-since been forgiven. But in the meantime Rose had been offered a job at the

Windmill Theatre in Soho, first as a dancer and later in one of the theatre's famous Tableaux Vivants – which basically meant standing around naked with other girls in 'artistic' poses. There she and Tilly and a host of other Windmill regulars had become good friends. It was such fun to see her again!

'Well, this is the place,' Rose said as they both walked out of the lane and into the clearing that contained Ten Bells Cottage.

Tilly had never been any good at hiding disappointment. Also, she was an urban creature who didn't really appreciate rustic settings.

'Well, it's ...'

'I know it's a bit rough but Dermot did build it all himself. Also, it's what he calls a "work in progress",' Rose said.

'It's quaint,' Tilly said after a moment's cogitation. 'That's what it is. Nice.'

'We do have a kitchen now and two bedrooms, one for us and one for Morry. And a lovely little living room where you can stay.'

Tilly smiled. 'I'm sure it'll be bona,' she said.

Rose walked onto the veranda and opened the front door.

Tilly put her head inside and said, 'Cosy.'

'Oh, and the lavvy's outside and, er, so's the water,' Rose said.

Tilly smiled. It wasn't as if she lived in luxury back in London but it had been a long time since she'd had to use a pump. Oh, well, all part of life's rich pattern ...

Heinrich had gone home early leaving Bernie in the office to finish up her paperwork. He didn't cope well with the heat of the Israeli summer and had returned to their apartment in the West Jerusalem district of Katamon to get some rest.

As afternoon had turned into early evening, most of the

staff of the *Jerusalem Post* had also left, with the exception of Bernie, Gibrail and old Saul the caretaker. Only very close friends knew that Bernie and Heinrich actually lived together and so, when the young Arab asked Bernie whether she would like him to escort her home, she said, 'No, thanks. I'll be fine.'

The Muslim evening call to prayer was winding its way across the city as she began to pack her papers away in her desk and so if she chose to walk home it would be dark by the time she got there.

Gibrail frowned.

'What's the matter?' she said.

'It will be dark soon,' he replied. 'It's not safe for you, I think. You know there are still people in this country who do not like British people.'

'I'm a big girl, I can take care of myself.'

It was sweet he was so concerned but also a little bit worrying too. It wasn't just Heinrich who had noticed the way the young Arab looked at her sometimes. Bernie could feel her cheeks burning underneath his gaze on occasion. Gibrail wasn't that much younger than she was and he was handsome. If she were honest with herself, his attention could sometimes be quite thrilling. Not that she took it seriously ... or at least that was what she told herself.

She picked up her handbag.

Gibrail said, 'Let me at least escort you to the end of the road. Or maybe I can get you a cab?'

He wasn't going to let it go and, quite apart from the notion that he might be sweet on her, he did have a point. Although Israel now had its independence, resentment about the years spent under British Mandate remained. And, of course, ownership of the land itself, particularly of Jerusalem, was still disputed by the Arabs, many of whom had been displaced when the State of Israel came into being. It was rumoured that this Colonel Nasser in Egypt had plans to one day take Israel on and reclaim the territory for his fellow Arabs. But that was only a rumour.

'Usually, I know, Mr Heinrich takes you home,' Gibrail persisted.

Did he maybe know they lived together? Whether he did or not, the young man was aware that European women rarely wandered the streets of Jerusalem alone at night. Even women like Bernie Lynch.

She lit a cigarette and said, 'OK, you can come and wait with me while I hail a cab.'

She was on the point of offering to drop him somewhere first when she recalled that being in a cab, effectively alone, with a young Arab man probably wasn't a good idea.

They walked down the stairs together and she, very briefly, felt one of his hands brush against hers.

Chapter 3

'I saw your girlfriend up the hospital,' Sharon said once her mother-in-law had gone to bed and she and her husband were alone.

Solly looked up from his newspaper and said, 'Girlfriend? What you talking about?'

'Rebekah Shapiro.'

But she looked away when she said the name because she knew it wasn't true. Solly went back to his newspaper.

Sharon picked up her knitting from behind the cushion. 'Well, ain't you gonna say anything?'

'Not unless you're finally gonna tell me what that doctor told you about Nat,' Solly said.

Knitting needles clacking, Sharon considered what he'd said for a few moments and then conceded, 'Said she could do with something called a nebuliser.'

'What's that?'

'Something to open up her airways when she has an attack. Won't cost nothing.'

Solly looked up again. With his heavily scarred cheek and

grey hair he looked older than forty, but he was still a handsome man and Sharon knew it. Other women looked at him even if she didn't. Not that it cured her jealousy of any female who came even close to her husband.

Solly said, 'Paying ain't the point. If we had to pay to make her better, we would.'

'Yeah, I know, but . . .'

'So it's good news.'

'Yeah,' she said. 'Gotta take her next week to pick it up and teach her how to use it.'

'Good.'

Solly went back to his newspaper. He knew when his wife was spoiling for a fight and that time was now. And all because she'd seen Becky Shapiro up at the London. The bloody woman worked there!

'Rebekah Shapiro come up and said hello to me and our Nat,' Sharon continued.

''Course she did,' her husband replied. 'She's been here more'n once for Nat. She's interested in her.'

'You sure that's all she's interested in?'

This time Solly put his paper down. Years ago, when he'd been sweet on Becky's friend Bernie Lynch, Sharon had made sure that Bernie lost her job. She was a vindictive woman and if she hadn't been the mother of his daughter, he would have told her the truth about their marriage: that he'd only proposed to her on the rebound from Bernie.

'Nurse Shapiro has saved Natalie's life more than once,' he said. 'We've a lot to be grateful to her for.'

'Oh, really?'

The look on Sharon's face combined with the irritating clacking of her knitting needles was too much for Solly. In spite of his artificial leg, he sprang to his feet.

26

'You stinking fucking moo!' he yelled. 'Why do you have to be so horrible about everyone all the time!'

He shook her shoulders. Sharon, her face going red with fury and fear, struggled to breathe.

'Not as if you want me yourself, is it?' he said. 'Off with anyone who'll have you whenever you get the chance!'

He bit down on the back of his own hand so that he wouldn't hit her.

Appalled, Sharon said, 'You mad fucking bastard! Do that again and I'll have you put away in the nuthouse!'

'And I won't be sorry to go!' he said as he threw himself back down in his chair. 'At least I'd get away from *you*.'

Sharon picked up her knitting again. They'd been here before. Not maybe in the same fashion, but they argued a lot. Solly's mother, Dolly, who lived with them, had warned her son about the effect their combative relationship was having on Natalie.

'You know she'll grow up hating the both of you, don't you?' she'd told him only the previous week after he'd had yet another screaming row with his wife.

Solly had alluded then to Sharon's well-known penchant for other men. But his mother didn't let him off the hook easily.

'So stop her going out!' she'd said.

'How?'

'I dunno, do I? Divorce her! Tell the judge she's always out *schtupping* other men!'

But Solly didn't want to do that. Decent people didn't get divorces, decent people worked their problems out. Except this one wasn't something that was going to work out any time soon.

Silence fell on them until Solly said, 'I don't want you mentioning Nurse Shapiro again. You hear me?'

He saw her shrug, but she didn't say anything.

'You hear me, Sharon?'

'Yeah,' she said. 'I hear you.'

'So don't do it and we'll all get on,' Solly said. 'You can take our Natalie to get this thing that'll make her better and then we won't have to have nothing more to do with Nurse Shapiro ever again.'

'If you like,' she said.

But inside Sharon seethed. She'd seen him looking at that bloody saint of a nurse and didn't like it. He'd mooned over that Bernadette Lynch woman for years and now he was hanging on her mate's every word. Not that she believed he was actually doing anything with Becky Shapiro. He didn't seem to have any sex drive these days, which was why Sharon went with other men. Or rather that was what she told herself.

Watching little Morry Lynch race around that enormous garden of theirs was bloody exhausting. Tilly gulped tea out of the old tin mug Rose had given her and looked out on what even she had to admit was an idyllic scene. Now the rain had stopped, Rose was cooking up a cauldron of something over an open fire while her husband chopped wood in front of a little copse of trees. The family looked, Tilly thought, rather like characters from that old book *The Swiss Family Robinson*. All tanned and a bit on the ragged side, they looked very fit and strong and happy. Although Tilly did wonder about that last bit. Sitting on the veranda wrapped in one of Rose's blankets, she wondered how things were between the couple. Really.

Because although Rose and her husband behaved very lovingly towards each other, Tilly wasn't so sure about Dermot. She knew what she'd seen that night Rose first brought him

28

to her flat and how he'd looked at the other men and the drag queens in the room. Subsequent encounters with him hadn't changed Tilly's mind . . . and then there was the fact that Rose still wasn't pregnant.

Morry wasn't Dermot's child. He was the son of a lecherous bastard theatre doorman called Kenneth who had raped Rose one night when she was drunk. It had happened during the Blitz in the basement of the Windmill Theatre. Dermot had taken Rose on in full knowledge of her circumstances. His name was given as the father on the little boy's birth certificate and he was a good dad to Morry. Watching them playing together when Dermot had first got home from work had warmed the cockles of old Tilly's heart. But . . .

Tilly finished her tea and lit a fag. Little 'Rosie Red', as she liked to call her friend, hadn't had an easy life. When she'd first come to the Windmill Theatre, she'd been on the run for stealing money from some old girl in the East End. Quite early on in their friendship, Rose had told Tilly she'd had an abortion when she was younger. She'd said then words to the effect that she never wanted to 'do it' again. She hadn't as far as Tilly knew, apart from that one time against her will.

Dermot took his shirt off and Tilly heard Rose say, 'Oh, Der! Make sure no one sees you!'

No one in this backwater would most probably. But Tilly looked and she liked what she saw. Not that she'd ever tell a living soul that. Working on the land obviously suited Dermot. His well-muscled body really was a sight to behold. He'd go down a storm with the punters down Piccadilly Circus. But then had he ever been with another man or not? A lot of men like him didn't for fear they'd be arrested and imprisoned and, now that he was a father, Dermot probably had even less incentive to risk it. Maybe he didn't even want to?

No. As a natural sceptic, Tilly couldn't believe that even though she hoped deep down that he didn't. The last thing Rose and Morry needed was any further instability; there'd been too much of that in their lives already.

The sky was full of stars. Maybe it was because she'd been brought up in London with its forest of buildings, its millions of people and its perpetual smog that Bernie considered the sky over Jerusalem to be so much more starry. When she'd first arrived in Israel it had been one of the things she'd noticed straight away. That and the terrible tensions that gripped this land, though it was holy to three different religions.

Heinrich had gone to bed hours ago and so Bernie was alone on the balcony drinking *arak*, the local aniseed spirit, and smoking a cigarette. Down in the street, nothing was moving except for a few mangy cats. Two years before she'd arrived, the old offices of the *Jerusalem Post* had been blown up by Arab terrorists and, even now, violent incidents happened as those who opposed the State of Israel continued their fight against what they called 'the occupation'. Although Heinrich, like most Jewish Israelis, saw the situation very much in black-and-white terms – the Jews had a right to their ancestral homeland, the Arabs did not – Bernie's opinions were more nuanced. A lot of Arabs had been displaced when the State of Israel had been declared back in 1948. War had raged between the infant Israeli state and its Arab neighbours resulting in an Israeli victory, what the Arabs called the *Nakba* or 'catastrophe'. Because for them it had been. Even the smart flat she lived in with Heinrich had belonged to Arabs once upon a time. She thought about how she would have felt had her old flat on Ten Bells Street been taken over by strangers. She would have done anything to get back what she believed belonged to her.

Her mind wandered to cub reporter Gibrail Khoury who had taken her to get a taxi earlier in the evening. Did his family originate from a place like this? Katamon had been a wealthy Arab district prior to the declaration of the State of Israel. As evidenced by the many churches in the area, Christians like Gibrail had once been numerous here. Bernie had heard that the young man's father had been a teacher and so he came from a background of learning if not money.

Had Gibrail maybe lived in Katamon at some time? She hoped not. She hoped his family had somehow not been displaced when the British Mandate ended. It was unlikely to be true but Bernie wished them well nevertheless.

It wasn't easy meeting Arabs and yet she knew that if she wanted to get a complete picture of the country, she had to find a way to do so. Heinrich, for all his kindness and his love for her, was definitely of the opinion that Arabs should be kept at arm's length. He freely admitted he couldn't forgive them for opposing the formation of his country and for precipitating the 1948 Arab-Israeli War. The Arabs themselves would say they were fighting for their existence, but Bernie knew so little about them, she thought that maybe not all of them were of that opinion. But how could she know for sure unless she asked?

She looked back inside the darkened apartment. Heinrich had been dealing badly with the heat for some time and often went to bed early these days. He also took the occasional day off work. Maybe, as the summer became hotter still, his absences might allow her the space to get out and meet some members of the Arab population? And maybe being amongst them would provide her with some new and interesting photographic opportunities.

*

'Kitty!'

She knew who was hammering on her front door but Kitty Lynch closed her eyes for a moment before getting out of her chair and answering it. She'd wanted a moment of peace not another crisis. But that was almost certainly what she was going to get.

'Nelly,' she said, as she opened the door to her neighbour. 'What do you want?'

Nell Larkin was drunk, but there was nothing new in that.

'When you going down Essex to see your Dermot?' she asked without preamble.

Kitty shrugged. 'Dunno, yet,' she said. 'What with work and my girls ...'

"Cause, if you're going, could I come with ya?' Nell asked. 'I can pay me own way.'

Not only was Nell Larkin drunk, she also had a cut on her cheek. Christ knew where she'd got that! She needed sorting out. Kitty held the door open for her and said, 'Come in and have a cuppa.'

'Oh, thank you, Kitty!'

She staggered into the flat and sat herself down in what used to be Kitty's husband Pat's old chair beside the range. Not that it was cold. It was just that being near the range, Kitty had noticed, even when it was unlit, instantly made people feel better.

She filled the kettle, lit the gas hob and put the water on to boil.

'So what you been up to?' Kitty asked her guest once she'd sat down in her own chair.

'Work an' that ...'

'You've got a cut on your cheek.'

Nell put a hand up to her right cheek.

'No, the other one,' Kitty said.

She felt her left cheek, and when her hand came away, could see blood on her fingers. 'Don't remember that ...'

Kitty shook her head, but she didn't say anything. She knew that Nell worked as a maid for some girl over in Stepney. Customers could cut up rough. But the chances were that Nell had tripped over. Drunks were never that steady on their feet.

'I'll give you a plaster and some TCP,' Kitty said as she got up and went to the cupboard under the sink. 'Come here and wash it first.'

Nell rose unsteadily to her feet and then let Kitty wash her face and cover her wound.

'You're ever so kind to me, Kitty,' she said when her neighbour had finished.

'Don't want you to get an infection.'

The kettle started to whistle then and Kitty poured boiling water onto tea leaves in her big, old, brown teapot.

'I know some people are using them teabags now,' she said as she fitted the knitted cosy over the pot. 'But I don't hold with it. The tea in them things is just the scrapings up off the floor.'

Nell said, 'So you going down the country to see your Dermot?'

'I will be, but I don't know when,' Kitty said.

It wasn't easy with work and her two remaining children to look after. Not that Marie and Aggie needed much assistance these days, but it was a right schlep getting out to Essex and, although Kitty did want to go, she dreaded the journey, which seemed to take forever.

'Well, when you do, could I come with you?' Nell asked again. 'I can't face all that on me own.'

She couldn't face it because she couldn't read. She might be alright getting to Liverpool Street Station but where she'd get out at the other end was anyone's guess. Not that Kitty would say anything about that.

'Yeah,' she said. 'Provided they can put us both up. Mr Shapiro's down there almost every weekend now, so we'd have to check with him.'

After all, the land, if not the little house on it, belonged to Moritz Shapiro and so he could go down there whenever he wanted. In one way, Kitty was grateful to him for giving Rose, Dermot and little Morry a home, but in another she was resentful. Having her boy and her grandson so far away was not what she would've picked. But she had to consider all the benefits of fresh air and freedom that it gave Dermot and his family. And it had at least got him out of the Docks. He'd been so unhappy there. Unlike his father, he'd never managed to stand up to the bullying and coercion that could go on down there. At least unlike his brother, Joey, he'd never joined in with it.

Kitty poured the tea.

'So why this sudden wanting to go out to Essex?' she said as she handed Nell a large mug of dark brown brew.

'Blessed said I need holiday,' Nell said.

'That the girl you work for?'

'Yeah.'

'So how'll she get on without you if you go away?'

Nell shrugged. Then she said, 'She's a good girl. Had to put up with nothing but shit since she come here. She's trained as a nurse, an educated lady. But all the work anyone'll let her do is on her back, poor little cow. Just because she's black.'

Kitty had seen the signs in houses with rooms to rent, reading 'No blacks, No dogs, No Irish'. They were everywhere. What her Pat, a life-long Socialist, would have made of it didn't bear repeating. As much as things had got better since the war – no bombing and free health care – some things had just stayed the same.

'I ain't felt well,' Nell continued.

'In what way?'

'Dunno. Women's problems.'

'You on your Change?'

'Nah,' Nell said.

'How'd'ya know?'

'Still bleeding.'

'You should go and see someone,' Kitty said. 'You don't have to pay now.'

'I ain't going down no hospital! I'll come out feet first!'

'Oh, you don't need to go there!' Kitty said. 'Just go down Dr Klein's surgery. Ask Becky to go along with you. If you don't feel right, then going down our Dermot's won't make you feel no better.'

Although Kitty had to admit to herself that in one way it might. If nothing else, Rose would ration her mother's drinking for a couple of days, which would probably make the world of difference. And it was doubtful to say the least whether Nell would ever go and see Dr Klein. And even if she did, he was often hardly any more sober than she was these days. When she'd gone, Kitty made up her mind to speak to Marie and Aggie about going down to Essex one weekend soon. And, yes, she would take Nell with her. God help her!

Life was changing around here. Moritz Shapiro knew the signs. As he looked out of his living-room window onto Fournier Street, he was struck by how empty it had become since the war ended. People were moving out of the old, battered streets of London. New towns were being built out in places he'd never heard of before – Basildon and Harlow.

And a lot of the Yiddisher people had gone to north London, where the bombing had been lighter and the streets were less dark. Some had even gone to the new State of Israel, like his daughter's friend Bernadette Lynch.

Moritz knew that Kitty didn't approve of what her daughter had done, but then the girl had always been headstrong. She'd do whatever she pleased. Secretly Moritz had always liked that about Bernie Lynch. In fact, his own daughter Becky and the girls' other friend little Rose both knew their own minds too. Bernie however had something extra, a questing spirit that had already taken her to mainland Europe and now the Middle East.

But it was dangerous out there. That was why, although he'd considered it for a while, Moritz had decided not to move to the land of his fathers. Just establishing Israel had necessitated a war between the new Jewish state and its Arab neighbours, and conflict, in the form of acts of terror perpetrated by Arab militias, continued. Why would he want to take his daughter into a situation like that?

And yet the streets around him were dying. There were rumours that, at some point, the whole area would be knocked down to make way for modern flats. It was what people wanted and Moritz couldn't blame them for that. His was one of the very few houses in Spitalfields that had a bathroom and electricity instead of old gas lamps. After five years of war people wanted and deserved better. What that would mean for an old man and his daughter living in a vast museum of a house, Moritz didn't know. Maybe, eventually, he'd have to move.

In the meantime, his customers knew where he was and work still flowed in and so he thanked God for that. When change did eventually come, he would be ready for it, unlike his forebears who had been chased out of their homes in Poland and the Ukraine by first the Tsars of Russia and then the Soviet Communist Party. So much hope had been invested in Communism when it had taken over Russia in 1917. One of the leaders of the Revolution, Trotsky, had even been a Yiddisher himself! But it had all gone bad somewhere along the line and, although the Soviets had helped the West win the war over Hitler, thoughts of what they did in their own country, and the others they had occupied after the war, made Moritz's skin crawl. There was talk of yet more pogroms and torture; of their leader Joseph Stalin's cruelty and spite. Moritz's old friend Patrick Lynch would have been horrified. In fact, many of the local Communists, with which the East End was once thick, had long ago surrendered their dreams of world revolution and unity between the working classes. Maybe the war against Hitler had knocked all the humanity out of people. But then again, maybe any scheme that aimed to make all men equal was doomed to failure.

Moritz closed the curtains on the darkening street outside and went to bed.

Chapter 4

Christmas Eve 1950

Gawd blimey, it was cold! There was ice not only on the outside of the windows but inside too.

Rose put her rubber boots on and went out to get the coal in. It wasn't far to the shed but it was far enough to take her breath away. When she came back in she had to jump up and down and rub her hands together to get warm. Only then could she start laying a new fire in the grate – breaking up bits of wood for kindling, making 'crackers' out of old newspaper and piling just enough coal on top so that the fire didn't die when she lit it.

Dermot, who had just got out of bed, walked into the living room, pulling his braces up as he did so, and made straight for the infant fire.

'Brass monkeys,' he said to his wife.

Rose pulled out the lever that activated the flue and stood away as some of the smoke came back at her into the room. That always happened.

'Be fine once we get the fire going,' she said. 'Is Morry still in bed?'

'Yeah.' Dermot lit a fag. 'Let him sleep. I think the poor little bloke's whacked out.'

They'd all been out to Maurice's school carol concert the previous evening. Little Morry had sung 'Once in Royal David's City' as a solo and then, after the show, they'd all had tea and cake in the school hall. It had been a late and exciting night for a little boy.

'Do you know what time they're all getting here?' Rose asked.

'Nah.'

Dermot sat down in what had become his chair.

'Such a lot of people!' Rose said. 'I still don't know where they're all going to go!'

Dermot rolled his eyes. 'I told you, I worked it all out. You, your mum and my mum can have our bed. Morry can sleep on a mattress in our room and Mr Shapiro'll have Morry's bed.'

'Where's Becky gonna sleep? And Aggie?'

'One'll have the sofa and we can push two chairs together for the other. I've got it all worked out.'

'And what about Tilly?' Rose said, since her old friend may or may not put in an appearance too.

'She can take her chances,' Dermot said.

Although he tried to hide how he felt, Dermot didn't like Tilly, or Herbert as he preferred to call her, purely to irritate. Last time the old drag queen had visited, she'd told Dermot that if she ever found out he'd been with another man, she'd chop his cock off. How she'd known about something Dermot had always kept to himself, he didn't know. Was it some sort of instinct?

Of course, he'd denied he'd ever had such feelings, but Tilly just scowled at him in disbelief. Had Rose maybe told Tilly how they lived together more like brother and sister than husband and wife? But then, why would she? It had been more her idea than his. She was the one who'd been raped and left pregnant with Morry for her pains. Not that Dermot was unhappy about his enforced marital celibacy. That suited him just fine. What he didn't need was Tilly turning up at Christmas of all times to check up on him.

Rose put some more coal on the fire, which was burning more brightly now. 'What about you?' she asked her husband. 'Where'll you sleep?'

'Oh, I'll make meself a bed in the tool-shed,' he said.

'But you'll freeze out there!'

'Nah! We'll have to build a fire outside for the cooking. The shed'll warm up and I'll take blankets.'

Rose shook her head. 'Why can't you sleep on the floor of Morry's room? I'm sure Mr Shapiro won't mind.'

'I'll be alright.' He looked up at her. 'Here, you look down in the dumps. What's the matter?'

She walked over and sat on the arm of his chair. 'Oh, it's just ... '

'What?'

'I've never done Christmas before,' Rose said. 'And we haven't even got a range! And your Marie's not coming because she's going to have Christmas with some girl she works with!'

He put his arm around her. 'Oh, cheer up, chicken!' he said. 'It'll be grand. I got us a big bird off the farm what'll come up lovely done on an open fire. You know it will because we done it before. And as for our Marie, I thought you was worried about having too many people in the house?'

'I am, but ... I still wish she'd come,' Rose said. 'It won't be the same without her.'

'No, but it'll be fine,' Dermot said. 'We've got plenty of grub and that wine what Mr Nice give me for a Christmas box is prop'ly strong. And Becky's bringing sweets.'

'I know. But . . .'

'But what?'

It was then that little Maurice came barrelling out of his bedroom, his face aglow with excitement, and said, 'Is it Christmas yet?'

The office was cold and made chillier still by Heinrich Simpson's displeasure. Most of the other reporters were out working, which left Bernie almost alone with her brooding lover. And so once Yael and Shimon had left to go to lunch together, she said to him, 'You know you're being ridiculous, don't you?'

Heinrich looked up from his typewriter. 'Oh, yes? You are going to spend Christmas without me and I am being ridiculous?'

'But you don't even celebrate Christmas,' Bernie said.

'You and I, we celebrated Christmas back in England!'

'For my sake, yes,' she said.

'I celebrated Christmas, I did! Back in Germany, we always had a big party.'

'Yes, but not really! Not like . . . Oh, for God's sake, Heinrich, leave it! I have the chance to go to Bethlehem for Christmas and I'm taking it. It's a brilliant photo opportunity.'

'You're going with that boy,' he said darkly.

Gibrail was taking her to Bethlehem, to attend Mass at the Church of the Nativity. They were going to stay with his elder sister and her family.

'Yes,' Bernie said, 'I am. And what of it? He's a work-mate who has very kindly invited me to share Christmas with his family, who are Christians.'

41

'He's in love with you.'

She shook her head. Not this again! Ever since the summer he'd not stopped. 'Will you listen to yourself?' she said. 'It's all bloody rubbish, Heine! Even if the kid does have a fancy for me, which I don't think he does, then he won't do anything about it. It's more than his life's worth and you know it!'

Heinrich didn't reply. They'd been here before. It irked Bernie that he appeared to have so little time for Israel's Arab population. On the one hand, having come through the war in Europe and all the absolute horrors Jews had suffered at the hands of the Nazis, she could understand how he found trusting anyone difficult. But Heinrich hadn't personally suffered in the concentration camps and so she couldn't see how he could justify having such extreme views.

Gibrail Khoury had asked Bernie if she would like to go to Bethlehem for Christmas back in November. Usually Israeli citizens were forbidden from travelling to Jordanian-administered Palestine. The only exception made to this rule was for Arab Christians resident in Israel who were permitted a laissez-passer at Christmas. And Bernie, with her British papers, was allowed access also. Not so Heinrich with his Jewish-Israeli citizenship.

'I know I can't go . . . ' he said.

'No, you can't,' Bernie said. 'But I can and so I'm taking the opportunity.'

He muttered, 'You're not even religious.'

'I'm going to experience what not many people can,' Bernie said. 'Which is an Arab Christian Christmas.'

'Why?'

'Why? Because it's my belief that these people are being squeezed out by both Israel and the new nationalism that is rearing up under people like this Colonel Nasser in Egypt,' she said. 'He and his people want a greater Arab nation, committed to Socialist values, not religion. There aren't many Christians left in these lands, I want to record their lives before they disappear completely.'

Heinrich didn't reply. She knew that in principle he agreed with her. If only she wasn't going with Gibrail!

After a while she went over to her lover and kissed him.

'Everything will be alright,' she said. 'I love you and that's the beginning and the end of it.'

But did he believe her? Sometimes she wasn't even sure she believed it herself.

Nell coughed up something that looked like a walnut: brown and knobbly. Kitty looked at it in her friend's handkerchief and said, 'Bloody hell, Nelly! That thing looks as if it's got a life of its own! How long you been bringing stuff like that up?'

Nell shrugged. 'I dunno,' she said. 'It's that rotten air in London what does it. Maybe out here it'll be better.'

She looked out of the carriage window into the frosty night. Out in the sticks there was very little in the way of lighting and all she could see was a sign on a station platform that she couldn't read.

'Where are we?' she asked.

'Wickford,' Kitty said.

'Where's that then?'

'No idea. But next stop's ours,' Kitty said. She took her small suitcase down from the rack above her head and then woke up her daughter. 'Here, Aggie, get yourself together, girl.'

Aggie opened her eyes and then pulled her bag towards her. The three women were alone in the carriage, which smelled of fags, Brylcreem and wet material. Lit by a single bulb in the ceiling it had a yellowish tinge, like a slightly infected lung.

43

'So the next stop's Hullbridge then?' Nell asked.

Kitty rolled her eyes. 'No, you soppy date! Next stop's Rayleigh. Then we have to get a bus to Hullbridge.'

'Fucking hell.'

Kitty shook her head. Nelly had been down to see Rose and family once, a long time ago, when Mr Shapiro had taken her. But clearly she'd not remembered anything about it.

Kitty lit a fag.

'We have to walk over a bridge to get to the bus-stop so you'll have to push yourself, Nelly.'

As well as suffering from phlegm, Nell was also often out of breath and her stomach still hurt.

'I'll be alright,' she said. 'As long as you give us a snout.'

Kitty passed her fag packet over and then, as the train began to slow, said, 'Come on then, girls. Nearly Christmas!'

Herbert looked down at the backs of his hands and wondered just how much longer Tilly de Mer could go on. Not only were there hairs on the knuckles, but the wrinkles and prominent veins on those hands made them look like they belonged to someone Herbert's mum's age. And she was over eighty.

Although he'd gone out in public dragged up in the past, and even sometimes now if he was in the West End, Tilly always travelled as Herbert these days. Just had to be sure no vestigial make-up was left behind after Tilly had been on stage. People would go bonkers if they saw a bloke out and about wearing eyeliner.

Tilly had caught the last train from Liverpool Street to Southend Victoria. She had to get off at a place called Rayleigh then catch a bus apparently. If only the Duchess of Greek Street had lent her the car! But she was using it herself to go and see her old mum up in Yorkshire. Of course, her need was greater, but Tilly still resented it. Hullbridge was the back of bloody beyond!

But it would all be worth it in the end. Being with Rose and little Morry was one of the great joys of Tilly's life and she'd spent a fortune on presents for the little boy. These included a couple of Airfix kits from Woolworths, a cowboy play-set from Hamleys and a platoon of lead soldiers all wrapped up in brown paper and string. She'd even had special gift tags made by some old girl in Berwick Street who was good at that sort of thing.

When the train reached Rayleigh, Tilly staggered off clutching her parcels and dragged herself over the railway bridge to the bus-stop. It was ever so dark out in the countryside! A bit like being back in the blackout. But Tilly was nothing if not a trouper and when she found the bus-stop, she resisted the urge to lean on it in exhaustion and lit a fag to bolster herself up while she waited. If a train had just come in from London then surely there had to be a bus soon? Not that there was anyone about she could ask. Beyond the station it was like the bleeding *Mary Celeste* – not a soul in sight.

Having finished her fag, Tilly dug inside her Gladstone bag for her hip flask. It was proper brass monkeys and so a quick swig of the good stuff'd do her no harm at all. She was just thinking how she really needed to get herself a new overcoat sometime soon, when she suddenly saw that she wasn't alone. A little old man, his head barely reaching her shoulder, had appeared close by and stood peering up into her face. 'You waiting for the bus, are you?' he said.

His accent was so countrified she had trouble making out the words.

'Yes,' Tilly said eventually. 'To Hullbridge.'

'Gone,' the old man said.

'Gone? How can it be? I just got off the train from London.'

'Gone an hour ago.' He shook his head. 'You want to get to Hullbridge, you'll have to walk.'

'Oh, for God's . . . '

'And no cussing,' the old man added over his shoulder as he walked away. 'Travel briskly and you'll be down by the river in less'n an hour.'

With so many parcels to carry? Tilly doubted it. But what else could she do? Rosie didn't have a telephone – who did? – and even if she had, what good would that have done? It wasn't as if bloody Dermot had a car or anything. All he had was some cart he sometimes brought home from that farm he worked on.

Oh, and now it was beginning to snow . . .

Bernie was accustomed to the way grand Arab houses were often accessed via very small and insignificant-looking doors. Gibrail's sister's house was no exception. Situated in the oldest part of Bethlehem, near the central Manger Square, from the street it presented to the outside world one wall, one small door and a barbed wire-laced window. And that was it.

Once inside a dark space that smelled of damp and what Bernie had come to recognise as the very distinctive smell of old stone, she took off her shoes and put on a pair of open slippers provided by her hosts. A short corridor then led her and Gibrail into a wide, colourfully tiled courtyard dominated by a central fountain in the shape of a tulip. No water was bubbling from its flowery mouth at the moment, but over the other side of the courtyard, half covered by a structure Bernie knew was called an *iwan*, she could see a large open fire surrounded by people reclining amidst large cushions. As they approached the fire, Bernie looked up into the cold December sky and saw that it was full of stars.

'We thought we would eat outside tonight,' a woman's voice said.

Bernie looked down. Tiny, almost childlike in stature, Gibrail's elder sister wore a long satin dress of many colours over which her long black hair flowed like a fountain.

'I am Rafka,' the woman said and held out a hand to Bernie, which she shook.

'Bernie,' she said.

Rafka kept hold of her hand and began walking towards the fire.

'Come,' she said. 'Leave my little brother and come and meet everyone.'

'Everyone' included Rafka's husband Issa, their daughter Maryam, a girl in her late teens, various 'uncles' – Arab families always seemed to have a lot of these – and an old woman called Magdelena who turned out to be Issa's mother. Informed by Rafka that Magdelena didn't speak any English, Bernie nevertheless paid her respects to the old lady by kissing her hand. Magdelena smiled.

'I hope you are hungry, Bernie,' Rafka said as she settled their guest down beside her daughter. 'The Midnight Mass celebrations always start with the arrival of our Patriarch from Jerusalem in Manger Square, which will be in about an hour. It is fun to be outside with the crowds, I think.'

And yet if Bernie knew anything about the Holy Land, she was also aware of the danger inherent in any form of public gathering. Some men would be carrying guns and if any sort of dispute occurred those weapons would be drawn.

Gibrail sat down on Bernie's other side. He said something

in Arabic to his niece and then smiled at Bernie. 'So how you like my brother-in-law's house?' he asked.

'It's beautiful.'

'You know, before the Israelis come, Issa owned many houses for pilgrims,' he said.

'Oh, so they could visit the church?'

'Yes. But now they are homes for poor people who run from the Israelis,' Gibrail said. 'Issa make not so much money now.'

Of course, Bernie knew that a lot of Palestinians had left their homes and run to the Jordanian part of the country when the new State of Israel had been declared. People like Issa's tenants were the fortunate ones. Those not so lucky lived in refugee camps, often living under canvas for years on end.

'And yet you didn't run. Why not?' she asked.

He shrugged. 'My mother has been sick for many years. I stay to look after her and my little sisters.'

It felt strange now to Bernie that she'd known so little about his life until this evening. She hadn't even known his mother was still alive. Even now she had no idea where he lived.

Rafka placed small glasses of tea down in front of her guests, which she then followed with a huge salver of rice, then baskets of unleavened bread and another salver of something that looked meaty.

Gibrail explained. 'This is called *Mansaf*,' he said as he pointed to the meat. 'Is lamb cooked in yogurt. It is very good on a cold night.'

Everyone tucked in, shovelling rice and then meat onto the bread with their right hands and then folding the whole thing into a parcel, which they ate from their hand. Bernie knew that most Arab families liked to eat like this and was fully aware of the prohibition on using the left hand, which was considered dirty. But she still found it difficult. Living as she did with Heinrich, eating by hand was something she just didn't do. Both Gibrail and Maryam helped her. The food was delicious, but when they kept on insisting she eat more after she was full, she had to refuse. Eventually they relented, but only once Rafka had told them to stop. Moving her daughter to one side, she said to their guest, 'My brother tells me you take wonderful photographs.'

'I try.' Bernie looked down. Self-deprecation was typical of Kitty and Bernie was nothing if not her mother's daughter.

'I have seen some of them and they are beautiful,' Rafka said. 'You will take some pictures tonight, maybe?'

'If I can, yes,' Bernie said.

'Oh, Issa will make that possible, so don't worry,' Rafka said. 'We may no longer be rich but we still have a position in this town that commands respect.'

Then she smiled and left. Bernie felt a tap on her shoulder followed by Gibrail's voice whispering, 'Many people here do not wish to make Issa angry. He will fix for you to take photographs but you must thank him, and in public. People have to see.'

See what exactly? Bernie wondered. The strange European woman elaborately thanking a powerful Arab? What was so great about that? But then she remembered that a lot of what went on here in the Middle East was about nothing more nor less than preserving face. Especially if one were 'powerful' in some way ...

Chapter 5

Because Ten Bells Cottage was made of wood, it got warm really quickly once a fire was lit in the living-room grate, and if the two bedroom doors were left open then it warmed those too. While Morry ran around being a Spitfire pilot, Rose brought out pies and bread from her larder and sat them in the grate in front of the fire to warm. Dermot had made a big bonfire out in the garden under which he'd placed some spuds to cook. But in the meantime bread and scrape and a good old helping of steak and kidney would keep them all going.

Nell Larkin had sat down beside the fire and fallen asleep as soon as she'd arrived. Rose let her get on with it even if the sight of his grandmother, snoring with her mouth open, did make Morry laugh. Becky and her father had arrived early in the afternoon, hours before Nell, Kitty and Aggie, who'd had a long and tiring journey by the sound of it. Tilly was probably coming too although she'd have missed the last bus now.

When she'd put the bread and pies in the grate, Rose went to sit down with her mother-in-law at the kitchen table.

'Your mum's got a right hacking cough on her,' Kitty said. 'I've told her to go and see the doctor.'

'She won't,' Rose said. 'She still thinks you have to pay.'

Kitty shook her head. 'I've told her enough times, you don't!'

'Me too,' Rose said. 'But you know what she's like.'

'Well, someone'll have to persuade her,' Kitty said meaningfully.

They watched as Morry joined Aggie in dressing the tree. It was only small but it was a real Christmas tree. Dermot had bought it off some bloke in the pub.

'I wish we had some more decorations,' Rose said as she watched her son gently place a few shiny baubles and some paper chains across the branches of the tree.

Kitty smiled. 'We used to make them out of old cards when the kids were little,' she said. 'When Pat was still alive.'

Rose put a hand on Kitty's and squeezed it. Patrick Lynch had died during the war. His illness had been in his chest, like Nell's was now.

Becky came and sat down with them at the table. 'Papa's asleep already,' she said.

'It's been a long day,' Kitty said.

'And he's old.'

They all sat in silence for a few seconds and then Rose said, 'I've got some ginger wine if anybody would like some.'

Kitty lit a cigarette. 'Oh, well, that'd be nice, love.'

For all their poverty, the Lynch family had always been open-handed with their drink at Christmas.

'Unless you've a milk stout,' she added.

'I've got that too,' Rose said. 'Do you want anything, Becky?'

She put her hands around her cup of tea. 'No, this is fine,' she said. Then she looked at Kitty. 'Have you heard anything from Bernie lately, Auntie Kitty?'

Bernie was always a sensitive subject to broach with her. Kitty had never approved of her daughter's involvement with a married man and, when Bernie had gone off with him to Israel, had been mortified. But Becky knew they wrote to each other. Not often, but they kept in touch.

Rose poured a bottle of milk stout into a glass and gave it to Kitty who looked deep into it as if seeking inspiration.

'I know Bernie intends to stay in Israel for now,' she said eventually. 'I wish she wouldn't . . . '

'But she won't always be there,' Becky said.

Kitty gave her a stern look. 'How do you know?'

'Well, I . . . '

'Could be gone forever for all I know,' Kitty spoke over her.

'She's taking the opportunity to travel . . . '

'With that man!'

If someone didn't change the subject soon, there was going to be a row. Becky had always supported Bernie in her decision to leave England and Kitty, who didn't, knew it. Luckily, it was at this point that the front door flew open and in walked Tilly de Mer.

'Hello, darlings!' she exclaimed as she staggered over the front doorstep followed by Dermot who did not look best pleased. 'Oh, I've had a hell of a journey!'

Rose ran up to her and gave her a hug. 'Oooh, you're so cold!'

'Had to bloody walk from Rayleigh Station, didn't I!' Tilly said. 'No buses. Blimey, it was endless! Like going on flippin' pilgrimage.'

Nell, awake now, looked up and said, 'Oh, it's you.'

'Yes, missus.'

Nell moved her chair away from the fire to make room for Tilly. 'Well, come on and get yourself warm.'

Tilly almost climbed into the grate.

Kitty, still smarting from what had almost been an argument with Becky, said, 'I'll put the kettle on.'

'Lovely.'

Tilly, who would far rather have had something stronger, warmed her backside by the fire and looked around the room, which was dimly lit with candles and hurricane lamps. Where the light caught the baubles on the Christmas tree, they shone silver and gold.

'Proper Christmassy this,' she said. 'You done us all proud, Rosie.'

Rose, blushing, said, 'Don't say too much. You lot don't know where you've got to sleep yet!'

The last time Bernie had been to Midnight Mass, her father had still been alive. It had been cold in the church that night and, as the incense had billowed around their heads, her dad had held her hand. Now that same smell brought the memory back and Bernie had to fight against bursting into tears. It was almost ten years since Patrick's death and she still missed him every day. She knew she always would.

The Church of the Nativity in Bethlehem was packed. All had passed through the small and very low door that led from the street into the church, made aware of their status as servants of God. Even if one wasn't religious – and Bernie wasn't – there was a power to be felt in this candle-lit, incense-shrouded place of holy icons, ornately dressed clerics and an atmosphere of worship carried out since the early days of Christianity. The original church had been built by the first Christian Emperor of Rome, Constantine the Great, which placed it in the fourth century AD. Just thinking about it made Bernie's head swim.

Sitting between Gibrail and his sister, Bernie studied their faces. Reflections of the candle flames on the High Altar illuminated their eyes, which looked towards the holy place with expressions of rapt fervour. Their faith meant so much to them! In fact, Bernie couldn't think of anywhere else she had been where faith had meant so much. It made her wish it meant something to her, but then how could she believe in any sort of religion that condemned her for her relationship with Heinrich?

As the choir raised their voices in praise of God, she wondered what her family back in London were doing. Becky had written to her a month ago to tell her that they might all be going to stay with Dermot, Rose and Morry in their little cottage in the country. But Bernie wondered whether her mother had been included in that. Kitty could be notoriously anti-social since her husband had died and Bernie knew that her mother probably wouldn't be able to get more than a couple of days off work. She was pretty sure that Aggie and Marie would go if they were asked. Part of her wished she was with them, but it was only a small part. Here, in Christ's birthplace, she felt privileged to witness an ancient people at prayer – an ancient people she knew were also very sad. For all the benefits to the Jewish people of the creation of the State of Israel, there had been losers from it as well as winners and she was among them now, praying for a better world.

'Our family always sat around a fire like this at the end of every day. Mum told me,' Rose said.

Everyone had gone to bed except for Rose and Tilly who now sat by the bonfire Dermot had built in the garden. After much shuffling about with blankets, Becky had joined Nell and Kitty in Rose and Dermot's bed, with Aggie on the floor, while all the men, her husband included, had bunked down in

Morry's little room. Tilly was supposed to have taken the sofa, but after everyone had finished their baked spuds and had a last nip of brandy, she'd chosen to join Rose by the bonfire.

'It's the Romany way,' Tilly said. 'I remember seeing them on the road when me and Mum used to travel down to Brighton by bus when I was kid. You ever see your dad now, Rosie Red?'

She smiled when Tilly used her stage name – Rosie Red the Windmill Girl.

'Not for ages,' Rose said. 'He sold a horse and wanted to give Mum the money for it, but she wouldn't take it.'

'Why not?'

Rose shrugged. 'I never asked. She won't talk about him.'

'Mmm. When girls get knocked up ...'

'They was both really young,' Rose said.

'Did he offer to marry her?'

'I dunno. Her mum and dad threw her out. Mind you, they come to see us when I was little.'

'Really?'

'The old girl, she read to me from a book,' Rose said.

'So your grandma could read?'

'Yeah.'

'Then why can't your mum or you?' Tilly asked.

'I dunno. Just looks like a jumble to me, writing does. Dermot tried to teach me when we was first married but I can't keep them letters in me head. Make no sense to me they don't.'

They sat in silence, watching the fire glow in the darkness. Eventually Tilly said, 'You are happy here, aren't you, Rosie?'

She smiled. 'I think so,' she said. 'Don't see no one much but Morry's doing well at school and Dermot likes his job. It's cleaner out here than it is in London.'

'Yes, but are you happy?' Tilly reiterated. On the one hand

Rose said she was, while on the other she seemed to be saying she was lonely.

'I do miss you and all the girls up Soho,' she said eventually. 'But I couldn't carry on with that life, not now I've got a kid.'

And yet she could have carried on if she'd done what she'd originally planned when she got pregnant, which was to go and live with Tilly. They would both have kept on working and shared the child-care. Tilly had felt rejected when Dermot had supplanted her. But she could see from the look on Rosie's face when she broke the news of her marriage that she was in love with Dermot. What a pity her husband was queer. And even though Dermot had promised Tilly, through gritted teeth, that he'd never do anything to put his life with Rose and Morry in jeopardy, Tilly knew just how hard that promise was going to be to keep. She knew more pretty young boys who'd vowed to be celibate because they didn't want to be caught by the police than she could number. Not one of whom had kept his promise.

'You should come up to my gaff and stay sometimes,' Tilly said. 'I'm sure your Dermot could look after Morry on his own for a couple of days.'

Rose frowned. 'Oh, I don't think he'd like that,' she said. 'And anyway, who'd make his tea?'

Thanks to Gibrail's brother-in-law Issa, Bernie had taken what she hoped were some brilliant shots of Midnight Mass at the Church of the Nativity. And even though she hadn't understood a word of what had been spoken or intoned, she'd found the whole experience profoundly moving.

Probably what had impressed her the most was the way that the faith of the worshippers appeared to be so strong in the face of their disrupted and, in many cases, impoverished lives. Her own experience of religion against a backdrop of want had been far more negative. Rather than sustaining their lives, the Catholic Church had, to Bernie's way of thinking, only ever oppressed her family with its rules and prejudices – many of which appeared utterly meaningless to her.

Now lying in an old-fashioned brass bedstead in a room Gibrail told her had once been used by Field Marshal Montgomery, Bernie looked out of the small window which gave a view down onto the big, central courtyard. A fire was still burning there and she could see several figures gathered around it. Were they telling stories to each other like the traditional Arab story-tellers of old? Or were they simply unable to sleep, like Bernie was?

The following day she would have to accompany Gibrail back into Israel. If she was lucky, she'd first have the morning free to wander around the streets of Bethlehem and see what people ate, drank and did there on Christmas morning. Not that Rafka and her family would leave her on her own for very long, if at all. Bernie knew that a huge breakfast had been planned, which could very easily take all morning to eat. There would also be present-giving, which made her feel anxious. Issa and Rafka might have a big, fine house but there was very little in it and money, she knew, was tight. She'd asked Gibrail what she might bring from Israel for his sister and her family and he'd replied, 'Candles, for the power cuts.'

She'd bought as many as she could, all wrapped in brightly coloured tissue paper. But still, it seemed such a little thing to give them. She just hoped they hadn't spent too much of their hard-earned money on presents for her. Although knowing Arab hospitality as she did, that seemed like a vain hope. Gibrail, she knew, had come with many, many gifts for his family and, he'd hinted, for her too. Seeing him watching Mass celebrated in the Church of the Nativity, she had been struck, not for the first time, by how joyful he always looked in the face of what had to be a difficult life. As an East Ender, Bernie knew all about making the best of a bad situation, but Gibrail seemed to go to a place way beyond that. He, she felt, actually relished his life, although it was so hard. He was also very handsome, which was something she found herself thinking about more and more.

If he'd ever come on to her, perhaps she wouldn't have been so tantalised, but he always behaved like the perfect gentleman, which only made it worse. Had she come here to Bethlehem not so much to take photographs as to be with Gibrail? It was a disturbing thought and one she didn't want to pursue. And yet it was part of why she stayed awake. Was he out there now, round the fire, telling stories with his family? Or was he lying in his bed somewhere thinking about her? After all Heinrich, who was nobody's fool, was of the opinion the young man was in love with her.

Christmas Eve and they were at it! Dolly Adler could hear the raised voices of her son Solly and his wife Sharon through two closed doors. Still rowing. If they carried on like this, they'd wake Natalie who was expecting a visit from Father Christmas.

Solly had piled up all his daughter's many presents in his mother's bedroom until they could be taken downstairs in the morning. Dolly switched her bedside light on and looked at them. Most were from her, Solly and her other son, Ben. Sharon hadn't contributed much, but then she never did. Selfish cow. The row this evening was about how she'd wanted to go out earlier and Solly had stopped her. She'd said she wanted to go down the Ten Bells with her cousin Helen, but she'd lied for Sharon in the past when she'd gone out somewhere to meet men. Because that was what Sharon did and, if Dolly wasn't too much mistaken, there was a particular man in Sharon's sights now.

It had been Dolly's sister, Evelyn, who had seen them together at the East Ham Palace, watching variety turns: Sharon and some bloke all dressed up like a dog's dinner. They were laughing and all over each other apparently. She hadn't told Solly, although he probably knew. He'd known about all the others. But what could he do? He'd known what Sharon was like before he'd married her and yet he'd gone ahead and now there was little Natalie to consider. But even so ...

People got divorced all the time and it was no bad thing, in Dolly's opinion. Not that she'd ever married Solly and Ben's dad. That bastard had already had a wife and kids! And although she'd wanted something better than a single-parent household for her boys, she had the feeling that kicking out Natalie's no-good mother could only be a good thing.

Suddenly the argument got much worse and she heard her son scream, 'So go to him, then! I don't fucking care!'

There was a silence then, followed by the slamming of an inside door closely followed by the front door. The sound of weeping accompanied this. Dolly left it a while before she went to see her son. Slumped in his armchair by the fire, Solly had his head in his hands. He didn't even look up when she put her hand on his shoulder. She doubted he even noticed.

Aggie was asleep and snoring like a train. Auntie Kitty looked as if she was asleep but Becky knew she wasn't. The body just lightly touching Becky's was tense and she wondered what was keeping her bedfellow awake. At Christmas time people tended to think about the year that was nearly over and their loved ones, especially those that were not present.

Although it was difficult to talk to Auntie Kitty about Bernie, mainly because she always lost her temper when the subject was raised, it was at least possible. Talk of her dead husband Pat always brought tears to her eyes but she liked it when people shared memories of him. The only person she never talked about was her eldest son, Joey.

As a child Joey Lynch had been a pleasant enough boy if never as chatty or funny as his brothers, Dermot and Little Paddy. It had been when he'd started working in the docks that things had turned sour for him. Becky had never known what really happened. Back in the thirties there had been whispers about how Joey had got in with Uncle Pat's old foreman, Artie Cross. Well known for his ability to get hold of goods other blokes couldn't, Cross was a thief and a bully and had a following of blokes who were both afraid of and admired him. Joey had been one of them.

When a local furrier's premises had been burgled, Cross and his mob had been in the frame for a while, along with Joey. In the course of the raid, a neighbour, Mr Lamb, had been punched about the head and subsequently died. Shortly after that, Joey Lynch had disappeared. Bernie had said very little to Becky about it and even less, she knew, to Rose. But deep in her soul, Becky felt that Bernie knew more than she was telling, which made her wonder whether Joey had killed Mr Lamb.

Artie Cross and his mob still worked in the West India Dock and nobody had ever been arrested for Lamb's murder. But then, even if people knew the truth, it was unlikely they'd tell. Nobody 'grassed' in the East End when all those involved were their 'own'. Grassing could kill off the standing of whole families and ruin businesses that had relied on local custom for decades.

Was Joey Lynch dead? He could be, although he could

just as easily be holed up somewhere in another part of the country. He may even be abroad. But Christmas was one of those times when people turned up unexpectedly. A lot of Christmas stories relied upon that notion and Becky wondered whether this year, or next year, or sometime soon, Joey might show his face to his mother and his siblings. Maybe he already had and she didn't know of it?

She turned over and heard Auntie Kitty's breathing finally change. Asleep at last, maybe she was dreaming about seeing her son again – or her husband – or Bernie …

Chapter 6

22 July 1952
Alexandria, Egypt

'Apparently there's going to be some sort of party here tonight.'

Bernie looked up at the palace overlooking the Mediterranean. This was the King of Egypt's summer home, the Montaza, and it was both beautiful and strange.

'It's amazing.'

Her guide, a middle-aged British Army officer called Captain Lennox, smiled at her. 'His Majesty King Farouk is a person addicted to parties,' he said. Then he added, 'Amongst other things.'

Bernie raised an eyebrow. Heinrich had told her that his old friend Malcolm Lennox was a respected 'Egypt hand' who knew all the ins and outs and gossip surrounding the British-controlled country. 'Oh?' she said, to encourage him to tell her more.

Lennox laughed. 'Oh, if I told you everything, Heinrich

would accuse me of corrupting you. Suffice it to say, old Farouk has an eye for the ladies and a very unfortunate relationship with gambling.'

'Still manages to keep palaces like this though,' Bernie said.

'For now,' Lennox answered cryptically.

With the help of Heinrich and his friends, Bernie had finally achieved her dream of visiting Egypt. As an Israeli citizen her lover couldn't accompany her because the two countries were still officially at war. But he'd made sure she wasn't going to be alone in what could be a dangerous country – there were rumours that certain military officers, including the glamorous Colonel Nasser, may be about to stage a coup against Farouk.

But that had been far from Bernie's mind when she had arrived at the Port of Alexandria the previous day to find her very smart, forty-five-year-old English escort waiting for her. So far Lennox had taken her to see the fifteenth-century Qaitbey Fort via a long walk along Alexandria's famous Corniche, plus the spooky Kom Ash Shuqqafa catacombs. Alexandria's seafront was like something she imagined one might see in the South of France. Elegant and thronged with smart cars carrying beautiful people, it was also the site of her hotel, the ornate and expensive Cecil.

Lennox, shading his eyes against the powerful afternoon sun, said, 'Do you fancy a drink before we shove off for Cairo? I know an excellent place five minutes away that serves the best whisky sour in the world.'

'I think I'd rather have lemonade in this heat,' Bernie said.

'Oh, they can trot out a soft drink at the old Cap d'Or.'

'Then yes,' she said.

He took her arm. 'Then let's get to it,' he said. 'I could do with a good snifter before driving down to Cairo.'

They began to walk. Cairo ... Just hearing the name made Bernie want to squeak with delight. Ever since she'd been a small child she'd been fascinated by Egypt. It had been a passion she had shared with her father, who had followed the excavations of Howard Carter at Tutankhamun's tomb fanatically back in the 1920s. He'd always said that one day she would visit the country and now she was here, albeit with a rather bitter taste in her mouth.

Things had deteriorated badly between Bernie and Heinrich in the past eighteen months. Ever since she'd gone to Bethlehem with Gibrail Khoury at Christmas back in 1950, in fact. Until Gibrail finally left the *Jerusalem Post* at the end of 1951, her relationship with her lover had been dire. Forever accusing her of pining after the Arab, he couldn't be persuaded that there was nothing between Bernie and Gibrail.

But then that hadn't been strictly true. Although the young man had never suggested anything inappropriate to Bernie, she had known she'd wanted him to. She'd also known that Gibrail wanted that too. But it had never happened and now, it was said, he was in Jordan with his family and good luck to him. Gradually things with Heinrich were beginning to improve, which made Bernie happy. She did love him. She just wasn't sure whether she was still in love with him.

Rose put a paper bag down on the cabinet beside her mother's bed.

'Them's some plums from the garden,' she said. 'You want to eat them to build yourself up.'

Nell Larkin turned her head to look at her daughter and said, 'Thank you, chavvy. I need a bit of good hobben.'

'They not feed you proper in here?' Rose asked.

'Like bloody shit,' Nell said. 'Wouldn't give it to the dog.'

When she'd finally been diagnosed with tuberculosis back in May, Nell Larkin had been sent to a sanatorium to recover. As in the past, treatment consisted of rest, plenty of fresh air and what was supposed to be 'good' food. Added to this regimen was a course of one of the new antibiotics, Streptomycin. It worked like magic on patients who hadn't had the disease for very long, but for someone like Nell, it was going to take longer. And although being treated out at Black Notley Sanatorium in Essex meant that she was closer to her daughter, she didn't like it at all.

'Bloody countryside,' she would grumble. 'Full of things as want to bite you and not a pub for miles.'

That said, the patients were given a bottle of Guinness once a day, but only one.

When Nell had first been admitted, she'd been on a 'complete rest' regime which meant that she'd had to lie flat on her bed and do nothing except eat, sleep and go to the toilet. As the antibiotics began to work, this changed to 'partial rest', which meant that she could sit up and be taken outside the ward in a bath-chair.

Nell's biggest problem had been the lack of cigarettes. But she'd eventually found a nurse willing to 'help her out', although she had to smoke her ciggies out of view of Dr Grainger, the consultant. This often necessitated hiding herself behind a large flower urn.

'You have to behave yourself, Mum,' Rose said. 'Or you won't get well and then they'll keep you in here.'

Nell shook her head stubbornly.

'I mean it, Mum,' Rose continued. 'Belly-aching about the food all the time and smoking – I know you do it.'

'I . . .'

'And when you get out, you gotta come home with me and

Dermot and Morry. There's bad air in London, it'll make you poorly again.'

Nell waved a hand. 'I won't need no looking after,' she said. 'Just got to get 'ome, that's what I need.'

'You can't go back to Ten Bells Street,' Rose said. 'That damp flat! That 'orrible lavvy! Ain't healthy, Mum!'

Nell crossed her arms over her thin chest. 'Gotta get back to work. My Blessed can't be left on her own forever. She'll look after me when I go home. Her and Kitty Lynch.'

'Auntie Kitty goes to work, she ain't got time,' Rose said. 'And you're supposed to look after Blessed, not the other way around.'

Nell shrugged. 'Dunno why you come if all you gonna do is nag at me,' she said. 'Don't even bring me grandson with you.'

'You know I can't bring Morry here 'cause of what you got!' Rose said. 'Don't want him catching it. Mrs Linden what lives down on Lower Road agreed to have him until I get home.'

'Why can't your husband?'

'Der's at work, Mum, don't be daft! Anyway, he's got to go up to his mum's when he finishes at the farm tonight.'

'What for?'

Rose shrugged. 'To see her,' she said. 'He goes up about once a month.'

'So why don't you and Morry go with him?'

'I don't go up that way much,' Rose said. 'Especially now you're not there. I see Becky when she comes down with Mr Shapiro. What do I need to go up London for?'

Nell could think of a few things, although she knew her daughter didn't like pubs or the sort of men who frequented them regularly. So she said nothing. But she thought lots – mainly about how drunk her son-in-law probably got when he went up to see his mum in Spitalfields. Rose had turned into a boring little housewife since she'd had Morry. Nell could understand why her old man might want to go out on the razzle once in a while.

Things were changing in Soho, so people said. But Tilly couldn't see it. Still the same old pimps walking up and down Rupert Street, the White Horse on the corner with Archer Street full of strippers getting a few G and Ts in before the evening's performances. The Duchess of Greek Street buying flowers for some boy she'd no doubt picked up on the Meat Rack at Piccadilly Circus. And then there was Dermot Lynch . . .

He came out of an anonymous-looking door next to the tobacconist's. Looking up at the building he'd come out of, Tilly realised it wasn't somewhere she knew, which was unusual. Tilly knew all the dives, strip clubs, brothels and private bars in Soho – or so she thought.

'What you doing slumming it here?' Tilly asked as she drew alongside Dermot.

He hadn't seen her approach. When he registered her, he sighed and rolled his eyes. 'Nothing for you to worry about,' he said.

'Big butch thing like you should be back on the farm, shouldn't you?'

Tilly could see loathing in Dermot's eyes. But also fear.

'I'm not here for sex if that's what you think,' he said.

'Really?'

'Really.'

'So what's so interesting about this gaff?' Tilly said, nodding her head towards the building Dermot had just left.

'None of your business.'

'Isn't it? I'd beg to differ. It is my business if it concerns my friend Rosie Red.'

'Well, it don't!'

He made as if to walk away. But Tilly grabbed the arm of his jacket.

'Oi! Let go!'

'Not until you tell me what you're up to,' Tilly said. 'Boys don't come round here unless they want something and I want to know what that is.'

Dermot leaned in close to his tormentor and whispered, 'Carry on like this and I'll shout me head off. I'll have the coppers do you for soliciting ...'

Tilly felt the wind go out of her sails. Although she should have done, she hadn't expected Dermot to react as he had. She knew he didn't like her, but she also knew that he put up with her for Rose's sake. Getting her friend arrested would definitely upset Rose. But then would he really do it?

'You tell me ...'

'One more word and every copper from here to Piccadilly Circus'll be on your tail,' Dermot hissed. 'I'm a married bloke, remember, and you're a washed-up old drag queen.'

And then he shook Tilly's hand off his jacket like it was dirt and walked away.

Alone and shaken, she made her way to the White Horse for a restorative gin. She would never have thought that Dermot Lynch had such spite in him! It had to mean that whatever he'd been up to was something really bad.

The man lurking outside his house was known to Moritz Shapiro. But the old man didn't offer to let him in, nor did the man on the pavement outside ask. He was waiting for Becky, was Solly Adler. Usually if he came to the house he had the decency to bring his little daughter with him. Although to be fair it was about Natalie that he came – humbly, cap in hand, asking for Becky's medical expertise. And yet even if his daughter couldn't see it herself, Moritz could see the light in Adler's eye every time he looked at Nurse Rebekah Shapiro. Her father didn't like it.

Moritz walked into his kitchen so he didn't have to look at Adler anymore. In his youth, when he'd been a leading light in the Communist Party, Solly had been passionate and handsome. Now, after sustaining severe wounds in the Spanish Civil War, and especially since he'd got married, the man looked worn out and broken. These days his face only lit up when he looked at Becky. Moritz knew he'd have to have words with her. Not that she'd do anything wrong, he knew that. But there had been a time when she'd been sweet on Adler who hadn't even noticed her back then. He'd only had eyes for Bernadette Lynch and she wasn't coming back to Britain any time soon.

Anyway the man had a wife now, for what she was worth, and more importantly a child. That said, Rebekah was vulnerable because she was lonely. Now that Bernie was overseas and Rose out in the country, his daughter didn't have anyone she was really close to nearby. And the district was falling apart. Spitalfields these days wasn't what it was either before or during the war. So many people had moved out and some of the flats and houses had been empty for over a year. Who would want to live in a house without a bathroom? And, in some streets still, without electricity. New flats were being built all over the country for people who wanted up-to-date services. They deserved them. The courage Moritz had seen exhibited by ordinary people during the war made him think that almost nothing the government could do for their poorest people would be too much.

And yet he stayed in the area and he knew he always

would. Admittedly he had a bathroom and electricity but what good was that if you were the only resident left on your street? But then it was his street. It was his house on his street and he knew he lacked the will and the strength to leave it . . . even if Becky did really need to move somewhere with a bit more life. Not that she'd ever said anything to that effect. But he was tired of seeing how sad she looked so much of the time. Whenever Solly Adler appeared, Moritz feared for his daughter.

It was about a hundred and forty miles from Alexandria to Cairo and although Lennox chatted companionably for most of the way, Bernie found herself drifting off. The heat and the ever-present dust were enough to knock the most hardened traveller flat and Bernie was hardly one of those. Although she loved living in the Middle East, the heat was hard for blonde-haired Bernie to bear. In the early days she'd tried her hand at sun-bathing but had just ended up with bright red skin, blisters and headaches. Now, wherever she went, she took a hat with her and covered her body in a loose shirt, her legs in long trousers.

Rolling down the car window to get some air, Bernie was nearly deafened by the sound of a truck overtaking them. She rolled the window up again.

'Sorry about that,' Lennox said. 'They don't take too many prisoners on the roads here and the horn is used as a lethal weapon.'

'It's so hot,' Bernie sighed.

'Can't be helped, old girl.'

They passed villages that were little more than collections of mud-huts. Bernie spotted many donkeys but not many women. Those she did see were muffled up in voluminous dresses and scarves, their faces all but invisible. Men dressed in long white or brown galabeyas carried large amphorae full of oil or water, their feet unshod, their faces weathered by wind and sand and time. Even Jerusalem didn't give Bernie the feeling of antiquity that every scene in Egypt evoked. Sometimes, if she half closed her eyes, she could almost imagine herself back in ancient times.

'Of course, we'll bypass central Cairo,' Lennox said. 'Be like bloody murder this time of day. Donkey carts and modern cars don't go well together, in my opinion.' He smiled at her. 'Giza's just outside the city so we'll go right there.'

'I do appreciate your taking time to show me around,' Bernie said.

'My pleasure,' he said. 'You know, Heinrich really looked out for me in the last days of the Palestine Mandate – the British squaddie not exactly being flavour of the month with the Israelis back then.'

Heinrich had been one of those who had opposed British rule in Palestine. But Bernie knew he had always shied away from using violence, unlike some of his fellow Israelis.

'He's a good man,' Bernie said.

'One of the best, I'd say.'

Within a few minutes she fell asleep again. She dreamed of home, which was rare these days, but then maybe dreaming about London made her cool down. When she woke, she couldn't remember what she'd dreamed about specifically. It was more of a feeling that she'd revisited home in her mind than an actual memory. And that would have made her sad had she not seen something that had been her heart's desire, from a child, right in front of her.

'Oh,' she said as the car pulled up beside her hotel. 'I can see the Pyramids!'

*

'She ain't getting on with it that well, to be honest,' Solly Adler said as he stood in front of Becky, clutching his cap in front of him.

'It's all down to persistence,' she replied. 'These new nebulisers are very good, but Natalie really must be encouraged to use it even if she feels she can't.'

He shook his head. 'She screams if we try to put anything over her face.'

'You and Mrs Adler should sit down with her calmly when she isn't having an attack and let her use it in a situation that isn't life-threatening,' Becky said. 'She needs to get used to it while she's calm, to learn that it isn't something that is going to hurt her.'

Solly shook his head. 'I don't know ... '

Becky took her house keys out of her bag. 'You're going to have to, Mr Adler,' she said. 'If you don't then Natalie isn't going to improve.'

'I know ... '

Becky put her key in the door. 'I'm sorry, I have to go.'

He took a step forward. 'Couldn't you ... '

'Mr Adler, I've no wish to cause trouble by coming to your home,' Becky said. 'Your wife has made it quite clear she doesn't trust me. Please don't pursue this. Speak to Dr Klein. He can arrange for a district nurse to come around. Now, excuse me, I have things to do.'

She left him on the doorstep, still holding his cap pathetically before him. Solly Adler had been such a fighter in his youth, it made her cringe to see what he had become. She walked into the kitchen where her father was making tea.

'Oh, a cuppa,' she said as she sat down at the kitchen table. 'That's just what I need.'

'Coming up,' her father said. 'Did you see Mr Adler outside? I think he was waiting to speak to you.'

'Yes,' she said. 'About Natalie. They're having trouble getting her to use her nebuliser.'

Her father put a big mug of tea in front of her and then sat down. While she took her first sip, he said, 'You know, Rebekah, you should stay away from that man. He has marital troubles.'

'I know,' she said. 'Sharon Adler doesn't like me and the feeling is mutual.'

'And the husband, he has eyes for you, I think,' Moritz said.

Becky sighed. 'Maybe,' she said. 'But you know, Papa, even if I felt the same way about him, I wouldn't do anything about it. I know his marriage is not a good one, but it's still a marriage and they have a child. He just asked me whether I would go around to their flat and teach little Natalie how to use her nebuliser. With the best will in the world, I had to say no.'

'Good.'

'I told him to go and see Dr Klein and ask for a district nurse to call.' Becky paused for a moment then added, 'I do know he's using his daughter as an excuse to come and see me.'

'It isn't fair on you,' her father said.

'It's not fair on anyone.'

'And there are stories about his wife ...'

'I don't listen to them,' Becky said.

Her father shrugged. 'I'm an old man. I hear things. Gossip. It's said Sharon Adler now has one special man in her life.'

Becky shook her head. 'It's not my business.'

'I only say it because knowledge is power,' he said. 'To know the true situation with Mr Adler and his wife will put you still more on your guard.'

'Don't worry about me, Papa,' Becky said. 'I am well and truly on my guard against Solly Adler.'

*

'Can you go out to the Pyramids at night?'

Bernie and Lennox had chosen to eat their dinner in the gardens of the Mena House Hotel, close to the swimming pool. And although the food hadn't been exactly exciting, the provision of a seemingly endless jugs of Pimm's was making up for it. She refilled their glasses.

'I'd counsel against it,' Lennox replied to her question. 'What with things being the way they are.'

'Oh.'

Alexandria had been full of rumours about a possible uprising against the King, but at the same time no one could quite believe that it would happen. King Farouk, a puppet of the British, must surely be a permanent fixture. A man who devoured bowls of cream and dancing girls with equal appetite, corrupt and gluttonous as he was, the idea of Egypt without him seemed impossible.

Lennox offered Bernie a cigarette, which she took, and then lit both their smokes. 'I wouldn't venture out there myself at night, much less with a lady in tow,' he said. 'We'll go in the morning. Tragically, every camel ride *wallah* and King Tut relic salesman will also be there, but we'll ignore them.'

Bernie smiled.

Somehow she'd thought that the Pyramids of Giza would be lit up at night, but all she could see of them now as the sun set were some indistinct outlines far into the desert. Although her first sight of the ancient monuments had been breathtaking, now she felt let down. She was also very tired.

'Do you think that any of the men who sell antiquities are actually selling the real thing?' she asked after a moment.

Lennox laughed at the idea. 'No,' he said. 'Certainly not stuff from Tut's tomb, that's for sure! Most of that tat comes from workshops in the backstreets of Port Said. Mind you, I do believe you can pick up some genuine mummy bandages from some of them.'

'Really?'

'Really. When the British first built the railways here in Egypt they ran on coal, of course. But when that was in short supply, the Egyptians used mummies ...'

'What?'

'Oh, yes,' he said. 'Not that we, the Brits, are any better. Apparently back in the nineteenth century, apothecaries at home used to sell something called "Mumia" that was supposed to cure something or other. Made out of ground-up Egyptian mummies.'

'That's terrible!' Bernie said. 'Those were someone's ancestors!'

Lennox shrugged. 'Needs must, I suppose,' he said. Then yawned. 'Oh, sorry! Long day.'

'You must be tired after all that driving.'

'Shattered,' he said.

She took a sip from her glass, watching as he poured his tumbler of Pimm's down his throat in one go. When he'd finished, Bernie said, 'Why don't you go and rest?'

'What? And leave you ...'

'I'll be fine,' she said. 'I know where my room is. I'd just like to finish my drink at leisure, have a few more minutes in the open air before I turn in.'

'Well, if you're sure?'

'I am.'

He rose to his feet. 'Then so be it,' he said. 'What time do you want to meet for breakfast?'

'Eight?'

'Eight hundred hours it is.' He saluted her, which made Bernie laugh. 'Tomorrow the Pyramids, the Sphinx ... and probably a rather dodgy ride on a camel,' he said then left her to it.

After he had gone, Bernie finished her cigarette, drank some of her Pimm's and then closed her eyes.

Chapter 7

Mrs Linden was a nice enough woman but her eldest kid, Stan, was a bit of a bully. And although Morry got on well with the other Linden boys, Stan gave them all a hard time, frequently cuffing them around the head and pushing them over whenever he could. Mrs Linden didn't see this as anything more than just kids mucking about, but Rose didn't like it because whenever Morry came home from there he was subdued. Hopefully, soon her mum could come out of the sanatorium and then she'd be able to stop Morry going to the Lindens' place. In the meantime, she hadn't much choice about it. Although she liked Hullbridge and people there were generally kind, nobody except Mrs Linden was prepared to look after Morry from time to time. Rose suspected it was because of Dermot. Just before they'd left London, notes had started to appear on flats for rent, saying 'No blacks, no dogs, no Irish'. Or so Dermot had told her and, although he didn't speak with an Irish accent, his name was as Irish as the colour green.

Morry went to bed without his usual story read to him by his dad. Rose knew the little boy, who had been able to read for three years now, found it hard to understand why his mother wouldn't read to him too. But try as she might, she just couldn't do it. Perhaps she was too old? That's what her mum always said if anyone asked her about reading and writing. *I'm too old for all that now.*

Once Morry was asleep, Rose went out into the garden and sat on the ground. She missed Dermot when he was up at his mother's place. Although they never had sex, she missed cuddling up to him in their bed. She loved him and he loved her and what they did or didn't do was their own business and didn't need explaining. Whatever the reason for it. Although people reckoned she didn't know about her husband, Rose thought perhaps she did. She'd been around men with eyes for other men often enough when she'd worked at the Windmill to know one when she saw one. But that didn't matter. Dermot provided for them, and he loved her and Morry, and she was glad that he never came to her for sex because she'd had enough of all that years ago when she'd first got pregnant at fifteen. That had ended in an illegal abortion, which was something she never even wanted to think about. Now it was just her and Morry and Dermot, as it should be.

Rose looked out towards the darkening river and thought about how much she missed her man.

There was a tingling feeling, as if someone was looking at her. Bernie opened her eyes and indeed someone was staring straight at her.

'Gibrail?'

Surely she'd had too much sun. The last time she'd seen

Gibrail Khoury had been the day he left the *Jerusalem Post*. Bernie blinked, but he still appeared to be standing before her. And he was smiling.

'Yes,' he said. 'It is me.'

Dressed in a light linen suit, Gibrail looked relaxed and, in contrast to the poor Arab trainee she'd known at the *Post*, prosperous.

Bernie indicated that he should sit down. The garden of the Mena Hotel was empty now, except for Bernie, Gibrail and a few wandering waiters. She looked at her watch and saw that it was almost eleven o'clock.

'I saw you across the garden, sleeping,' he said. 'At first I wonder whether it really is you – and it is!'

Bernie shook her head. 'It's amazing!' she said. 'What are you doing here?'

'Ah, you first,' he said.

Bernie offered him a cigarette and they both lit up.

'I've always wanted to visit Egypt,' she said. 'Of course, Heinrich couldn't come, which is why I've never been. But a friend of his, an English officer, agreed to show me around for a few days.'

'So you are tourist?'

'Yes, I suppose so,' she said. 'And you?'

'Business,' he said. As he spoke he touched the very ornate watch on his wrist. The way he was dressed, the way his hair was brilliantined to within an inch of its life, this wasn't the Gibrail Bernie first knew. She was a little ashamed of how much she liked this new appearance of his.

'What kind of business?' Bernie asked.

'I have an uncle in Cairo,' Gibrail said as if this in some way explained his presence.

'What does he do?' Bernie asked.

And then Gibrail changed the subject. He said, 'How would you like to see the Pyramids now? At night?'

'You're pissed.'

'Yup.'

Dermot staggered across the threshold and cuddled his mother.

'Christ!' Kitty said. 'You smell like a bleedin' brewery! Where've you been?'

'Nowhere.'

She was on her own. Both Marie and Aggie were out. This meant she could let rip at her son without anyone else having to put up with it. So she did.

'Don't give me that!' she said as she pushed him away from her and reared back her head to look at him. 'God Almighty, you look as if you've been beaten up!'

'Then maybe I have,' he said, smiling.

There was no reason for Dermot to smile and he knew it. Although he hadn't been beaten up, he'd been roughed around a bit by some tosser in Dirty Dick's up by Liverpool Street Station. Bloke had called him a 'poof' and so technically Dermot had started it. He'd won too. The other bloke wouldn't be calling anyone anything until he got some new teeth.

Kitty pushed him into his father's old chair and put the kettle onto the range to boil.

'What you doing getting into fights?' she asked.

He shrugged.

'Don't give me that, silly bollocks!' Kitty said. 'You, a husband and a father, scrapping and drunk as a fucking sack!' She lit a cigarette.

'Gi' us a smoke?' Dermot held out his hand.

'Get your own!' Kitty said. But then relented and gave him a cigarette.

When she'd made tea and poured it out into cups, Kitty sat down next to her son and said, 'Why'd you come up here if all you do is get pissed? You were hammered last time you come to stay too. What's going on? You got something you want to tell me?'

'No.' He sipped his tea.

'Remember, I am your mother and so I know when you're lying,' she said.

'I'm not lying.'

He sounded fourteen years old again and they both knew it.

'Ah, grow up!' Kitty said. 'This is me you're talking to, not some daft bleeder in a pub! You and Rosie having problems, are you?' She crossed her arms over her thin chest. 'You should have another little 'un. Put a stop to all this nonsense, that would! Focus your mind, do kids. I should know ...'

'It's got nothing to do with Rosie or Morry,' Dermot said.

'So what is it then?'

What indeed? He'd have liked, in a way, to be able to say it was the simple fact that he was a homosexual man living in a heterosexual world. But he knew that would send his mum over the edge – and it wasn't even the whole story. Because that was far worse than his just being what they called in the East End, an 'Iron Hoof'. That was nothing at all compared to what Dermot was involved in.

It wasn't called the Great Pyramid for nothing. Even in the dark, Bernie could see that the structure before her was massive.

'You know it is Egyptian Christians who look after the ancient things?' Gibrail said to her as she stroked one of the enormous stone blocks at the bottom of the pyramid. 'Not the Muslims ... Egyptian Christians, called Copts.'

'What do you mean, look after?' Bernie asked.

'They guard the ancient places, Karnak and the Valley of the Kings.'

'So are they here somewhere?'

She'd seen him pay a man in a turban when they'd first approached the Pyramids.

'No,' he said. 'He is gone now.'

So he'd paid the man off. But why? They were just looking. That said, it was an odd thing to be doing so at night, with no lights around. If she thought about where they were too hard, Bernie found herself feeling slightly spooked.

'There are some people who say that the Copts still worship the old gods in secret,' Gibrail said.

'Do you think they do?'

'I don't know,' he said. 'People say the Copts are the real Egyptians, the children of the Pharaohs. If they are ... '

If they were then Bernie knew she'd like to meet them. Thousands of miles away in London in the 1930s, she had devoured library books about the old Egyptian gods, Hathor and Horus, Isis and Osiris. Gods so powerful they weighed the hearts of even the Pharaohs themselves as they decided who was and was not pure enough to proceed to eternal life in the Afterlife.

Gibrail said, 'How are you?'

'Me? Fine,' Bernie said. What else did you reply to a handsome man in the dark outside a pyramid that was thousands of years old?

'And Mr Simpson?'

She said, 'Heinrich is fine too.'

'You wish he was here?'

She felt a sudden chill. 'He's Israeli so he can't come.'

'That's not what I asked.'

She'd avoided the question and he knew it. But why?

'It's not possible, so I haven't thought about it,' she said.

'Yes, but if it were possible?'

He had moved closer to her now. She was almost as tall as he was and after a tough East End childhood more than capable of looking after herself. That said, this was Gibrail. He'd never hurt her. So why did she suddenly feel threatened and was it by him or by the strength of her own feelings?

Eventually she said, 'Yes, that would have been nice, but . . .'

Gibrail took one step closer and kissed her. For a moment her mouth resisted his, but then it didn't.

When he eventually drew away from her, he said, 'And now?'

Bernie didn't even have to think. This time she moved towards him, took his face in her hands and kissed him with a passion she hadn't felt for a very long time.

Taking off their clothes and lying down together in the cool sand felt like the most natural thing in the world, as did the urgent way they made love.

She thought he was asleep as she crept into their bedroom. But Solly Adler was awake and he could smell the sex on her. As Sharon attempted to slip silently into bed beside him, he sat up and put the light on. With her lipstick smeared all over her face, she looked like a cross between a clown and some broken-down old alcoholic.

'Have you seen yourself?' he asked as she blinked under the pale light of the single bulb above her head.

When she spoke, her voice was slurred. 'I thought you was asleep.'

'You look like an old tom,' he said.

She laughed.

'Funny, is it?' he said. 'Where you been? I won't ask who you been with because it's this same fella you're always out with now.'

Sharon pulled the front of her dress down to expose the tops of her breasts and said, 'My lover! And we've been up West. That's where he lives, up West.'

'Oh, well, good for him!'

'Yeah, and he is good,' Sharon said. "Specially when it comes to getting it up!'

For a moment she carried on laughing then she stopped.

Solly, enraged and afraid of what he might do to her, turned away.

She said, 'Is that the best you've got? Bloody nothing?'

'Shut up,' he murmured.

But she was not to be silenced.

'Why'd'ya think I go elsewhere, eh?' she said. 'You don't love me, you never have. Thinking about that Lynch girl and now her mate, Nurse Shapiro.'

'I've never done nothing . . .'

'No, but you'd like to,' she said. 'I bet you'd get it up for her!'

Solly knew he was being taunted and so he said nothing. How he'd 'get it up' for anyone these days was a mystery to him. He hadn't had sex for years.

Sharon lurched towards him across the bed. 'He's like a ramrod, my bloke,' she said. She licked her lips. 'Bloody great big mouthful . . .'

Solly said, 'If you like his cock so much, then go and live with it!'

'I will,' she said. 'Can't take no more of you. You're fucking mad!'

'Yes, I am,' he said. 'I married you!'

He threw the dressing-gown she kept at the bottom of their bed at her.

'Take that and all your other things and get out my flat,' he said.

For a moment, she said nothing. In the past he'd always stopped short of chucking her out because of Natalie. Sharon used their child now to save herself.

'And what about our daughter?' she said. 'What's she going to do without her mother?'

'Oh, so you're not taking her with you then?'

Sharon felt her face turn pale. She'd never even considered leaving with Natalie. What would her Ronnie think about that? Not much, she imagined. She certainly couldn't turn up at his gaff with the girl in tow.

'Not thought about that, have you?' Solly said. 'But then you don't have to, because if you attempt to take Natalie out of here, I'll fucking kill you.'

For a moment they stayed where they were until Solly said, 'Well, go on then! Get your things and sod off.'

Sharon put as many clothes and as much make-up as she could squeeze into the old suitcase she'd brought with her when she'd first moved into the Adlers' flat. She thought about maybe saying something bitter about how her husband could be with Nurse Shapiro now, but then decided against it.

Once Sharon had shut the front door behind her, Solly heard his mum knock at his bedroom door.

'Son . . .'

'It's alright, Mum,' Solly said. 'Go back to bed. I'll tell you all about it in the morning.'

And then he cried. Not because Sharon had gone, but because his humiliation had lasted so long.

*

He walked her back to her hotel. The lights in the gardens were supplemented by what looked like fireworks in the sky. Bernie, in spite of the guilt that had overtaken her as soon as they'd got dressed, smiled. Gibrail did not.

'I will take you back to your room,' he said as they walked past the deserted swimming pool.

Heinrich had been Bernie's first and, until this meeting with Gibrail, only lover. This young man had showed her a passion she'd not witnessed before. Although she felt guilty about betraying Heinrich, she was also elated and, if she were honest, in love. Because finally having someone like Gibrail in her life was a revelation. It had been something she had missed out on so far. Real romantic love between her and a man near her own age, not someone old enough to be her father. Someone who wasn't too tired, too hot, too cold, worn out, infirm ...

'What ...' she began.

Gibrail put a finger to her lips.

'I will have to go from here tomorrow morning and so will you,' he said.

'Lennox is taking me to the Pyramids then,' Bernie said.

'No, no.'

'Yes!'

'No,' Gibrail said. 'No, tomorrow will be different. You see those lights in the sky?'

'The fireworks?' Bernie said.

'They are not fireworks, Bernie,' he replied. 'They are from tracer ammunition. Tonight the revolution begins and the Arab nation finally seizes its destiny.'

And when Bernie really looked at the lights in the sky, she could see that these weren't fireworks. She felt her heart begin to pound.

'Tomorrow the army under Colonel Nasser will take control of Egypt. Then we will make war on Israel.'

And with that he left her. At the main door to the hotel, he walked away and she knew, deep in her soul, she would never see him again. At that thought she had to stop herself from screaming.

Back in her hotel room, Bernie watched the lights in the sky and listened to the gunshots from nearby Cairo while sitting on her bed in a daze. Had Gibrail always been an Arab nationalist or had that happened since he'd come to Egypt? And what had their love-making meant? Heinrich had always said that Gibrail fancied her and Bernie, if she was honest with herself, had long had eyes for the handsome Arab. But was what had happened between them real or just a way for Gibrail to get back at the people who had 'taken' his country via Heinrich?

'Dermot?'

When they'd all been kids, Bernie had thrown stones up at Becky's bedroom window to get her attention without her father knowing. Now, it seemed, Bernie's brother was doing the same thing.

'Let us in!' Dermot said, keeping his voice as low as he could to avoid waking any of the neighbours up.

'It's two o'clock!' Becky said.

'It's important!' Dermot countered.

Putting on a candlewick dressing-gown, Becky crept down the stairs to the front door and let Dermot in. Then she led him through the house to the kitchen and shut the door behind her.

'Blimey, Der, what's going on?' Becky said as she filled the kettle at the sink and then put it on the stove to boil. Whatever it was, a cup of tea wouldn't hurt.

'I need to tell you something,' he said. 'I've thought and thought and I don't know who else I can turn to.'

Becky sat down. She pushed an ashtray across the table to her guest and Dermot lit a fag.

'Is it about Rosie?' she asked. 'Or Morry?'

'No, no.' He shook his head. 'They're both grand. It's just ...'

He was clearly struggling with whatever it was he had to say and so Becky took one of his hands.

'Just tell me,' she said.

He sighed and then he said, 'I've found our Joey.'

Becky felt her heart jolt. Like most people in Spitalfields, she had imagined that Joey Lynch was either dead or in prison.

'How?'

'When I brought Mum and the girls back after Christmas last year, I went up West to see whether I could get Rosie something nice in the sales,' he said. 'I saw him then.'

'Where?'

'Leicester Square. He was just leaving his gaff, which is near there. Can't tell you exactly where because, well, I promised him I'd not let on to anybody.'

Becky sat back in her chair and sighed.

'What's he doing?' she said.

'When I met him that first time, he was working for some Maltese bloke running books.'

'Betting?'

'Yeah. Up Walthamstow Dogs mainly. It's hooky, but then how could Joey get any other sort of work?'

'I don't know,' Becky said. 'He was never convicted of murdering Mr Lamb, was he?'

'No, but he run away and so ...' Dermot shrugged. 'I've tried to persuade him to come home, but he won't.'

'Do you think that Auntie Kitty would accept him?'

'I don't know. Every time I've come up to see Mum, I've been to see Joey too. But he's mixed up in some stuff . . . '

'With these Maltese men?'

Dermot shook his head. 'Yes and no,' he said. 'I don't know exactly what they do, but I know it's bad. They have girls, you know . . . '

'Working girls?'

'Yeah. On the streets. Joey does a bit with them too.'

'So he's a pimp?'

He shrugged.

'Dermot, you can't get involved in his life,' Becky said. She stood up because the kettle was boiling and made a pot of tea. 'You've got your own family now, Rosie and Morry.'

'Yeah, but Joey's family too.'

'Is he?'

Dermot looked up at her. 'He's me brother,' he said. 'I know you ain't got no brothers and sisters, Becky, but we're all joined by blood, you know?'

'I understand that you love Joey but if he's involved in bad things, you can't let him drag you down with him.'

'He wants to set up on his own, away from these Maltese fellas.'

'Doing what?'

Dermot shrugged. 'Same,' he said. 'Running girls, books . . . '

'Illegal things.' Becky shook her head. 'Dermot, you can't do that.'

'I know!'

'So?'

'If I leave Joey on his own it'll be much worse,' he said. 'If I'm there maybe I can . . . control him . . . '

Becky shook her head. 'Der, you won't be able to,' she said. 'What I remember about Joey is a young man who went his

89

own way. Uncle Pat didn't want him mixed up with Artie Cross and his gang of dishonest dockers, but that's the direction he took. He'll drag you down ...'

'Yeah, but if I can stop him ...'

'You won't be able to,' she said. 'I think you already know that, Der.'

He said nothing. Becky poured them each a cup of tea.

'You won't tell Mammy or the girls or anyone, will you?' he asked as she set his drink down in front of him.

Becky thought for a moment and then she said, 'I won't, provided you don't get mixed up in his life. If you do ...' She sat down. 'Even if you do, I won't, but I'll try and stop you. If not for your sake then for Rosie's and Morry's. They don't deserve to have your Joey in their lives and I think you know that.'

Bernie didn't know whether she'd slept or not when she left her room and went to meet Lennox for breakfast at eight. She'd heard some vehicles pull up outside the hotel in the early hours of the morning but, in spite of what he'd said about a 'revolution', the Gibrail who had made love to her was the one who would not leave her mind now. What they had experienced together had been so loving and so magical, he could not possibly have just used her, could he?

But Gibrail was nowhere to be seen and neither was Lennox. Instead Bernie found herself face to face with a man who said his name was Colonel Mostafa. Stern and abrupt, he told her that Egypt was now under a new administration. It was one, he said, that had no place in it for people, even non-Jews, visiting from the State of Israel.

'You will come with me now,' he said, 'and be repatriated back to Britain.'

'But I don't live in Britain!' Bernie said.

'You have a British passport,' Mostafa continued. Then he eyed her closely. 'Why you want to go back to the Israeli State?'

Was it a good idea to tell this stern and rather frightening-looking man that Israel was where she worked? Where she lived with her Jewish lover?'

Mostafa grabbed her arm. 'Come now,' he said. 'Your things will be sent on later.'

In spite of the fact the colonel was surrounded by a group of young soldiers Bernie imagined were his men, she pulled away from him.

'No!'

'You will do as I tell you!' he roared. 'You are a foreign national, you must leave this country at once!'

'And have you steal all my things?' she said. 'No. No, I will go and get my things and ...'

'Miss Lynch will accompany me back to my car and I will drive her to an appropriate border crossing,' Lennox said. Quite where he'd materialised from Bernie didn't know, but she was grateful for the intervention.

Mostafa said something in Arabic to which Lennox replied, aggressively, in the same language. Mostafa then told them both to go.

When they finally got away from the Free Officer colonel and his squad, Bernie said, 'What did you just say to him?'

'I told him you are one of Winston Churchill's nieces,' Lennox said. 'I pointed out it would be very unwise for a new, young country like Egypt to get involved in a diplomatic incident involving a relative of a British national hero.'

Bernie's mouth dropped open. 'Blimey, you've got a nerve!' she said.

Then she laughed and went on laughing as they grabbed her things from her room and drove away from the Pyramids.

Chapter 8

October 1952

Kitty was cleaning the kitchen floor to within an inch of its life. Marie, on her way to work, said to her, 'Mammy, why are you doing that? Our Bernie won't care if your floor's a bit iffy.'

Kitty, fag hanging out of the corner of her mouth, headscarf covering her rollers, rolled her eyes. 'This lino was put down before any of yous was born,' she said. 'If I don't scrub it every day it'll stink. Not that you and Madam Aggie'd ever notice.'

Marie left her mother to carry on scrubbing the unscrubbable. The flat hadn't changed a bit since Kitty and Pat had moved in back in the twenties. There was still no electric or hot water and the khazi was still out the back in the yard. Not a stick of new furniture had come into the place since 1930 and the lino she was insisting upon scrubbing wasn't much more than broken fragments. But she had to do something to keep herself entertained while she waited for her eldest girl to come home.

Ever since she'd left for Israel, Bernie had written every

week and even telephoned, via the Shapiros, a couple of times. But she'd never visited and, although Bernie had assured Kitty she was simply coming home for a holiday, her mother wondered. Her bloke had to be getting on a bit now and Kitty wondered how her daughter was doing, living with a man old enough to be her father. It was dangerous out there in the Middle East too. Bernie had been in Egypt when there'd been a military coup and they'd got rid of their King. Kitty was glad she'd thought her daughter safe in Israel at the time. Apparently, the girl had had a wonderful time in spite of the violence and even managed to get to see the Pyramids.

Kitty had always been too busy with the younger kids, the housework and the sewing she used to do at home when the children were too small, to take any interest in reading about things like that as Bernie loved to do. She'd never really understood what her daughter had seen in a load of old tombs. No doubt Bernie would tell her when she got home. If the two of them managed to get any time together.

As well as Bernie's own sisters, Becky Shapiro was mad to see her too; then there was Little Paddy and his tribe coming over from Tottenham at some point. At the end of the week Bernie was off to Essex to see Dermot, Rosie and Morry. Even Nell Larkin, Rose's mother, knew she was coming and had asked whether, if she had time, Bernie would visit her in the sanatorium. Everybody loved Bernie Lynch and everybody wanted to hear stories about her adventures abroad, because no one else was doing anything exciting in their lives that was for sure.

The car pulled up beside him but Dermot ignored it. He knew who was driving. He heard the window being rolled down.

'I ain't interested,' Dermot said without looking at the occupant of the vehicle.

The car moved along beside him, down the road leading to the old Anchor pub.

'Well then, you're gonna miss out,' Joey said.

'That's what you said when you conned me into doing the furrier's place over,' Dermot replied. 'Remember? The night Mr Lamb died?'

'That was amateur stuff,' Joey said. 'Artie Cross and his mob was just playing at it. This time I've got the right crew and the money's big.'

'I don't care.'

There was a woman in the back of Joey's car, but Dermot couldn't see her face. One of his tarts.

'So you go off and do your job and forget about me,' Dermot said. 'I ain't stopping ya. '

'Ah, Der, come on!' his brother called after a minute. 'Don't you wanna have enough gilt to buy a proper house for Rosie and young Morry? Do you wanna work baling hay and milking sheep the rest of your life?'

'You milk cows, bell-end!' Dermot said.

'How should I know?'

Dermot kept on walking and the car kept on following until finally he put his hand on the edge of the open window and looked into his brother's face.

'Me answer's no,' he said.

'Weren't when we first started talking about it,' Joey said.

'No, well, that was then,' Dermot said. 'I've had a chance to think since and the answer's still no.'

Joey shrugged. 'Your loss.'

'You'll find another driver,' Dermot said. 'Ten a penny we are. See ya around.' Then he looked into the back of the car and tipped his head at Joey's passenger. 'Miss.'

It was only when his brother had driven off that Dermot

realised he knew Joey's latest tart. It was Solly Adler's wife, Sharon.

Bernie flew into Becky's outstretched arms.

'Oh, God, it's so good to see you!' she said.

She buried her face in Becky's hair, only just managing not to cry, grateful that the first person she'd met 'back home' had not been her mother. Unlike Kitty, Becky didn't bombard a person with questions. When they'd finished hugging, she held her friend away from her so that she could look at her.

'You look fantastic, Bernadette,' she said. 'Oh, blimey, do you have a tan?'

'Inasmuch as a blonde can tan,' Bernie said.

'That is so fashionable!'

Becky had seen Bernie walking along Fournier Street and had run out to greet her. She'd known that she was coming but actually to be with her friend again was an emotional moment for both of them.

'I've been so looking forward to seeing you,' Becky said. 'I've got a few days off work and I've been looking out of the window every five minutes! How long did it take you to get here?'

'What, from Israel or up from Southampton?'

'Southampton!'

'The ship docked this morning and so it's taken me all day,' Bernie said. She let her small suitcase drop to the ground.

Becky picked it up. 'Well, let's get you over to the flat. Your mum'll be so pleased to see you. I think she's been cleaning the place since before dawn!'

Bernie shook her head. 'Oh, Mammy! She never changes.'

'Thank God!'

Arm in arm, the girls began walking towards Bernie's old home.

'How are you? How's Israel? And Egypt! Oh, I bet that was wonderful, wasn't it?'

'It was interesting,' Bernie said.

'You always wanted to go there. I remember you talking about it years ago.'

'I'll tell you all about it once I've freshened up and had some rest,' Bernie said. 'And what about you?'

'Oh, nothing much. The job is never-ending but now people don't have to pay when they get ill, it's much easier. Mind you, it still took a bit of persuasion to get Rose's mum in the sanatorium. No matter what we said, she was terrified she'd have to pay.'

'How is she?'

'She's getting better, but you know, with TB, even with antibiotics, it's a long road.'

'Der said she'd like to see me in his last letter.'

'Yes.' Becky gripped her friend's arm tightly. 'Everybody wants to see you.'

'It was definitely her.'

Rose shook her head.

'You have to stay away from the both of them, Der,' she said to her husband. 'I know Joey's your brother and everything but he's trouble too.'

'I know.' He put his arms around her. 'I'm sorry I kept that I was seeing him from you, but I didn't want you to worry.'

'I know. But you can't save him from himself, Dermot, no one can.'

Rose went back to her chair and picked up her knitting. 'Poor Solly,' she said. 'I wonder if he knows his missus is messing around with your Joey?'

Dermot sat down beside her. 'I dunno,' he said. 'Poor

bugger. Not that anyone could ever understand why he married her. Should've married our Bernie ...'

'She had her adventures to go on too,' Rose said. 'Can't wait to see her!'

Dermot smiled.

Then Rose said, 'Do you think that Bernie and Becky ever think about having babies?'

'What, them career girls? I dunno,' he said. Then, because it had been on his mind lately, he added, 'Do you? I mean, I know we don't ...'

'I'm happy with just Morry.' Rose smiled at her husband. 'We don't need none of that between us to show we love each other, do we?'

She was, in so many ways, the perfect wife for him. She was kind and tough, loving and beautiful – but Dermot, even knowing what she'd been through as a teenager, couldn't fathom her complete lack of interest in sex. He wished with all his heart he could be the same. But he couldn't. Infrequent though they were, his secretive trysts with other men provided relief he knew he couldn't do without.

Ever since his old school friend Chrissy Dolan had moved down to Southend-on-Sea, Dermot had gone there for the occasional evening. Chrissy knew where all the boys met and Dermot had experienced several encounters in the semi-dark underneath the famous Pier. He tried to limit it, but sometimes 'it' just came to get you.

A new hand, Raymond, had started on the farm where Dermot worked in the middle of June, a young lad with blue-black hair. The first time they'd looked at each other, Dermot had known. The first time they'd had sex was in the cow byre. Now they had it anywhere they could be alone. The boy was beautiful and he knew it. Dermot knew he was properly in

97

love, which was awful, not just because of Rose and Morry but because Raymond was not a good person. Sex with him came at a price – be it fags, drink or joining in with the three-somes Raymond liked so much involving the farmer's bored daughter, Viv. But in spite of that, Dermot knew he couldn't give Raymond up. He didn't want to hurt Rose and Morry but he also didn't want to hurt himself. And being away from Raymond for any length of time would hurt him.

Breaking into her husband's train of thought, Rose said, 'I wonder what she looks like now?'

'Our Bernie? Same, I s'pose.'

'With posher clothes,' Rose said.

'Maybe.'

There was a pause and then Rose said, 'I've never had posh clothes much, but I did have a few nice dresses when I worked at the Windmill. Don't know where they went.' She smiled lovingly at him. 'Don't matter, though. Our family is all that matters to me.'

Being back in the flat was everything Bernie had dreaded it would be. Damp, shabby, dark, the drains smelled something rotten and Mammy, after a cursory hug, continued to clean around her. Bernie, sitting with a cup of tea in one hand and a cigarette in the other, wished that Kitty would just sit down, but knew she wouldn't.

'So how's your Mr Simpson?' Kitty asked as she cleaned invisible specks off the front of the kitchen range.

'Heinrich is fine,' Bernie said.

'He's not . . .'

'No, his wife still won't give him a divorce, Mammy. That's not changed.'

Her mother looked up at her. 'Don't be proud of that,

Bernadette,' she said. 'I love you, you're my daughter, but I'm also ashamed of your situation.'

'Which is why you tell people that I live on my own,' she said. 'I know, Mammy, Marie told me.'

'I'm not ashamed of saving face,' Kitty said. 'What am I supposed to say?'

'The truth?'

'That you're living in sin! Time was, I wouldn't talk to you because of it. I've treated you as fairly as I'm able.'

And Bernie knew that was probably true. Her mother was never going to accept Heinrich Simpson's presence in her daughter's life. But then again, she probably didn't have to.

'Where are the girls?' Bernie said, asking after her younger sisters.

'Marie's working ...'

'Still driving?'

'Oh, yes. Still going on about the Knowledge and never doing it. And Aggie's on her way home. They're both looking forward to seeing you.'

Bernie opened her suitcase and took out a small parcel wrapped in thin, brown paper.

'This is for you,' she said to her mother.

Kitty stopped what she was doing and looked at the parcel. 'What is it?'

'Open it and you'll find out.'

Kitty had always told her children that she didn't like surprises and so she frowned as she looked down at the package. 'What's that written on it?' she asked. 'What language is that?'

'It's Arabic,' Bernie said. 'Open it.'

'Alright then.'

She unwrapped the package remarkably quickly for one who didn't like surprises.

99

'Ah, now look at this ...'

It was a Rosary. The beads were large and made of what looked like wood.

Bernie explained, 'It's olive wood. From the Mount of Olives.'

Kitty wiped a tear away from her eye while Bernie pretended not to notice.

'Well, that's very thoughtful of you, girl. Very.'

'I got it from an Arab shop,' Bernie said. 'A lot of them are Christians.'

Kitty nodded. 'That's ... That's really thoughtful.'

She put the Rosary in the pocket of her apron. Bernie knew she'd say no more about it and probably wouldn't even tell anyone she had it. What she would do was look at it when she went to bed and then she'd probably cry again. Bernie smiled to herself, knowing that her tough old mammy was pleased even if she didn't show it.

Sometimes when you heard things on the grapevine, you couldn't wait to pass them on. But there were other things, overheard in shops or on the street corner, that you knew you had to keep to yourself.

Dolly Adler's daughter-in-law Sharon had been gone three months now without a word as to where she might be. Dolly had even asked her uncle, the sweat-shop owner Sassoon, but he'd said nothing. Solly and Sharon had married in synagogue and so her family had to be ashamed of her behaviour. But then they were probably also worried about whether Solly might pursue his wife for money. Not that he was like that. Even though he could have done with a few bob to help with feeding and clothing young Natalie, he was too proud to ask.

Dolly had been getting fish and chips for their tea when she heard about Sharon. Although the area had changed a lot in recent years and many of the former residents had moved out, there were still enough old timers to provide a decent flow of gossip across the manor.

Old Angie McGuinness was several people behind Dolly in the chippie queue. With her arms crossed over her massive chest, she was gossiping to Mrs Digby, the priest Father Aiden's housekeeper. They both had terrible reputations for spreading outrageous tales about people and, to begin with, Mrs Digby had swung into a story about a girl called Michelle who, it would seem, had 'yo-yo' knickers. However, expanding on the topic of girls who were no better than they should be, old Angie began talking about Bernadette Lynch and Dolly's ears pricked up.

'Kitty Lynch likes to say the girl's just working abroad.'

'Which she is.'

'Ah, yes, but what Kitty won't own up to is that her girl went off with a man.'

'Who?'

'Dunno. Posh bloke. Jewish.'

'Ah, well,' Mrs Digby said, 'another case of a parent trying hard and then losing their child to this wicked world.'

'Yeah, but she's coming back home apparently,' Old Angie said.

'Who?'

'Bernadette Lynch, you soppy date!'

'When?'

'I dunno.'

'Who told you?' Mrs Digby asked.

'My sister's girl works up the London Hospital and knows one of the other Lynch girls, Marie. She told her. Don't know if Bernadette's staying or just visiting. But fancy having her in the house! I mean, you'd've thought that someone like Kitty Lynch'd keep her away, wouldn't you?'

Mrs Digby tutted. 'The things as go on!'

'What you 'aving, Mrs A?'

Dolly, shaking her head to dispel the thoughts raised by the women's conversation, looked up into the face of Stan the fish and chip man and said, 'Oh, sorry. Two rock and three chips, please, Stan. And I'll have a wally for our Natalie.'

'Comin' up.'

While she waited for her fish and chips, Dolly thought about what Angie and Mrs Digby had said about Bernie Lynch. If she was coming home for good then Solly would find out about her soon enough. But if she was just visiting then it was best he wasn't troubled by the news. Her son had held a torch for that girl for years and, if Dolly was honest, she believed he'd married Sharon on the rebound from Bernie. Now, however, it seemed he had taken a fancy to Bernie's friend, Nurse Rebekah Shapiro. A Jewish girl from a good family, she was a career girl, so people said, and Dolly didn't want to get her hopes up too far. Besides, for the moment, her Solly was still married to Sharon who, it was whispered, was living with some gangster bloke up West.

Rose slipped into bed beside her husband and blew out the candle on her bedside table. For a moment she tried to settle then she gave up and lit the candle again. Dermot turned over and said, 'What's the matter?'

'I was thinking,' Rose said.

'Oh, blimey, watch out!' her husband replied.

Rose nudged him in the ribs with her elbow. 'Give over,' she said. 'Listen, Der, I know that your Bernie's coming down here Friday, but I'd really like to see her with Becky. She's back to work Wednesday night so, if I can get Morry picked up from school tomorrow, I was thinking . . . '

'You'd like to go up to London tomorrow?' he said.

'Yeah, well, if we can afford it, I'd . . . '

'Well, we can't really,' Dermot replied. 'But then I expect if you . . . Look, you take your fare out of your housekeeping and I'll have a word with our Bernie on Friday.'

'What – ask her for money?'

'Yeah. She's a famous photographer out there,' he said.

'You can't ask her for money, though . . . '

'I can. She's me sister. Anyway, she'll be over the moon to see you early like.'

'You think so? I mean, there ain't time for you to telephone Mr Shapiro or nothing, not now.'

Dermot shrugged. 'Don't matter,' he said. 'They won't be going far, will they?'

'No.'

He kissed her on the cheek. 'You go, love,' he said. 'I'll be alright. I'll pick Morry up from Mrs Linden for you.'

'Provided she can have him.'

'Take everything you need for the trip with you when you take Morry to school tomorrow. Then I'll come home from work by Mrs Linden's and pick him up.'

Rose knew she was desperate to see Bernie with Becky so that the three of them could all be together again, but she also felt a bit bad about leaving Morry and Dermot too. Not that Dermot seemed too worried. In fact, if she didn't know better, she might have thought her husband wanted to get rid of her.

Chapter 9

Aggie put her head around the curtain that surrounded Bernie's bed. In the old days this cubby hole had been where Joey and Dermot had slept.

'You gonna be home tonight?' the girl asked her sleepy, tousle-haired sister.

'Yeah,' Bernie said. 'Gonna spend the day over with Becky but I'll be back here for tea.'

'I'll see you tonight then,' Aggie said.

'Yeah.'

She heard her sister open and then close the street door behind her. She'd been vaguely aware of Marie coming home in the early hours and then her mammy leaving for Tate's at six. The Lynch household was always busy whoever lived there.

With the place almost to herself, Bernie got up and went out to the lavvy in the yard. Although her mammy and one of her sisters were out, she had to queue because of the family upstairs. Indians by the look of them, there were two women and a little girl waiting for yet another woman to finish. Bernie smiled at them, but they didn't smile back. Not that there was too much to smile about what with the autumn weather rolling in and the stink from the drains.

Once she'd 'been', Bernie put some water on to boil so that she could have a strip wash in the sink. To everyone around her, this was just normal. Who, after all, had a bath? Apart from the Shapiros. But in Jerusalem she'd got used to a shower. What was more, unless there was a sudden water-cut she could shower every day. Wash over, she got dressed and then lit a cigarette. She'd got used to having coffee instead of tea since moving to Israel and felt she couldn't face Mammy's dusty old tea-leaf canister. She wasn't bothered. She'd had a drink of water and anyway was keen to get out of the flat in case she woke up Marie.

Still driving ambulances, the older of her two sisters showed no sign as yet of settling down. Kitty was worried about her, but then Kitty worried about everybody. That Marie didn't 'have someone' bothered her mother intensely. But Bernie knew that her sister didn't want to marry. She hadn't said why, but she had said in one of her letters that marriage was not something she would ever consider because she liked her freedom. Bernie could understand that. Being with someone wasn't easy. Compromises had to be made and things sometimes happened that threatened the strongest relationship. Frowning, she left the flat and walked out into the street.

God, the old place looked bad! Run down, the road covered in litter, parts of it looked as if the war had only just ended.

The train was due to get into Liverpool Street at half-past ten. Then it was only a short walk to Fournier Street and Becky and Bernie.

Rose still had a key to her mum's old flat and so she'd pop in there just to make sure everything was alright. The girl her mum worked for, Blessed, was paying the rent for Nell until she came out of the sanatorium, which was nice, but Rose still worried about the place as the whole area was alive with rats and mice to say nothing of the damp.

Although the thought of living with Nell again made Rose anxious, she did wish that her mum would come and stay with them for a while after she got out of hospital. But she knew she wouldn't. Nell liked working for Blessed. The girl was funny and kind, and working for a prostitute was familiar territory for Nell. Then there was her drinking. No doubt that would all start up again once she was out. Rose knew she couldn't tolerate all that around her son. If only her mum could give it up!

The train pulled into Stratford, which meant that there was only about ten more minutes to go. The steam from the locomotive as well as the smoke from all the factory chimneys made it look as if there was fog outside when there wasn't. The sun, high in the sky, tried to shine through all the muck in the air but without much success. After living in the countryside for so long, Rose wondered how she'd put up with all the filth in London. Coming back to it now made her cough.

But that would soon be forgotten when she saw Bernie. Rose couldn't actually remember the last time she'd seen her and found herself thinking about how her friend would look. Would she be brown from the sun? Would she speak with another accent? Would it feel the same between her, Becky and Bernie?

Rose felt her stomach turn over as she considered the possibility that Bernie might now be an entirely different girl.

*

'Well, that's Auntie Kitty for you!' Becky said after Bernie had told her how her mother had received the gift she'd brought her from Israel.

'I searched high and low for a Rosary made of wood from the Mount of Olives and she just puts it in her apron pocket,' Bernie said.

Becky laughed. 'If she hadn't you'd've wondered what was wrong with her!'

Bernie drank her tea. 'This is true.'

Sitting in Becky's kitchen brought back a lot of memories for Bernie – not least of her brother Dermot's wedding to Rose.

'We all got together loads of food for Rosie and Dermot's wedding in here, didn't we?' she said.

'It was a great day.'

'Until Rosie went into labour.'

Becky laughed again. 'Ah, yes, little Morry's entry into the world,' she said. 'You know Papa had Mama's old wedding dress cleaned after Rosie went into labour in it, but it's never been the same since. Don't tell her.'

'I won't.' Bernie smiled. 'It's so good to see you. It's been such a long time. What have you been doing?'

'As I told you before, working,' Becky said. 'There's not much time for anything else, although I also find I have to do more and more for Papa now he's getting older.'

'Where is he?'

'Out,' she said. 'He goes for long walks these days, mainly to West Ham to the cemetery where Mama is buried.' Her face fell. 'I think he feels he might die soon.'

'No! You think so?'

'Yes,' Becky said. 'Not that he's particularly ill, as far as I know. Just old and tired. To be honest with you, Bern, I know he worries about me and whether I'll ever marry.'

'Wants to know you're settled.'

'Yes. I wish I could reassure him I'll be alright whether I have a husband or not.'

Bernie paused before she answered, then she said, 'You know, Becky, the world is changing. I've come to know quite a number of women who don't want marriage and kids. We want more ...'

'Oh, I'd like to marry one day,' Becky said. 'But not yet. Not until I find the ...'

'Right one? Not sure he exists,' Bernie said. 'But I know you mean someone you can love and who loves you. You want respect too.'

'I do.'

'We were lucky with our dad,' Bernie continued. 'He was a good man. Never knocked Mammy about or any of us kids. He liked a drink but he was no drunk and he worked his bloody socks off all his life. Your papa's a good 'un too. But they're rare. Look at that pig Rose and her mum used to live with, knocking Nelly about all the time and then what he did to Rosie ...'

Becky shook her head. Len Tobin had been Nell Larkin's common-law husband all the time Rose had been growing up. He'd sold first Nell on the streets and then Rose to his sailor mates from the pub. She'd been fifteen at the time.

Changing the subject, or so she thought, Becky said, 'So what about you and Mr Simpson?'

Bernie took a deep breath. 'Well ...'

And then the doorbell rang.

'I'd better get that,' Becky said. 'Back in a mo'.'

Sharon was busy filing her nails.

'Don't get all that muck over the sheets!'

She looked up at the man who'd just got out of bed beside her and said, 'Who rattled your cage?'

Joey Lynch, or 'Ronnie' as he was known in and around Soho, looked down at her.

'And get up, you lazy mare!' he said.

'Why?'

'Because I've got business,' he said. 'And I want you with me.'

'Don't know why.'

'To sit about and look pretty, what do you think?' he said. 'And put on something nice. Fuck knows, I've spent enough money on your clothes. Wear that red dress.'

Sharon swung her legs out of the bed and stood up. 'Where we going?'

'Mile End.'

'What, down that snooker club ...'

'Just get yourself ready!'

Before Sharon had moved in, Joey's bedsit in Rupert Street had been quite enough for him. There was even a sink in the corner and, although he had to share the bog with the other residents, he had his own cooker. Not that he or Sharon used it that often. They usually went out to eat. He did, after all, have to show off her and all the dresses he'd bought her.

'Fucking clothes all over this gaff!' he said as he pulled his braces up onto his shoulders. 'Like a bloody jumble sale!'

Sharon sauntered over to the sink behind the battered Chinese screen they used to give their ablutions some privacy. 'Don't you call my clothes jumble!'

'You know what I mean.'

She shrugged. 'Anyway,' she said, 'what's got under your skin this morning? Like a bear with a sore head.'

Joey put on a jacket and lit a cigarette. 'Dermot,' he said.

'Your brother? What about him?'

'I want him with me, on this job.'

'I know. But he don't want in.' Sharon washed and then rinsed her face. 'He won't grass. Don't know why you're so bothered. You've got Ted and Stu, and them blokes down Mile End'll sort you out with a driver. What do you need Dermot for?'

'Never you mind,' Joey said. 'I just need him.'

Sharon washed underneath her arms and then threw her flannel in the sink. If she didn't know better, she'd be inclined to believe that Joey was dependent on his brother in some way. But that wasn't the case at all. If anything, Dermot's need to see Joey was greater. But then, when she thought about it, Sharon wondered whether Joey really wanted his brother in on the job he was planning just to prove to himself he wasn't the only bad apple in the Lynch family basket.

When Becky brought Rose into the kitchen Bernie shrieked with delight. All three girls instantly reverted to their fourteen-year-old selves and jumped up and down with excitement as they hugged each other.

Once the questions about how Rose had got there and why she'd come had been answered, they settled down to more tea, beigels and even a few glasses of Becky's father's kosher wine.

'It's not strong,' she said as she topped up their glasses for the second time and made her friends giggle.

'You could've fooled me!' Bernie said as she lit a cigarette.

Rose made a face when she attempted to get the sweet wine down. 'This is ...'

'Oh, chuck it down yer neck!' Bernie said. 'You only live once!'

'If I go home pissed ...

'If you go home pissed and my brother says a word, you tell me and I'll sort him out!' Bernie answered.

They all laughed.

Becky held hands with both her friends. 'It's so good we're all together again!' she said. 'We can almost kid ourselves it's like the old days!'

They all fell silent then as the implication of what she had just said sank in. Eventually Rose said, 'You mean, like when we was kids?'

'Yeah,' Becky said. 'I s'pose so. When we were kids we all used to run about together, didn't we? Spend all our summer holidays together ...'

'Then the war came,' Bernie said.

'Yes.'

'Mum always says we was lucky to get through all that,' Rose said.

'She's right.'

'But it's a different world now from what it was before,' Becky said. 'Some good things, some bad. You must've seen so much change in Israel, Bern ...'

'I'm pregnant.'

For a moment, Rose at least felt as if she'd misheard.

'Beg pardon?' she said. 'You're ...'

'I'm pregnant,' Bernie repeated. 'About three months gone.'

Unsure how to respond, Becky said, 'Well, a baby, as Matron Mary always says, is a blessing ...'

'Yeah, but it's not for me, is it?' Bernie said. 'I'm not married and got no prospect of being married.'

Becky said, 'What does Heinrich say?'

'He doesn't know.'

Becky looked at Rose whose face was inscrutable. All the levity had gone out of their meeting and Becky, at least, began to feel cold. She got up to put some more coal on the kitchen fire.

Rose, who was often more acute in her observations of others than people gave her credit for, said, 'Is it his – Heinrich's?'

'Rosie!'

'No,' Bernie said. She shook her head. 'Happened when I was in Egypt.'

'Who with?' Becky said.

Bernie smiled. 'I met that Arab boy who used to work at the *Post*, the one that Heinrich always reckoned fancied me. He lives in Egypt.'

'So Heinrich was right.'

Bernie sighed. 'Yeah. In a way. What Heinrich has never known is that I had a few feelings of my own for this Gibrail. We made love at the Pyramids.'

Becky put a hand up to her mouth.

'Yeah, what a bloody cliché, eh? And I can say all I like about getting carried away by the moment, but I also know I wanted it to happen,' Bernie said. 'I wanted him and he wanted me and so it happened. Me and Heinrich, well, there's not been much or any of that, in fact, for the past year. Even if I wanted to lie to him about who the father is, I couldn't. He ain't a fool.'

Rose took a swig from her wine glass. 'So what you gonna do?' she said.

Bernie shrugged. 'Get rid of it.'

Becky took her friend's hand. 'Oh, Bern, that is so dangerous!' she said. She looked at Rose who knew first-hand how risky an abortion could be. 'Rosie ... '

'Nearly killed me,' she said. 'But it's up to you, Bernie.'

'Rosie!'

'No, Becky,' Bernie said, 'Rosie's right. It is my decision. And I have to make it while I'm home. I either get it sorted here or I go back to Israel and face the music.'

'But if you go back to Israel, how will you work?' Becky asked.

'I'm not showing yet but when I do ...' Bernie shrugged again. 'There's women in the *kibbutzim* who have kids without no men. Maybe I could go and live on one of them? Pick oranges and live in a commune.'

'But what about your career?' Becky said. 'Yes, I've heard of *kibbutzim*, farms basically where everyone shares the work and lives as an extended family. I know you're a Socialist, but could you live like that?'

'I dunno.'

'And also, you're not an Israeli citizen.'

Rose, who had been thinking about the problem from a different direction, said, 'I know people who'll help.'

'Help?'

'That girl me mum works for, Blessed, she gets caught sometimes,' Rose said. 'She uses a woman up Poplar somewhere. Used to be a nurse. Knows what she's doing. Blessed ain't never got sick after.'

The Shapiros' kitchen fell silent again as all three girls fully absorbed what Rose had just said. Of course, getting a professional abortion in hospital was impossible unless there was a medical reason for it. Abortion otherwise was illegal and so the only way to procure one was to do so illegally. There were people all over London who, for a consideration, would oblige. But few of them had any actual medical knowledge and the whole undertaking was very risky.

'I'll have to think about it,' Bernie said. 'I go back at the end of next week.'

'You'll need time to recover if you ...' Becky looked down at her hands.

'I know,' Bernie said. 'We'll have to see, won't we? Have to see ...'

*

113

The older brother was called Charlie while the younger one was Reg. There was a third brother somewhere, Reg's twin Ronnie, but he didn't make an appearance this time. Reg and Ronnie Kray were both on the run from the army, Joey had told her.

The snooker club, which was run by the brothers but owned by someone else, was dingy with peeling wallpaper and carpets that were sticky and covered in dog-ends. The whole place stank of damp. When Sharon sat down at the scarred and greasy bar, the older brother smiled at her while Reg looked her up and down as if she were a piece of meat. She found it rather sexy.

It was he who poured her a port and lemon while Charlie and Joey sat down at a table at the back of the hall.

'Here you are, darlin',' Reg said as he plonked the glass down in front of her.

'Ta.'

Sharon wiggled her shoulders as she spoke, coming on to him. But when he grabbed one of her breasts she regretted it because he squeezed so hard, Sharon had to stifle a scream. As he walked back towards Joey and his brother, Reg looked over his shoulder at her and leered.

Sharon knew all about Joey's 'job'. He'd always, so he said, wanted to do a jewellery shop and had some time ago identified his target, Mappin & Webb, on a street called Poultry in the City of London. Easier, he reckoned, to get away from there than any of the jewellers he might target up West. Joey even had a couple of fences lined up to shift the goods once the job was over. This Reg and his brother, rising stars in the East End underworld, had got involved somewhere along the line and the men were now discussing who might drive Joey's getaway car.

'Your boys going in tooled up?' she heard Reg ask Joey.

'Yeah.'

'What – all of ya?'

She saw Joey shrug. 'Maybe. Why not?'

He always kept a gun beside the bed. He'd told Sharon it was just in case his old bosses 'the Maltesers' came to call. She remembered how, back in Spitalfields, it had been rumoured that Joey Lynch had killed the old weaver, Fred Lamb. He'd disappeared for years after that. Then out of the blue she'd met him one night while out with her cousin, Fat Helen. Up the Hammersmith Palais they'd been, when a familiar face had asked Sharon to dance. Back then he'd still insisted she call him Ronnie even though she told him she knew who he was.

Ronnie/Joey had been all over her during that first dance. Halfway through the second, they'd had to go outside and find a back-alley. That night he'd taken her to his place in Soho. From then on she'd been obsessed. Whereas her husband found her repulsive, Joey could never wait to give her one. The feeling was mutual and when they had sex he was fond of calling her 'juicy Lucy'.

But just recently the shine had started to come off things between them. He was still eager but she'd seen him looking at some of the younger tarts and wondered whether he was getting a bit extra elsewhere. Joey was a good-looking bloke who was no slouch in bed and so she knew he had to have offers. She saw that Reg turn around to look at her again and felt herself flush.

Chapter 10

Rose didn't say anything about Bernie's pregnancy to Dermot. She still hadn't told her mum and it was up to Bernie to tell her family or not. Besides Dermot had been in a funny mood when she'd got home from London the previous evening. Quiet and sort of tense. When they'd gone to bed that night, he hadn't even kissed her cheek. He'd gone to work early too and Rose found herself wondering what had happened.

Although she'd never said a word to him about it, Rose knew all about the young man he was seeing on the farm. She knew that some of their money went that way from time to time and, although it didn't please her, she wasn't prepared to argue with her husband about it. That was Dermot's 'other' life, and while it didn't impinge upon her and Morry, it was alright by her. Or rather, she could put up with it.

Having dropped her son off at school, Rose was walking down the towpath beside the river. It was cold but bright and it was very pleasant just to walk and look and think her own thoughts. She was quite unaware of the two young women walking towards her until the one with the long red hair said, 'You're Mrs Lynch, ain't you?'

'Do I know you?' Rose said.

'No, but I know you,' the redhead said.

'Oh, yes?'

There was a smugness in this young woman's tone and Rose fully expected her to have a go on account of Rose being a 'pikey', which was what they called Romany people out in Essex.

'You're Dermot's missus,' she continued.

'Yes?'

The other girl with her, a brunette, laughed.

'I've had your old man,' the redhead said. 'I sucked him off!'

Rose didn't think, she just acted. First, she punched the redhead in the face, then she kicked her while she was on the ground. The brunette, terrified by the sudden violence, ran away.

'Did you sleep last night?'

Bernie shook her head.

'I thought not,' Becky said. 'You're very pale, you know. You're not being sick, are you?'

'No.'

They were going to the Italian cafe, Pellicci's, on the Bethnal Green Road.

'Can we talk about something else?' Bernie asked as they passed Spitalfields Market.

Becky squeezed her arm. ''Course,' she said. 'It was nice to see Rosie yesterday, wasn't it?'

'Yeah. Seeing her again on Friday,' Bernie said.

'She just couldn't wait!'

'I'm looking forward to seeing Morry.'

117

'Oh, he's quite a big boy now,' Becky said. 'And bright. He read me a story at Christmas. It helps a lot that Dermot can read with him.'

Bernie shook her head. 'I wish Rose'd give it a go again,' she said.

'Yes, but you and I have both tried to teach her without success. And so's Dermot,' Becky said. 'It's as if she doesn't see what we see.'

'Maybe by the time you've grown up it's too late to learn how to read and write?'

'Maybe.' They'd just passed a couple of costers Becky knew by sight when they saw Kitty Lynch walking towards them.

'I thought your mum was at work today?' Becky said to her friend.

'So did I,' Bernie said. 'Blimey, she looks cross about something!'

Reg had come to see Joey, who was out. Sharon, still in her dressing-gown, said she'd let him know that Reg had called. But then, just as she was shutting the door, she saw a look in the big boy's eyes that made her invite him in.

For a few moments they stood looking at each other. Then she said, 'Do you want a drink? I've got Scotch.'

'Ta.'

He sat on their bed. He was a bit like a dark young bull. Sharon poured him a Scotch and then gave it to him. She saw him watch the front of her robe as she leaned over to give him the glass. She had nothing on underneath and, when one of her breasts touched the side of his face, she leaned in still closer. His mouth opened and she sat on his lap so that he could lick her cleavage. His breath was hot and short and she could feel him harden underneath her.

When he finally raised his head he said, 'I could tell you were a dirty bitch.'

'I could tell you had a big cock,' Sharon said.

She ground herself against him and Reg groaned. Eager fingers fumbled to undo his fly and then he said, 'Joey wouldn't like this, would he?'

'I don't care about Joey,' she said as she pushed him inside her.

He was good, hard and brutal, and when he came inside her he bit so hard on one of her nipples he made it bleed. When she'd made him hard again, he asked her to go down on him, which she did. Watching her with dead, cold eyes, he said, 'You're good at this, girl.'

She was – with the right fella. Sharon had always used sex to boost her own self-esteem. Any man who looked at her and could hardly control himself was a catch in her eyes. She had a feeling this great brute would do just about anything to get inside her knickers again and the thought turned her on.

When she'd finished, Sharon sat on his lap again and said, 'You know I'd do anything for you, Reg. You're something else, you are, boy.'

It was unusual for Kitty Lynch to apologise to anyone. But on this occasion she said to Becky, 'I'm so sorry, love, I have to speak to our Bernadette alone. It's been driving me mad all morning and I can't bear it no longer.' Then she took hold of Bernie's arm and dragged her back to the flat without a word.

Once the street door was shut behind them, however, the yelling started.

'When was you going to tell me you're up the stick!'

Bernie couldn't speak. Who had spilled the beans?

'Well?'

Eventually finding her voice, Bernie said, 'Who told you?'

'No one,' Kitty said. 'But when you start putting on weight in a certain place and you're back and forth to the khazi, then it's not difficult to work out.'

'I thought I didn't show ...'

'You don't much,' Kitty said. 'But when you've had as many kids as I have, then you know. What's he think about it, eh? Your bloke?'

Bernie sat down. 'He doesn't know.'

'Well, don't you think you should tell him?'

She couldn't let her mother know that the child wasn't Heinrich's. She couldn't.

'His wife won't divorce him.'

'Well, something'll have to be done,' Kitty said. 'What was you thinking?'

Bernie shrugged.

'How far gone are you?'

'Three months.'

Kitty shook her head. 'So what you doing here ... travelling all that way?'

She shrugged. 'I wanted to see everyone.'

'Well, now you're here, you'd better stay and have it here. Far as I know they don't have no National Health in Israel.'

'No. But I can't stay. I have to get back to my job.'

Kitty shook her head. Then she sat down. 'Another massive journey while you're like this?'

Bernie looked at her mother whose eyes were blazing. She still hadn't made contact with anyone who would give her an abortion. Was she going to do that? Was she going to tell her mother that was the plan? If it was.

'I'm going back Saturday week,' she said.

Her mother lit a cigarette. Bernie saw her take a deep

120

breath before she said, 'So next question has to be, are you keeping it?'

'I know you'd want me to ...'

'Not what I'm asking. Do you want to keep it?'

'I don't know,' Bernie said. 'My head's all over the place.'

'Pity it weren't more together when you got knocked up. But there it is.' For a while Kitty smoked in silence and then she said, 'God forgive me, I can't hold with killing babies but if you need to find someone ...'

The next silence hung between them like smog – foul and impenetrable.

Eventually Bernie said, 'I have to think, Mammy.'

'Well, you'll need to do it fast, my girl,' her mother said. 'Because you can't go off on no ship if you're sick. I told work I had a dodgy stomach but I spoke to one of the other girls before I left and she give me this.' She handed over a piece of paper to Bernie. 'If you decide to go and see her, you say you're a friend of Verna's.'

Bernie looked down and read the name 'Dot' followed by an address in Poplar.

'Used to work up Whipps Cross Hospital,' Kitty continued. 'Helped Verna out twice and she had no problems. It's up to you but I'm off back to work tomorrow and so you need to sort yourself out.'

He was only a lad of twenty-one, but Raymond Warner knew all the moves. Once he and Dermot were alone in the bottom field, Ray pulled him into one of the hedgerows and kissed him. Taken unawares, Dermot fell over backwards and landed with the boy on top of him. Ray, laughing, began to undress.

'Hey! Hey, we've got work to do!' Dermot protested. But Ray

121

just carried on undressing until Dermot could do nothing else but make love to him.

When they'd finished and lay together, smoking cigarettes in the grass, the boy said, 'What do you think of Viv?'

This was the farmer's daughter, a sullen young woman of twenty Raymond sometimes included in their sex games. As much as he could, Dermot tried to stay clear of her.

'She's alright,' he said. 'Why?'

'Thinks she might be up the duff,' Ray said.

Dermot sat up. 'What?'

'Oh, it's alright. I told her if she is, I'll marry her.'

'You'll . . .'

'What else can I do?' he said. 'Farmer Nice'll sack us if I don't – so Viv says.'

'Then get another job!'

'Can't. Anyway, it don't mean *we* can't carry on as we are. Viv says she likes it when we all muck about together.'

'But you'll be married.'

'I'll still want cock.' Raymond winked at him. And once again Dermot allowed himself to believe that what he and this irresistible boy did together would have no repercussions for the two most important people in his life: Rose and Morry.

Becky hadn't felt like continuing on to Pellicci's now that Bernie had been dragged away from her by Kitty. At a loss as to what to do next, she finally decided to make her way back to Fournier Street. Bernie was still nowhere to be seen and Becky feared that her mother had somehow found out she was pregnant. Auntie Kitty rarely skipped off work on a whim.

When Becky got home she found that her father was in but not alone. Someone she hadn't seen for a very long time was with him, taking tea in the front living room.

'Ah, Rebekah darling!' said Mrs Rabinowicz the matchmaker when she saw her. 'Excuse me if I don't get up, love, but my legs have gone.'

Back before the war Mrs Rabinowicz had tried to make a match between Becky and the jeweller Chaim Suss. But at the time she'd been obsessed with Solly Adler and so eventually her father had called the whole thing off. Now that Solly was married with a child her old fixation seemed silly, but she was still glad she hadn't married Chaim even though, at the time, Mrs Rabinowicz had been furious.

'How's business at your hospital?' the old woman asked.

Becky looked at her father who shrugged and said, 'Mrs Rabinowicz was passing, Rebekah ...'

'Your father asked me in for a cuppa,' she said.

Someone here wasn't quite telling the truth. Becky feared it was her father. When she'd turned down Chaim Suss he had accepted her decision and had supported her while she trained as a nurse. But time had moved on and she knew that the fact the area was changing so rapidly was worrying him. She knew that ideally he'd want her to settle down somewhere more salubrious.

'I thought that you were going to be out with Bernadette,' said Moritz as he poured his daughter a cup of tea. Becky noted he was using their best china.

'Oh, she had to go home.'

'Nothing wrong, I hope,' said the nosy matchmaker.

'No, Mrs Rabinowicz,' Becky said with a smile. 'Bernie's fine.'

'Lovely girl that Bernadette Lynch,' Mrs Rabinowicz said. 'Working in Israel now, I hear, taking her photographs.'

'Yes.'

'I remember when that Communist boy, Solly Adler, was sweet on her,' the old woman continued. 'I said to the

Rabbetzin Cohen at the time, I said: "The girl's a *shiksa*, there's no future in it." And there was not. Then Solomon married Sharon Begleiter and now they've got a little daughter, so it all ended well.'

Becky wondered whether Mrs Rabinowicz had heard that Sharon had left her husband and child, but didn't say anything.

'So how are you then, Rebekah?' Mrs Rabinowicz said. 'You happy in your hospital and all that?'

'Very,' Becky said. 'You're learning every day, meeting new people all the time ...'

'Young men?'

She heard her father clear his throat. She wasn't supposed to be here.

'I work on the maternity ward, Mrs Rabinowicz,' Becky said. 'The only young men I get to see are the ladies' husbands.'

'Doctors?'

'Oh, we see them, but they don't take a lot of notice of us nurses.'

Mrs Rabinowicz shook her head. 'That's a shame.'

'Why?'

The old woman looked surprised. 'Well ... nice girl like you meeting a young doctor ... Marry one and you never have to worry again.'

'I disagree,' Becky said. 'Marry a doctor and you'd be forever worried – when he gets called out at night, when he has to attend patients in road accidents, when he has to deal with violent people in his clinic. More often than not a doctor's wife ends up being his receptionist. A waste of a nursing training if you ask me. And anyway, I don't want to get married.'

An embarrassed silence fell and then Becky put down her teacup on the table and got up. 'Anyway,' she said, 'nice to see you, Mrs Rabinowicz, but I have things to do.'

And she left them to it. She'd speak to her father about this later.

Solly Adler's sister-in-law, Evie Newman, née Begleiter, lived in Hackney. This was why he was standing on the steps of a dilapidated house in the De Beauvoir area of that borough.

Eventually a small, fat woman with bottle-blonde hair came to the door and said, 'Whadda you want?'

In the background Solly could hear a baby crying. Evie must have had another child since he'd last seen her.

'I need to contact Sharon,' he said.

'How should I know where she is?' her sister said.

'You're family. I need to find her, to tell her something.'

'What?'

'Natalie's got to go into hospital,' he said. 'To have her tonsils out. Doctor reckons it'll help make her asthma a bit easier.'

'Sorry to hear it,' Evie said. 'But I can't help you with Sharon.'

'I heard she was up West ... '

'Maybe,' she said. 'But then wherever she is, there's bound to be a bloke involved, so I shouldn't worry about her if I was you.'

'I don't.'

He left, no closer to finding out where his wife was, and returned to Spitalfields. He got off the bus on the Bethnal Green Road opposite Pellicci's Italian café. On a whim he decided to go in and buy himself a cup of tea. He saw Becky, sitting in a corner looking miserable, before she saw him. He walked over to her table and said, 'Mind if I join you, Nurse Shapiro?'

'Oh, er ... ' She appeared to struggle to decide how to reply for moment and then said, 'Yes. Please do.'

Solly sat down.

'I promise I won't ask you about anything medical,' he said. Then he called up to the counter for a cup of tea.

Becky smiled. 'Oh, that's the least of my worries!'

'Oh, what . . . '

'So how are you, Mr Adler? And Natalie?'

'Oh, I'm carrying on as usual and Nat, well, she's got to have her tonsils out next month.'

'That might make her breathing easier,' Becky said. 'And it's done very quickly these days so you don't need to worry about the operation.'

'Doctor's explained it to me,' Solly said. Then he smiled. 'We still ain't got our Revolution but at least we've got free medical treatment, eh?'

For a moment he looked just as he had back in the thirties when he'd been a firebrand young Communist. Becky was dazzled.

'Indeed,' she said.

'Lot of water under the bridge since then,' he said. His tea arrived and he loaded the cup with sugar.

'I don't know what's ahead,' Becky said. 'But at least we're no longer at war and, as you say, we can take care of our health without having to sell everything we possess. I'm sure that Natalie will be fine.'

'She will. She's a good kid,' he said.

Everyone knew that Sharon Adler had left her family, which had to have had an effect on Natalie. But Becky didn't broach the subject. Solly Adler, for all his romantic past, looked a little fragile these days.

Chapter 11

Rose didn't always get up with her husband when he left for work. But this morning she did, mainly because she couldn't keep how she felt inside to herself anymore. Also Dermot must have found the silent treatment she'd given him at supper the previous evening strange.

Outside in the garden, shaving over the pump, he looked away when she approached him.

Without preamble Rose said, 'You've been having it off with some local girl, I hear.'

She watched his face go white underneath his shaving soap.

'So that's yes then,' she said. 'I can take lads, but a girl ...'

'No ... No ... What?' He dropped his razor on the grass and put his hands on her shoulders. 'What ... What's happened?'

'Some girl with red hair up on the towpath yesterday,' Rose said. 'Laughing at me, saying you give her one.'

'No! What did you ...'

'I punched her and called her a liar,' Rose said. 'Dirty

country bumpkin! First I thought to myself that you being how you are, it had to be a lie. But then I got thinking . . . '

'It *is* a lie!' Dermot said. 'Of course it is!'

'I know we don't do nothing, and I don't want to, but that don't mean you can shame me with some other woman.'

'I never! I didn't!'

'So why she say it then?' Rose said. 'I never seen her before so how'd she know me? I keep meself to meself, apart from talking to Mrs Linden. Who is she, Der?'

'I don't know,' he said. 'Why d'you think I might know her?'

'I dunno, but she knew you all right.'

'I've no idea what's going on!'

Rose shook her head. She didn't believe or disbelieve him. Men were, as her mum had always told her, born liars. Rose had thought that Dermot was different. All she did know was that encounters like the one she'd had with the young woman on the towpath didn't arise out of nowhere.

Rose walked back into the cottage to get herself ready and make breakfast for her son.

'Blimey, girl, what you been eating?' Joey asked Sharon as he lay beside her in their bed. 'Oysters?'

Sharon smiled. The only aphrodisiac she'd needed was to think about Reg while Joey gave her one. Thinking about him had made her hot and wild and she'd done some things she'd never done with Joey before, which had put a smile on his face.

'Didn't realise you were quite such a dirty cow,' he said.

'Happy to oblige,' she said.

As soon as she was able, she'd get down Mile End and have that Reg all over again. It was all she could think about. After Reg had left she'd replayed the whole thing over and over in her mind until, just before midnight, Joey had come in. But he'd been drunk and so she'd had to wait until the morning.

'Cheered me up, to tell the truth,' Joey said.

'A bit of hanky-panky'll always do that.'

'Yeah,' he said. 'Out with a couple of faces from Bethnal Green last night ... told me them Kray boys got picked up at their snooker gaff yesterday afternoon.'

Sharon felt her heart miss a beat. 'What – Reg?' she blurted out.

'And his brother Ron,' Joey said. 'That was Charlie you met. Ron and Reg went AWOL from the army and now the MPs have been in to collar the pair of them. But it's alright, I know the geezer Reg had lined up to drive for us. Just a bit of a shame as I liked them two.' He got out of bed. 'Going to the khazi.'

When he'd gone, Sharon lay back down as she took in the news. No more bunk-ups with Reg then, which was a proper shame. And him gone into the army too. What a fucking waste!

Dorothy Anstiss was a thin woman in her fifties. She lived in a small flat in a damp bomb-damaged house in Crisp Street, Poplar. When she first opened the door she looked at Bernie with suspicion, but when told she was 'a friend of Vanda's', broke into a wide, toothless smile.

Sitting Bernie down in the only chair in a room that contained one small bed and a scarred sideboard, she said, 'It can happen to anyone, love. Happened to me once, donkey's years ago.'

When she laughed, Dorothy or 'Dot' sounded like a strangled owl. It didn't put Bernie at her ease.

'So how far gone are you, sweetheart?'

'Three months.'

'Oh, we can deal with that,' she said. 'So, look, you sure, are you?'

Bernie still didn't know. Maybe if she talked to this woman she might be able to make up her mind.

'I'm with this fella,' Bernie said. 'Been with him a couple of years now.'

'Get careless, did he, love?' Dot said. 'Men do. Want to "feel" you, you know, down below. None of 'em like using a letter. Selfish bleeders! Why don't you lay down on the bed so I can have a look at you?'

Bernie got up and walked over to the bed.

'Take your knickers off, that's right,' Dot said.

'But what I'm saying is, it's not his,' Bernie said. 'My fella's. It's someone else's.'

'Oh. Bit of a pickle you're in then. Can't you pass it off as his?'

'No.'

Bernie didn't want to go into the whole story about Heinrich being a very white Jew and Gibrail a dark-skinned Arab.

But Dot said, 'Not a black man, this other bloke?'

'No ...'

''Cause that *is* a problem,' she said. 'But if you say it's not then ... Now let's have a look at you, love. Just open up your legs, that's it.'

Bernie looked at the ceiling. The woman's fingers felt cold and callused; somewhere else in the building another woman shouted at her kids that they were all 'little fuckers'. Was she doing the right thing? When she'd got up that morning it had felt right, but now she wasn't so sure. And what about her visit to see Rosie and Dermot out in Essex? She had to be there on Friday. Would she be well enough to go?

Dot put her hands on Bernie's stomach. 'There shouldn't be

too much pain,' she said. 'But I got a drop of something you can sniff to get rid of that.'

Something she could sniff. What was that? Bernie began to feel afraid.

'Something to sniff?' she said.

'Ether,' Dot said. 'Used to work up Whipps Cross so I know what I'm doing.'

'What did you do there, Mrs . . .'

'Dot.'

'Dot . . .'

Bernie looked up into her folded toothless face.

Dot said, 'I was a cleaner, love. But they trusted me to take the amputations down the furnace.'

'Penny for 'em.'

Raymond put an arm around Dermot's shoulders and nibbled his ear. But Dermot pushed him away.

'What's up with you?' the boy said.

In the barn while they were feeding the cattle, Ray had noticed that Dermot seemed distracted.

'What's up with me?' he said. 'I'll tell you what, shall I? Fucking Viv telling my missus I've been with her, that's what!'

'Viv? Our Viv?'

'Who else?' Dermot said. 'Met Rosie on the towpath yesterday. Just started on about how her and me had been at it. Rose hit her.'

'Christ!'

'But she believed her too! Fucking hell, I don't even like the woman! If it hadn't been for you . . .'

'I'll talk to Viv,' Ray said. 'Sort it out. Surprised she ain't been down here if that happened. You sure it was her?'

'Who else could it be?'

Ray snaked a hand round to the front of Dermot's trousers.

'Fuck off!'

'Oi! Warner!'

They both looked around and saw the farmer, Bill Nice, standing at the entrance to the barn.

Ray let go of Dermot and said, 'Yes, sir?'

'I wanna word with you,' their boss said.

'Oh?'

'Yeah. I want you to come up to the house with me now,' he said.

Suddenly Raymond looked afraid.

'Oh, what's it . . . '

'Never you mind what it's about, I'll tell you when we get to the house! And you, Lynch, you get on with your work.'

'Yes, sir.'

Ray left with Farmer Nice, his head held low and, Dermot observed, his hands shaking.

Her father always managed to be out when he knew that Becky needed to talk about something he didn't want to discuss. This time was no exception and so, instead of waiting for him to creep home, she went out to look for him.

He was likely to be either lurking in Bloom's, nursing cup after cup of lemon tea, or walking around a graveyard – Jewish or Christian, he didn't discriminate. The churchyard at the end of the road was the obvious place and so she began to walk towards Christ Church.

Moritz Shapiro didn't really have friends and so it was almost certain that she'd find him alone.

Becky waved to Mr Nadel the furrier whose business was based beside the side-gate into the churchyard. She turned left to go inside, which was when she found herself face to face with Solly Adler.

132

'Oh,' she said. 'What ...'

As was his custom, he took off his cap to her.

'Nurse Shapiro.'

'Mr Adler, I thought you'd be at work.'

For years he had worked for his wife's uncle in his sweat shop.

'I've got a new position,' he announced. 'In the post office.'

Solly's brother Ben was a postman. It was very likely he'd fixed this up.

'Postman,' he confirmed. 'So start early and finish early too, which is handy. I can be at home for our Natalie when she comes home from school.'

'That's good.'

They looked at each other. Everyone knew that Sharon Adler had taken off with some bloke up West. Unlike when they'd met at Pellicci's, Becky decided to just come out with it.

'I heard that your wife ...'

'Yeah,' he said.

'I'm sorry.'

Solly shrugged. 'Better really. Means I can spend all me time with the little 'un.'

She smiled. 'So ...'

'Just going up the Lane for some beigels.'

'Oh, have you walked across the churchyard?'

'Yeah.'

'Didn't see my father there, did you?'

'No,' he said. 'Why?'

'I need to speak to him,' she said. 'But he's done a runner.'

Solly laughed. 'Parents, eh?' he said. 'My mum's always on the missing list if there's something important going on.'

'If you do see him, could you let him know I'm looking for him?'

"Course.'

Solly made as if to leave and then he said, 'I don't mean nothing by this, nurse. I mean, it'd only be as friends, but if you have some spare time at the weekend, I wondered whether you'd like to come with us – me and Nat that is – to Victoria Park. Just for a stroll like . . . '

She did like him. Even after all these years, there was definitely a soft spot deep inside her for Solly Adler. But he was still married. She said, 'I don't know . . . '

'We're taking a picnic,' he said. 'Mum'll make it, so it won't be horrible.'

She laughed.

'I mean, as a bloke I'm a bit . . . '

'Of course I'd love to come,' Becky said.

'Oh, that's . . . ' Clearly, he had thought she would say no. But now his face lit up.

'How could I not?' Becky said. 'Your mum used to work at Lyons Corner House, she must make the best sandwiches in the world.'

'I dunno about that . . . '

'So what time?'

'I was thinking about one in the afternoon,' he said. 'Me and Nat'll come and pick you up. Get the train from Liverpool Street.'

'I'm not at work until six so that'll suit me fine,' Becky said. 'I look forward to it.'

'Me too. Thanks.'

And then he left her, scuttling away towards Brick Lane, his face very slightly red. It was strange. They were both adults and yet they'd spoken to each other as if they were a couple of kids again. Becky walked into the graveyard and made her way down towards Commercial Street.

*

St Anne's Church was on her left as Bernie walked down the Commercial Road on her way back to her mum's flat. As she passed by she looked in to catch a glimpse of the strange pyramid that stood in the graveyard. Nobody knew why it was there except that it had been deliberately constructed by the church's architect, Nicholas Hawksmoor. He'd also built Christ Church at the bottom of Fournier Street and, according to her late father, there had been rumours about Hawksmoor being some sort of magician.

Thinking about Pat Lynch made Bernie smile. He wouldn't have wanted her to risk her life having an abortion. She'd felt sick as soon as old Dot had touched her. Even with ether on hand, Bernie had known she couldn't go through with it. The old girl had been very understanding, even made her a cup of tea.

'It ain't for everyone,' she'd told her as they'd sat in her damp, greasy flat drinking very sweet tea. 'I know it'd put me out of business but I think they should make it legal. So many girls get in trouble these days, it's like a flood.'

Bernie knew what she meant. Including Rose, she knew eight girls who'd had illegal abortions. Two of them had died.

'I'm sorry I wasted your time,' she'd said.

Dot had waved this away. 'No need. Lot of girls can't go through with it,' she said. 'I'd never make no one. You thought about what you might do now?'

Bernie had shaken her head. 'Not really.'

But now she had to think about it. Her mammy wouldn't be home for hours, but she'd known where Bernie intended to go and would want to know what had happened.

If she went back to Israel, she'd have to tell Heinrich about the pregnancy. He'd know it wasn't his because they hadn't made love since the beginning of the year and she was only three months pregnant. She'd couldn't cover up her infidelity.

What she did then would depend upon what he decided to do. They couldn't marry because his wife wouldn't give him a divorce and it was a big commitment to raise another man's child as his own. He could easily chuck Bernie out and, if he did that, she'd have to leave Israel and come home. He'd go mad once he knew it was Gibrail's baby, but Bernie couldn't do anything about that. She owed it to Heinrich to tell him the truth and so that was what she would do. Her mammy wouldn't approve and would worry furiously, but there was nothing Bernie could do about that.

Raymond's face was white and his eyes stared into the distance as if he'd seen something truly terrible on the horizon. But the fact that he had returned at all was a good sign.

Dermot grabbed his shoulders and led him behind the stables. He said, 'What happened? What did he want with you?'

The boy had been in with Farmer Nice for well over an hour. The old man was not given much to conversation and so Dermot had wondered what he'd been on about all that time. Dermot hoped the lad hadn't mentioned his name at all. The less Farmer Nice knew about his workers' private lives, the better.

Eventually, when he was able to speak, Ray said, 'Viv told her old man about her being up the stick.'

'Christ!'

She'd not told Rose that when they'd met on the towpath, thank God.

'So I've said to him I'll marry her,' Ray said.

'Did he give you a choice?'

'Not really.' He shook his head. 'Give her two black eyes he has. She was crying.'

136

'She was there?'

'Couldn't go out looking such a sight. Anyway, it's what she wanted all along.'

'What? To be married?'

'I told ya, she's right got the hots for me,' Ray said complacently.

'And you? Do you want to get married?'

He shrugged. 'Don't mind, do I? I mean, won't mean nothing can't still happen with us.'

'But you'll be married!'

'Well, you're married.'

It was a fair point.

'Farmer's gonna give us that old cottage out by the road down to the river,' Ray said. 'Then we're on our own. I'll have to keep her and the kid and ... ' He sighed. 'Ain't got no gas or 'lectric that old place. Viv ain't used to living like that.'

Dermot ignored this hard luck story. He had other worries. 'My name come up at all?'

'Nah. Kept you out of it.'

'And Viv?'

'Her too.'

'And yet she told my wife ... '

Raymond laughed. 'That was just her having a bit of a laugh,' he said.

'My Rose ain't no fool.'

'Yeah, but so what?' Ray said. 'You can tell her Viv's marrying me because I got her up the stick. Ain't lying. Only person what can't know about what we all done together is Farmer Nice 'cause then you'd lose your job.' He paused for a moment. Dermot could feel the boy's mind turning over.

'Well, of course, we'll need a bit of help, Viv and me,' he said.

'Help? What exactly do you mean by that?'

'Money, ' the boy said. 'A bit extra. Be hard for us on my wages.'

Dermot had always known that Raymond was a mercenary little swine, but he also knew that he was besotted with him. Ray only had to touch him and Dermot was lost.

'Are you blackmailing me?' he said with a creeping sense of dread.

'Only sayin',' Ray replied. 'Be a pity if Old Farmer Nice found out you'd shagged his darling daughter, wouldn't it? Be a bit of a mess if your wife got to know too.'

'But I haven't . . . I just played around a bit with her because you said to.'

'Yeah, you keep saying that, Der,' Raymond said. 'You try and prove that one, son.'

And there it was. Dermot felt his heart sink. He'd always known that Ray was a selfish little shit with no morals. Had he always known that the boy would blackmail him if he could? Of course he had, Dermot was no fool! But he and Rose and Morry were skint most of the time anyway, how on earth was he going to pay to keep this evil little bastard's mouth shut?

Dermot looked away.

He felt Ray put a hand on his buttock. Then it moved around to the front of his trousers. Dermot didn't push him away.

'Call it payment for services rendered,' Ray whispered to him. 'Because there will be services . . . '

Then he kneeled down in front of Dermot and began to unzip his fly.

Her papa arrived home just after Becky had seen Bernie return to her mum's flat and decided to go over and talk to her. But she needed to have a word with Moritz first.

He was surprised to see her in the kitchen.

'Ah, Rebekeh-leh,' he began.

Becky didn't wait to launch into her question.

'What was Mrs Rabinowicz doing here?' she asked.

'Ah . . . '

'Yes, ah. I'm not about to forget she turned up here when you thought I was going out with Bernie,' she said. 'What's happening, Papa?'

'Happening?'

He put his Homburg hat on the kitchen table and sat down. 'What do you mean?'

'We all know what Mrs Rabinowicz does for a living, Papa,' Becky said.

'Ah, yes, but we were just talking, she and I . . . '

'About what?' Becky said. 'I remember when she invited you to listen to the King's Coronation on her wireless and you were horrified. You had to sit in her stuffy drawing room with all those other people aching for the *shadchan* to fix their sons and daughters up with potential matches. You hated it.'

'I did.'

'And so why invite her in – as if I hadn't worked that out . . . '

He sighed. Then shrugged. 'What can I say? I see you working all these hours, getting thinner and, yes, getting older, and I think, "Rebekah should be taken care of." What father doesn't think like that? And now this area is so rundown and everyone is moving away, what kind of future do you have here?'

'I don't know,' Becky said. 'Who does? We live in a world full of change, Papa. At the moment, I'm happy. I like living here with you and working at my hospital.'

'But you are so alone, my daughter!'

'Papa, I've got loads of friends at work! We go down to see Rose and Dermot every month and, don't forget, my job is

139

tiring. I don't want to live miles and miles from the hospital, this place suits me fine.'

'I will die soon.'

'No, you won't!'

'Everyone dies.'

'Yes, it's called being human! Papa, I could die tomorrow . . .'

'God forbid!'

'We learned that in the war,' she said. 'But there's no point in worrying about it.'

'I want to see you settled,' he said. 'Happy.'

'I am happy! I love my job, I have friends and . . . Papa, even if you do die, I won't be out on the street, will I? You own this house and one day it will come to me. I'm very lucky.'

Moritz didn't say anything for a while. She was right, she was lucky. Most of the people they lived amongst were in circumstances that were far more precarious and impoverished. Becky didn't need to be married. He simply felt that it would be better for her if she was.

'So anyway, let's have an end to matchmakers, OK?' Becky said. 'If I marry, I marry. And if I don't, never mind.'

Her father shook his head mournfully.

'And think of it this way, Papa,' she said. 'If I marry, I'll have to give up nursing. And I can't think of anything that would make me less happy than that.'

Once she'd put Morry to bed, Rose went and sat down beside the fire with Dermot. They'd barely spoken since he'd got in from work, but now she had things to say to him.

'I spoke to Mrs Linden about that girl I met on the towpath and she told me she's Farmer Nice's daughter. Called Vivian, Mrs Linden said, and no better'n she should be for a twenty year old. You know her, don't you?'

'I've seen her,' Dermot said. 'Matter of fact, just heard today that she's going to be marrying one of the other farm hands.'

'Oh?'

'Lad called Raymond. Got her up the stick.'

'And yet she told me ...'

'She lied to you, Rosie,' he said. 'If I'd known it was that Vivian you'd met, I could've put you straight this morning.'

'I don't understand why she'd say that if she's in the family way by this boy,' Rose said. 'What's that got to do with you?'

'Nothing,' he said.

'You know this other hand, though? The one what got her in trouble?'

'A bit,' he said. 'Honestly, Rosie, it's nothing to worry about. Now let's have an end to it.'

He could see she was still disturbed by what had happened but he also knew that she'd let it be. Rose was basically a trusting soul and Dermot always felt bad about not telling her the whole truth. But what else could he do?

Yes, he'd reluctantly played sex games with that girl but now she was marrying Raymond. That made him feel jealous and slighted, but he couldn't do anything about it. Ray had said the two of them would carry on anyway and so it wasn't as if the boy had entirely rejected him. And then there was the money. If nothing else that would keep Ray close to him, but how was Dermot supposed to get hold of cash he didn't have?

Chapter 12

December 1952
Jerusalem, Israel

'How are you feeling now?'

Bernie came out of the bathroom with a face the colour of ash.

'Not at my best,' she said.

'Do you feel up to going to work?' Heinrich asked.

'I'll go mad if I stay in the flat,' she replied.

He shrugged. 'Well, if you're coming, we'd better get going or we'll be late.'

Bernie had told Heinrich about the baby as soon as she'd returned from her visit to England. He had been hurt but not surprised. She was young and beautiful while he was, as he put it, 'old and tired'. That notwithstanding he'd agreed to raise the child as his own, even though it would be born a bastard. Sometimes Bernie wondered whether he ever thought about Gibrail and what would happen should the young Arab appear in their lives again. Since he was caught up in the turmoil of the rise of Arab nationalism in Egypt, it was unlikely, but not impossible.

'Are you out today?' Heinrich asked her as they left the flat and began to walk down the stairs to the front entrance to the block.

'Yes,' she said.

'Where?'

'The Dead Sea.'

'The Dead Sea is a big place.'

'There's a new hotel being built near the rock of Masada,' she said.

Heinrich frowned. 'That's in the middle of nowhere!'

'It may be, but Gershon wants it covered and who am I to argue with our editor?'

'Who's reporting?'

'Ari Yaffe,' she said. 'The owners of the hotel want some publicity shots too so it'll be worth my while.'

'I hope Ari's driving,' Heinrich said.

'Absolutely not!'

'You're driving?'

'Have you seen Ari drive?' she said. 'I'd be safer in a lake full of sharks! Drives as if he's on fire!'

'Oh.'

Having reached the front door, the two of them walked out into a cool winter's day and got in Heinrich's car.

Once inside he said, 'Well, just be careful, alright? Remember . . .'

'I'm pregnant, yes,' she said, and then squeezed his arm affectionately.

It was good he was so involved in anticipating this baby even if it wasn't his.

*

The first smell that hit you as soon as you closed the street door was cigar smoke. That and a strange concoction that seemed to be made up of coffee, bacon and garlic. Dermot didn't like it but he knew why Joey insisted they meet at the Bar Italia. It was full of wrong 'uns.

Apparently, at any time of the day or night, you could see representatives from most of London's crime families in this small coffee bar on Frith Street, Soho. Also Joey lived just around the corner and so it was convenient for him.

He and his boys had spread out along a bench table. Sitting behind them was an extraordinary character who wore a deep burgundy velvet jacket and had a purple rinse on their hair.

Dermot went up to the counter and ordered a frothy coffee before joining his brother and his 'boys'. There were four of them – Ted who was about sixty and looked as if he'd been hit in the face with a concrete block, ex-soldier Stu, border-line out of his mind, and the Craxi brothers, Italian and little more than kids. They'd all done time except for Joey and the younger Craxi, Vincenzo.

'Glad you could make it,' his brother said when Dermot came to join them.

'Tube was murder,' he said and sat down.

Around them, conversations – urgent or strained – resounded against the walls, the buzz of sound obscuring all but the loudest exclamation.

'The shop starts packing up at five so we go at quarter-past,' Joey said.

Dermot had begged his brother to let him in on this job. He hadn't wanted to but Raymond was pressuring him for money. Joey had taken him on as driver, thanking the Krays very much for their bloke, but turning him down on account of the fact that Dermot was family.

Family! What the rest of them would say if they knew, especially Mammy, didn't bear thinking about. Dermot knew she'd never forgive him if she found out. He knew he'd never forgive himself for doing this but then that was yet another cross he'd have to bear. And all because he loved men – something he couldn't help.

Joey looked at his brother. 'All you have to do is pick the car up from Tatty Mick's and then drive it to Grocers' Hall Court for quarter-past five. Then you wait there.'

'What if you don't turn up?'

'We will,' Joey said.

'How can you be so sure?'

Old Ted piled in. 'I know he's your brother, Joey, but do we need this kind of talk?'

'Shut up,' he told Dermot. 'I've sorted it. Right?'

'Right.'

Dermot lowered his head. Either the next day would see them dripping in knocked-off jewellery or else they'd all be inside. The way he felt, it didn't matter either way to Dermot. What with Raymond's demands for money and the fact that Rose didn't trust him anymore, what was the point? Even his mammy looked at him askance these days. But then there was Morry. How would it be for him if his father was inside? He'd already let the kid down, doing what he'd done with Ray, but things could get so much worse if he ended up in prison. What would Morry make of him then?

'Mick's expecting you at midday,' Joey said. 'So don't be late.'

Mick Hanrahan, known to just about everyone as 'Tatty' on account of his terrible clothes, lived in Wapping. Dermot had arranged to stay with his mother the night before and it was just a twenty-minute walk.

'I won't. So what ...'

'You don't need to know nothing about the job,' Joey said. 'So don't ask.'

Dermot shut up.

'You'll get your money as soon as it's over, unlike the rest of us,' his brother said. 'So button it.'

Dermot was going to get a hundred pounds for driving the gang away from the scene. That was all he needed to know and all, apparently, he was going to be told.

When the other blokes had gone and it was just Dermot alone with his brother, he said, 'There won't be no shooters, will there, Joey?'

'I told you once, I won't tell you again.'

'You promise?'

Joey ruffled Dermot's hair in the same way he'd done when they were both kids.

'Would I lie to you?' he asked.

And Dermot knew the answer to that question. It made him feel cold.

For a moment, Becky didn't know where she was. This wasn't her bed! This wasn't her room, which was so much bigger than this cold little shoe-box! She sat up and automatically looked at her watch. God, it was ten o'clock! She was just swinging her legs out of bed when she realised that she wasn't on shift until the evening. Then she remembered where she was.

The bedroom door opened and a fully dressed Solly Adler came in bearing a cup of tea. He smiled at her. He'd put on a little weight lately and it suited him. These days he looked a lot happier.

'Sleep well?' he asked her as he placed the cup and saucer down on the bedside cabinet.

'Yes, thank you,' she said.

'I'll leave you to get dressed,' he said.

As she sipped her tea, Becky recalled the events of the night before. Dolly Adler, Solly's mum, had invited her the previous week.

'Come round ours next Thursday night,' she'd said. 'We're having a bit of a knees-up.'

Apart from Christmas at the Lynches, Becky had never been to an East End knees-up. It was the kind of raucous party of which her father had always disapproved. But now that she was an adult she could make her own choices. Also she was seeing a lot of Solly Adler these days. So far they'd been on two picnics with Natalie and four other 'dates' – walks by the river and a couple of trips to the pictures. They were friends and so last night Becky had stayed in Solly's bed, quite alone, once the last of the other guests had left in the early hours of the morning.

Her papa had known that Becky was going to be staying there. Dolly Adler had sought him out and told him herself.

'Becky needs to get out while she can, Mr Shapiro,' she'd told him. 'Soon enough she'll be at home with a husband and babies, good-looking girl like her.'

She'd said nothing about how close her son and his daughter had become recently, but both Dolly and Becky knew that her father was aware of it.

Ever since that first picnic back in October, Moritz had watched the relationship deepen without comment. Becky wondered how he'd feel if he knew that she and Solly hadn't even kissed as yet.

They'd come close to it. The knees-up in Dolly's cramped living room, around her ancient out-of-tune piano, had been riotous. Solly's Uncle Mervyn had come over from Wanstead with enough beer to sink a ship while his cousin Stephen had provided a lot of vodka and lime which, to Becky, had tasted a bit like she imagined petrol would. But she drank it anyway – hence her taking over Solly's bed. Hence her almost kissing him.

But he had, gently, pushed her away. The last thing she remembered from the previous night was a vision of Solly tucking her into his bed and then chivalrously leaving. The memory of it made her both smile and want to cry at the same time. Was she falling for him all over again?

She'd seen it before, but this time, looking up at the huge rock of Masada made Bernie think about Rose.

Situated on the shores of the Dead Sea, it was a bleak place, freighted with a history that summed up the tragedy of the Jewish nation. Masada had been the location of the Jews' last stand against the Roman invaders in AD 73. After that the Twelve Tribes had forever wandered – to Europe, Asia, the Americas, Australasia. Now she was back in the Land of Israel, Bernie finally understood why all the Jews she knew were so passionate about this tiny country in the depths of the Middle East.

Rose, too, came from a wandering tribe, but hers was of a different sort. Where the Romany people came from and why they travelled was a mystery. Some said they had come originally from Egypt while others pointed to an Indian heritage. Bernie didn't know the truth of the matter, but what she did understand was that Rose and her mother were restless souls.

Nell Larkin was due to come out of the sanatorium at Christmas. And although she had finally agreed to go and stay with her daughter while she continued to recover, Bernie also knew that Nell was gagging to go back to Blessed and her old job. She learned all this from letters received regularly from Becky. Bernie's brother Dermot was also cause for concern, it seemed. Back in October he hadn't seemed like himself. Now Becky confirmed that he 'looks thin and tired'. What was going on there?

It had been hard for Bernie to tell Heinrich about Gibrail and the baby. When she'd first spoken of it, he'd left the apartment and disappeared for two days. When he'd returned, he'd cried.

She had expected him to be bitter and blame her for succumbing to Gibrail's obvious charms but he hadn't. Instead he'd said he was sorry he hadn't loved her enough and had asked what he could do to make things work again between them. She hadn't known how to reply and so she'd remained silent. Ever since then they had both behaved as if the child were his. In a way it was, inasmuch as it would never know its real father. Not now.

As far as Bernie knew, Gibrail was still in Egypt. After the King was sent into exile in Europe, Colonel Nasser and his Free Officers were put in charge of the country, which had to be music to Gibrail's ears. Arab Nationalism was a rising force in the region and one Israel felt threatened its existence. The whole notion of 'homeland' was, Bernie had come to see, a very fluid one.

Still looking at the massive rock above her, she wondered what childbirth would be like. Becky had sent her a long list of things she should ask about before she was admitted to the hospital Heinrich had selected for her. Called the Bikur Cholim, it catered largely for Orthodox Jewish women, but gentiles were permitted on its wards too. Bernie's main worry was that she wasn't married. Of course, the hospital administration would know, but would the nurses and the doctors? And what about the other women on the ward? Although Bernie had some grasp of the Hebrew language she was by no means fluent. Would she even be able to exchange pleasantries with the other ladies?

But it was pointless speculating. For the time being she had simply to enjoy her last months as a woman without children and keep her fingers crossed regarding the future. Whatever happened, she had seen the Pyramids and so she'd achieved her daddy's goal for her. Thinking of Pat Lynch always made Bernie smile.

'Something's up, I know it is,' Kitty said.

She was on her tea break with her youngest Aggie, who had come to work at Tate & Lyle's with her mother two weeks ago.

Aggie, who looked both sweet and glamorous in her work overalls, her hair tied up in a colourful and elaborate scarf, said, 'Oh, you worry too much, Mammy!'

'Your brother's never been so keen to be popping back home all the time as he is now,' Kitty said. 'Christ knows what Rose thinks about it all!'

'I think Rosie's got enough on her plate with little Morry and her mum,' Aggie said. 'Maybe Dermot don't want to be around too much when Nelly gets out.'

'Oh, he can handle Nell Larkin,' Kitty said. 'And if he can't then he knows he just has to have a word with me and I'll sort her out. No, he's up to something. Staying over again tonight! When's he at work, for Christ's sake?'

Aggie shrugged.

Realising she was boring her own daughter, Kitty said, 'So tell me about Becky Shapiro and Solly Adler? I hear they've been seen stepping out together.'

Aggie laughed. 'Stepping out together? Who are you, Mammy, Queen Victoria? Yes, Becky and Solly have been seen going to the pictures. What of it?'

'He's a married man.'

'Married to a tart who's buggered off!' Aggie said. 'Anyway, what's it to you, Mammy? Our Bernie's long over Solly and especially now she's ...'

'Don't say it!' Kitty held up a warning finger.

'Especially now she's pregnant ...'

Kitty swiped her youngest round the side of her head.

'Ow!'

'Don't you say that!' Kitty said. 'Not outside our home!' She lowered her voice. 'Your sister's keeping her shame concealed out there in the back of beyond – let it stay there!'

'Mammy!'

'No,' Kitty said. 'I'll not have it spoke of, you hear?'

Aggie became silent and the two of them didn't speak again until much later on that day. The world was changing with regard to what was 'shameful' and what wasn't. Aggie knew this and was annoyed that her mother didn't. When Bernie had been at home back in October, her 'shame' had almost ruined what should have been a good time for the whole family.

Fashion wasn't something Becky Shapiro had ever really paid a lot of attention to. During the war, clothes had been hard to come by and had consisted mainly of the make do and mend home-made variety. Material, such as it was, had been in short supply and anything approaching a 'style' had been non-existent.

But ever since glamorous new lines had been produced in Paris back in the late forties, women in Britain had started to feel the effect of what was known as the New Look. This was basically a very feminine silhouette, comprising full skirts, cinched-in waists and, often, sweetheart necklines. Becky had bought her first, full-on New Look dress for Dolly's knees-up and it had made an impression.

When Becky left Solly's bedroom and walked into the Adlers' booze-scented living room, she once again caught Dolly's eye.

'You look a right treat in that, Rebekah,' she said as she nursed a glass of sparkling Andrews liver salts. 'And I say that as a woman who's disgustingly hungover. Don't judge me!'

Becky smiled. 'I won't.'

'And I should add that black and white is really you,' Dolly said. 'Do you want some of this, girl?'

She held out her glass of liver salts to Becky.

'No, thanks.'

'Well, you've a head for that vodka better'n I have,' Dolly said. 'Blimey! Feel as if I've been kicked in the skull.'

'I'm sorry.'

'All me own fault, love. All me own fault.'

'Well, I'd best go now,' Becky said.

'Oh, our Solly's doing some breakfast,' Dolly said. 'Bacon and eggs.'

Becky knew that the Adlers didn't keep kosher but she still found the casual way they sometimes talked about food a little bit shocking. Even though she and her father had stopped eating strictly kosher during the war, they still drew the line at bacon.

'No, I must get home, thank you,' Becky said.

As she was leaving the flat, she saw Solly moving things round in a hot, smoky frying pan.

'I'll see you, Solly,' she called out as she left.

Because he couldn't abandon the hot frying pan, he just blew her a kiss.

Chapter 13

'If you wanna see the future then you should go and see your Dermot's missus,' Sharon said as she watched Joey pace the floor at the end of their bed like a caged tiger.

'What?' he said. 'What you talking about?'

'You,' she said. 'I know what you're like. Thinking about all them things that could go wrong, or might go wrong. Want a crystal ball, you do. Why I suggested you go and see that Rosie Larkin.'

He shrugged.

'Gyppos, wasn't they?' Sharon said. 'Her and her mum. Can look into the future the gyppos can.'

Joey lit a cigarette. 'Don't be so daft.'

'I'm not daft,' she said. 'Look, if it works out it works out and ...'

He leaped over the end of the bed and took her by the throat.

'You the one taking risks, are you?' Sharon attempted to speak, but couldn't. 'I thought not,' he said. 'Me, ain't it? Yeah!'

He let her go and she gasped. 'Shut yer yap unless you know what you're talking about!'

He was always anxious before a job. But knocking over a post office in Epping was a long way from doing over one of the biggest jewellers in the country.

When she'd finally got her breath back, Sharon said, 'I'm sorry, babe. I know it's ...'

'If this goes to plan we can sod off,' Joey said. 'Italy, South of France, anywhere you like. A million quid's worth, my boy reckons, a million fucking quid.'

Through judicious use of alcohol and dope, Joey had got close to one of the young shop assistants at Mappin & Webb on Poultry. A clearly very, very secret homosexual, Ernest Waits possessed a love of Soho coffee joints and an ambition one day to go to Morocco. Joey, who liked the odd frothy coffee himself, had promised Ernest enough money to *buy* bloody Morocco provided he did as he was asked. Ernest had almost bitten his hand off.

Sharon, who'd been unimpressed by twenty-year-old, Ernest kept *schtum*. She'd said her piece when Joey had first cultivated the lad and he hadn't listened then. He certainly wouldn't now the job was imminent.

'Mummy?'

'Yes, darlin'?'

'Will me dad be back tonight?'

Dermot's latest visit to his mother was a two-day affair and so Rose said, 'No, love. Tomorrow.'

'What's he doing?' Morry asked.

'He's up with Nanny Kitty,' she said. Then looked at her mother who was sitting across the breakfast table from them. Nell made a face, but she said nothing.

Although she'd never told her mother the truth about Dermot, Nell knew. If questioned, she'd say it was because of her gypsy second sight. What was probably the truth of the matter was that Nell was and had always been a keen student of the weaknesses of men.

When the little boy left the breakfast table to go to the toilet, Nell said, 'Why don't you and Morry come back and live with me? Blessed'll take me back and you can get some cleaning work. We'll manage.'

Rose rolled her eyes. 'Why would I wanna do that, Mum?' she said. 'If Der is playing around then he should be the one to go and he should be the one who supports us.'

'Stuck out here in the middle of nowhere,' Nell grumbled. 'Come home! We'll go today!'

'No.'

'Why not?'

"Cause I don't like it up there no more,' Rose said. 'I like it here, Mum.'

'I don't like it here.'

'No, but you're gonna be here until you're strong enough to go back to London. You promised.'

Nell put her head down, grumbling to herself.

Morry came in from the toilet and put his coat on.

'Now I've got to take the little 'un to school,' Rose said to her mother. 'You wait in the warm and then you and me can go out and look for mistletoe for Christmas.'

Nell couldn't think of anything worse. As a child she'd been sent into Epping Forest with her brothers to collect mistletoe and holly to sell door to door for Christmas. She'd hated it. There had never been much mistletoe and the holly had shredded her fingers. But she didn't say anything.

As she watched Rose and Morry head down the lane

towards the child's school, Nell thought about Dermot again. She had a bad feeling about him.

Mick Hanrahan was a tall, thin bloke with curly fair hair and a smell all his own. A car mechanic by trade, he'd always lived on Wapping High Street with his mother and four sisters. Who their father was was anyone's guess, but the Hanrahans were a lively bunch, with the exception of Tatty.

'It's a Sunbeam,' Mick said.

Dermot looked at a big black car that could do with a polish. 'Where's it come from?'

Mick looked at him and then away. It was not a question that warranted or even deserved an answer.

'If you can trace them plates, I'll eat me 'at,' he said after a pause. Dermot nodded. Mick was a bloke of few words.

He handed over the keys. 'I've filled her up,' he said.

'So where'd I take it ... after?'

He shrugged. 'Wanstead Flats.'

He walked back into his house, which was also his garage. One of the sisters came out from somewhere at the back of the building and said, 'You wanna cuppa, Mickey?'

'If you like.'

Dermot, left alone in the street with the car, walked around the vehicle to familiarise himself with it. What he was supposed to do between picking the car up and doing the job, he didn't know.

When Becky got home there was a letter waiting for her from Bernie. It was folded inside a Christmas card. Her papa was with a client in his work-room and so she sat down at the kitchen table to read it.

Dear Becky

Hope this letter gets to you before Christmas so that you can display a card that actually comes from Jerusalem on your mantelpiece! It's a photograph of the Church of the Holy Sepulchre, which won't mean much to you, but if you show it to Mammy, she'll be really impressed.

I'm still working hard despite my condition and things are alright between Heinrich and myself. I will have the baby in a hospital here in Jerusalem in April. It's quite a religious one and so I don't know how I'll get on with the other ladies.

It seems strange to be pregnant. I never thought I'd have children, but what do I know, eh? Any news on your side? You never mention any young men and so I just assume you're still on your own. You shouldn't be. Not unless you want to be.

Have you heard from Rosie? I do wish that she could write, but I don't suppose that will ever happen now. Dermot sent me a photo of little Morry, who is growing up fast. I hate to miss so much, but until this baby is born I can't really plan. I know that Heinrich wants us all to stay here, but I really don't know these days. In one way this is a lovely, sunny country, perfect for raising children, but it's also really dangerous. Only last week a bomb went off underneath a car right outside our offices. Don't tell Mammy or the girls.

Anyway I must go now, dear Becky. Love to your papa and big hugs and kisses to you.

All my love,

Bernie

Becky stood the Christmas card on the table and put the letter in her pocket. She missed Bernie so much! And yet she was also painfully aware of the fact that she wasn't telling her friend the truth about herself. There was someone in her life. Although she and Solly weren't sleeping together, they saw each other almost every day.

She knew that Auntie Kitty, Aggie and Marie knew about her and Solly and they all wrote to Bernie from time to time. If Becky didn't tell her soon, someone else would. She could just go to bed after her night-shift and put it to one side, or she could get on and write to Bernie about it now.

Becky walked out of the kitchen and into the living room. She sat down at her papa's old writing desk and took out two sheets of paper and a pen. Then she paused. What exactly was she going to write? What, in fact, was she to Solly and what was he to her? And because he was married, what did that matter anyway?

Feeling deflated, she sat back in the chair and chewed on the end of her pen. It wasn't only Bernie who was uncertain about her future, was it? And anyway, what future? With a married man in tow, some would say there wasn't one. Then she heard a knock at the front door.

There were a lot of guns on the streets of London. Most of them had been brought back by soldiers returning from mainland Europe after the war. Although the Military Police had tried to limit the number of weapons entering the country at the ports, thousands had got through. A lot of them were German.

Joey Lynch had bought his Walther P38 pistol from a bloke who'd needed the money to pay off some tart he'd got in trouble. The Craxis were tooled up as well. They had their old Enfield service revolvers. Stu was too off his head to be tooled up while Ted was too bloody old.

The city was at its most typical – dank and grey, with fog hanging low over the river. Joey stood outside the Mansion House, the Lord Mayor of London's residence, and looked across the road to his target.

The Mappin & Webb building on the city street called Poultry had been built in 1870. A Victorian Gothic design, it occupied a wedge-shaped piece of land. It looked like the famous Flatiron Building in New York – if more ornate. But this was all just tiresome detail to Joey Lynch who simply looked upon the building as a source of money.

Because all the bankers, brokers and other city toff types bought their wives and their secretaries jewellery around Christmas time, Mappin & Webb had more stock than ever in December. Young Ernest reckoned they carried about double the normal amount.

At five o'clock, the staff would start emptying the windows and putting the display cases into the safe, which was in an office at the back of the showroom. Assistants would go backwards and forwards, filling up the shelves until there were just the contents of the cash registers left, which would be packed away last by the manager, Mr Evans. This would take approximately half an hour and so by five-fifteen the staff would be following their usual routine and not expecting the unexpected. Or so Joey hoped.

Of course, he hadn't just taken Ernest's word for this. He'd been in at the end of the day a couple of times himself, being that annoying customer who just can't decide what his wife might like. While attempting to serve him, Mr Evans always made sure that what Ernest called his 'system' for loading the safe carried on without a hitch. And it always did, except that today it wouldn't. And what was more, Ernest would make sure no one sounded the alarm.

Joey looked at his watch and hoped that his brother had picked the car up from Tatty Mick's. He had no idea where the motor came from but, knowing Mick, it had probably been nicked somewhere out in the sticks. He might look like a pile of rubbish, but Mick was no fool – unlike Dermot. Stupid bastard didn't even want to be in on this job, which clearly frightened the shit out of him. Joey didn't know the details, but the stupid tosser owed money to someone. Joey smiled. Dermot had always been a prat. When he'd refused to get involved with Artie Cross's mob down the docks, when he'd run off like a girl when they'd done over the furrier's place . . .

The other dockers had always believed that Dermot was a poof. If he were honest, Joey hadn't even tried to protect him, mainly because he hoped it wasn't true. But the way his brother used to hang about with that little perv Chrissy Dolan hadn't looked good. Now, of course, he had a wife and a kid so there was no more of that talk even though Joey wondered. What could a farm worker living in the arse-end of nowhere owe money for? And to whom?

'What's Granny doing?' Morry asked as he pointed out into the darkening garden.

Rose looked out of the window and peered into the thicket at the river's edge.

Her mother was kneeling on the ground there, a small pile of things beside her. Rose couldn't see what they were but thought she knew.

Wiping her hands on her apron, she said to her son, 'You wait in here and I'll go out and get her. There're some biscuits in the tin on the table.'

The boy went straight for the food. Rose ran out into the garden.

'Mum, what you doing?' she said as she approached her mother.

Nell's eyes were closed and she was muttering something. At her side was a cloth doll wrapped in leaves.

'You cussing someone?'

Rose had seen her lay curses before – mainly on her old lover Len Tobin who had raped and brutalised both of them.

Nell opened her eyes.

'I got a bad feeling about your Dermot,' she said.

'So why you putting your curse on him?'

Nell didn't speak for a moment. She picked up the doll.

'Mum?'

'Don't want him to cause you no harm,' she said.

'He wouldn't.'

'Not saying he'd do it deliberate, but I think that boy's in trouble and I don't want it spreading to you and our Morry.'

Rose sat down beside her and said, 'Mum, please don't do nothing to Dermot. I love him.'

She put a hand on her daughter's shoulder.

'It's done now, girl,' she said. 'You and me, we move amongst these gorgers but we have to protect ourselves from them. Your man's not a bad 'un but I think he have secrets as can bring harm. All I care about's you and the boy. Can't change now, chavvy.'

Rose watched the last rays of the sun disappear behind the trees and felt tears run down her cheeks. Things had been wrong in her marriage for a long time and she had begun to live with an unnamed fear she couldn't express. Had Dermot really had sex with that red-haired girl? She was the daughter of the farmer he worked for. Rose had also heard that the girl was to be married to one of the other farm hands. What, if anything, did that mean for Rose and her family?

When the light had gone completely, she helped Nell back to her feet and they walked together back to the cottage.

Becky tucked herself tight in at Solly's side. It was freezing cold but she was still glad that he'd brought her here. She'd never before seen the huge Christmas tree that the King of Norway sent every year to Britain in thanks for liberating his country from the Nazis. Covered in lights, even through the smog it shone like a beacon of hope for the future.

'It's more wonderful than I imagined,' she said as she held her hat on with one hand, and gripped Solly's arm with the other.

'I'd love to see the forests of Norway,' Solly said. 'Imagine acres and acres of ground covered in trees as beautiful as this?'

She smiled. 'Thanks so much for coming to get me,' she said. 'I would never have come up here on my own. It was a lovely idea.'

'I knew you'd like it,' he said. 'And if you're really good, I'll take you to Lyons for a cuppa and a bun.'

She stayed close by his side. 'Well, now you're talking,' she said. 'Because although I could probably look at this tree all day long, it's really too cold now.'

He patted her hand. 'Then let me escort madam to the nearest Lyons,' he said.

Trafalgar Square was full of people looking at the tree and feeding the pigeons. Later there would be carols but for now all Solly and Becky wanted was tea. Although that wasn't quite true. As they walked across the square towards the National Portrait Gallery, Solly suddenly stopped and looked at her.

Confused, Becky said, 'What is it?'

And that was when, for the first time, without a word, Solly kissed her. And she kissed him back.

Chapter 14

It was cold but Dermot Lynch, muffled up in his greatcoat, hat and gloves, was sweating inside that car. It was ten-past five and, according to Joey, the gang should be preparing to go into Mappin & Webb, their faces covered with stockings. Dermot knew they were armed, whatever Joey said. Why would anyone do what was basically a smash and grab job without taking weapons?

Men in bowler hats and women teetering on high heels, their gloved hands full of Christmas-wrapped boxes and big, overflowing handbags, passed him by without a second glance. A scruffy bloke in a car was nothing to write home about.

Grocers' Hall Court, where the car was parked, led into the precincts of the Worshipful Company of Grocers. The road was narrow and largely deserted as the city emptied out after the working day.

It took quite a while for Dermot to realise that another car had come in and parked behind him. It didn't matter. He could go forwards and still reverse out easily. And at that moment there was no hurry.

'Sir, I'm sorry, we're just about to close . . . '

'Oh, no!'

'Sir . . . '

Joey pushed his way past the little man and into the shop.

'It's me wife's birthday!'

He had a scarf wrapped around his face. The Craxis and Stu wore stocking masks.

'Sir!'

The boys were already in the display cabinets, grabbing diamonds, rubies, gold, anything, smashing glass if they had to.

Joey looked at Ernest who was watching from over by the front door.

'Down on the floor, all of you!' Joey shouted. He waved the pistol above his head. 'Anybody wants to be a hero'll get to meet his maker!'

There were five members of staff, including the manager, all male. Two young men hit the deck and covered their eyes. The manager, Ernest and another man just stood, undecided.

Joey grabbed Ernest and thrust a bag into his hands. 'You! Fill that up!'

The boy moved slowly.

'Quicker'n that!'

They came from two sides – the front entrance and from the back of the shop. Coppers. Loads of them.

'Put the gun down, Lynch!'

Dermot lit another fag. It was a quarter-past five and so the job was now underway. He checked the car's fuel gauge, yet

164

again, and gunned the engine, yet again, just to make sure that it still worked.

He had his route all worked out. Back towards the East End via Leadenhall Street, past Aldgate and then off down the Commercial Road to disappear in the small streets and bomb-sites of Limehouse. There was a dirty great crater opposite The Grapes which they'd push the motor into and then they'd disappear.

Joey had said that Dermot could have his money as soon as the job was over, so with any luck he could head off back to Essex that night and give Raymond his bloody money in the morning. Married now, the boy was kept on a tight rein by that Viv. All Dermot got was the odd fumble with Ray in the cow-shed. The boy wasn't even that enthusiastic any longer. The time was coming when they'd have to pack it in altogether.

Dermot looked in the car's rear-view mirror and saw a pair of eyes staring back at him. Cold and relentless, they made him shudder. London was full of mad bastards these days. Blokes back from the war carrying guns and grudges and a need to get ahead in spite of lost homes, lost limbs and lost hope. Dermot knew how they felt. He knew, in a way, why Joey had never even shown signs of changing his ways. Being honest and careful hadn't ever helped their dad. Pat Lynch had lived and died in poverty, his wife was still there ...

The first gunshot rang through the cold winter air like a muffled bell. The shots that followed sounded like the breaking of branches on a desiccated tree. Dermot felt his heart race, his hands go cold and clammy.

The man with the cold eyes in the car behind got out, accompanied by three others.

*

It was one of the Kray boys' relatives who'd come up with the idea that a Job was a performance. An old travelling man, this uncle or whatever he'd been, had said to Joey, 'It's a magic show is a Job. You have to take the audience with you or you're fucked. And if some cunt interrupts or you forget what you're doing, that's it.'

He'd known it was over when the coppers arrived. In spite of the shooters. What were they for if you didn't intend to use them?

Vincenzo Craxi had dropped his piece as soon as the coppers burst in. Without even being told, the cowardly twat. His brother had followed suit. But Joey couldn't let it go. If this show didn't go on, he had nothing. He shot into a bunch of the bastards coming at him from the back of the shop. Someone had dobbed them in! One of the coppers fell to the ground. For a split second he saw Ernest's face, smirking at him, and aimed for the little grass but by that time the coppers from the front door had him down.

Joey struggled, effing and blinding as they tried, and failed, to get the cuffs on him, and then suddenly he was shot. They weren't armed and so it had to be his own gun. Not once, three times. Once he could and maybe did do himself by accident but the rest ...

No one except the Filth piled on top of him could see what had happened. No one but coppers watched his blood pump out onto Mappin & Webb's expensively carpeted floor. The last thing Joey Lynch saw were the people he'd tell St Peter at the Pearly Gates had murdered him, just as surely as Artie Cross had murdered Fred Lamb in front of Joey's eyes all those years ago back in Spitalfields.

The policeman with the dead eyes patted him down against the side of the car.

'I'm not armed,' Dermot said.

'We have to check you ain't lying, son,' Inspector Bridges said.

'What's happened? I heard loud bangs.'

'That's for you to tell us, I imagine,' the inspector said. 'Mappin & Webb mean anything to you, son?'

'No …'

'So why say you're not armed when my oppos have just attended a scene over at Mappin's involving shooters?'

'I …'

'Best button it until you get yourself a brief, son,' the copper said.

'Yeah, but …'

The policeman moved in close so that none of his colleagues could hear and whispered, 'Your brother Joey's done a right number this time, pal.'

Dermot closed his eyes. Someone had grassed. The car containing the coppers had arrived before the Job had started, so they'd known it was happening. Who would have done that?

'I heard …'

'Never you mind what you heard,' Bridges said. 'Never you mind nothing except taking care of number one, boy. When we get down the station, I want to know all about what you was doing here. And "no comment" ain't gonna cut it. You and me both know what's going on here and the only way you're gonna get yourself any sort of clemency is if you come clean.'

When she thought back on it later, Becky realised that it had been her inability to respond to Bernie's letter that had finally made up her mind for her. Solly Adler wasn't just a friend and it was disingenuous to say that he was – especially after their kiss in Trafalgar Square. But, the way things stood then, he wasn't anything more than that either. Except in Becky's head – and Solly's.

There had been a reason why she'd invited him back to her house that evening. She'd known that her papa would be out doing a fitting for a customer in Finchley. And so when they'd arrived back from central London she'd asked Solly in.

Neat and smart, he had looked so handsome when he'd come to pick her up to take her up West. So accustomed was he to his prosthetic leg that he hardly even limped at all these days. Not that it mattered. More to the point was how happy and even young he looked now. Becky hoped she had something to do with that but reasoned that it probably had as much if not more to do with the fact that Sharon had gone.

When they got in, she'd settled him in the drawing room and then she'd heated some scones and made tea. There was no cream to be had anywhere and so they had to make do with some of the home-made jam that Rose had produced in the summer.

'It's strawberry,' Becky had said as she'd placed the tea-tray down on the table.

He'd said, 'Handsome.'

She'd poured and then made up a scone for him. Then they'd chatted. Did he know, she wondered, why she'd invited him back to her house when her father was out? And if he did, did he think she was a tart?

He'd said, 'You'll have to tell Rose her jam's really good next time you see her.'

'Why don't you come and see her too?' Becky had said. 'It's beautiful out in the country. I know Natalie would love it. Be good for her chest.'

He'd said he might well do that. Then she'd made more tea and while she'd been in the kitchen he'd come in and watched her with a smile on his face. How soon after that they'd kissed she couldn't now recall. What she did know was that they'd gone to her bedroom almost immediately. And, although she'd been scared, she'd also been excited.

As he began to undress her she'd said, 'I've never done this before.'

But he'd just smiled. Of course she hadn't. Anyone could see that Nurse Shapiro was a virgin. Why had she said that?

But she knew why. She didn't want him to hurt her and, although the first time wasn't as earth-shattering as some people insisted it would be, it wasn't painful either. And when he made love to her a second time, it was perfect.

Kitty had just put a batch of mince pies in the oven when she heard a knock on the door.

'Oi, Marie!' she called out to her daughter. 'Get that, will ya!'

'Alright.'

Kitty flung the tea towel she'd just used into the wash basket and then washed her hands at the sink.

'Who is it?'

Usually her girls would answer her immediately, but not this time.

'Marie?'

The young woman wasn't alone when she came back into the parlour. There was a man with her, a tall chap, in a uniform. What did the coppers want here?

'Mrs Lynch . . . '

His voice was deep and slightly muffled by his walrus moustache. He was an old copper, probably around Kitty's own age. She felt herself begin to go dizzy but pulled herself together.

'Yeah,' Kitty said. 'You are?'

'Sergeant Pond,' he said. He looked at the kitchen table which, thankfully, was clear of dirty plates for once. 'Can we sit down, Mrs Lynch?'

'You can,' Kitty said. 'I've got too much to do.'

'I think it might be a good idea if you sat down,' Pond said.

Kitty felt her face drain of blood. This was bad, whatever it was. But if she just kept on acting normally maybe it wouldn't be as terrible as she thought it might.

'Sit yourself down then,' Kitty said to the officer. 'Can I get you tea or ...'

'I'll put the kettle on, Mammy,' Marie said. 'You sit down.'

'No ...'

'Sit down, Mammy!'

Her daughter was holding in something so terrible, Kitty could almost see whatever it was wriggle like a snake behind her eyes.

Kitty sat. Marie put a hand on her shoulder and then filled the kettle and put it on the range.

'Mrs Lynch, I've come about an incident as happened on Poultry in the City an hour and a half ago,' Pond began.

'I work down Silvertown,' Kitty said. 'Tate's. I never go up the City.'

'This isn't about you,' Pond said.

'So who is it ...'

She knew what he was going to say next though. She'd been expecting it for years.

'Your son Joseph,' Pond said, 'was apprehended while trying to rob a jeweller's.'

Nobody spoke. Kitty looked at Marie, who turned away.

'I see.'

'Together with his associates, Joseph was loading bags with jewellery. Our officers intervened.'

'So he's arrested?'

The pause told Kitty everything she needed to know. She said again, 'I see.'

'Your son had a gun,' Pond said. 'He shot one of our officers. He couldn't be disarmed without the use of force. I'm sorry.'

Sorry? Kitty felt her head go all over the place. She said, 'Sorry for what?'

'I'm afraid that your son died during the course of being disarmed, Mrs Lynch.'

The kettle began to whistle as it boiled on the range. Marie took it off and put it on the drainer.

Kitty had always known it would end like this. Joey had left the family a wanted man when Fred Lamb had been killed. Pat had always believed the boy was innocent; that Artie Cross had killed Fred the weaver, not Joey. But her son had protected Cross and, despite what Kitty knew about the East End code of never 'grassing', she hadn't been able to forgive Joey for that. So much so that on the few occasions he had tried to come back to her, Kitty had sent him away again.

Eventually she said, 'He was always gonna sort his problems badly.'

Pond didn't comment. Marie put her arms around her mother's shoulders, her own eyes full of tears.

'I'm afraid there's more,' Pond said.

'More?'

Her son was dead, how could there possibly be more?

'Your younger son, Dermot . . .'

Kitty felt her heart miss a beat and she screamed. Not Dermot too! No! Not Dermot, he didn't go about with Joey, he . . .

'He's alright,' Pond said. 'But he has been arrested on suspicion of driving the getaway car for his brother.'

And so that was what Dermot had been up to lately, was it? Kitty put her head in her hands and said, 'God forgive me. God forgive me.'

The grey blanket they'd thrown around his shoulders reminded him of the old army blankets he'd always had on his bed as a kid. Because he'd been the eldest, Joey had been allowed to have the only coloured blanket in the flat. It had been red.

'So?' Inspector Bridges repeated.

Dermot shook his head. They'd told him that his brother was dead, but that couldn't be right. The coppers didn't have guns and this Bridges had told him Joey had been shot dead.

'Ever hear of Ted Moore, Stuart McColl, and Vincenzo and Maurizio Craxi?'

Dermot kept *schtum*.

"Cause let me tell you, son, them boys are singing like canaries,' Bridge said.

Dermot looked away. Every time he thought about Joey being dead his eyes filled up with tears. He'd been a mad bastard and in many ways Dermot had hated him, but he'd loved him too. Joey was his brother!

'With or without you, we'll get all the gen on who did what and when,' Bridges said. 'Don't you worry about that, son. But if you help us, it'll go easier for you. Also, I wouldn't trust them other faces to tell the truth about what happened here today. You're a nice lad with a clean record. The rest of them are scum, I won't sugar-coat it. Moore's done two ten-year stretches and McColl should've been banged up years ago, the mad bastard!'

Still Dermot said nothing.

Even if Joey was dead, which Dermot prayed he wasn't, he

was going to do a stretch of some sort just for being where he was in a hooky car when the robbery went down. Had Tatty Mick grassed? Dermot couldn't see it, but then again maybe the coppers had paid him off? Maybe the Italian boys? Maybe that kid Joey had on the inside? And then he thought about Raymond and the money he would now never be able to give him. Not that it mattered anymore in terms of his job with Farmer Nice. Ray could tell the old bastard anything he liked now, it made no bloody difference to Dermot.

But it would make a difference to Rose and to Morry, and the thought of them was what finally made him cry.

Rose opened the door and rubbed her eyes. Was she seeing things?

'Marie,' she said as she pulled her nightie tightly around her body against the cold. 'What you ...'

It was then that she noticed her sister-in-law wasn't alone.

'We need to come in, Rosie,' Marie said as she and the copper behind her pushed through the front door.

'What's going on?'

Nell, holding a candle aloft to light her way, looked like a ghost in her thick, white nightie.

'Marie?' she said. 'That you?'

'Yes, Nelly, sit down. You too, Rosie,' Marie said.

'What you got a copper with you for?' Nell asked.

Marie led her to the table in the middle of the room and sat her down, then she did the same thing to Rose.

'What's going on?' Rose repeated.

Marie took her hands. 'It's Dermot,' she said.

'I knew it!' Nell interjected.

'Mum!'

'He's been arrested.'

'What?'

'Back home in London,' Marie said. 'He was driving for a job organised by Joey.'

'Joey?'

Marie wiped a tear from her eye. 'I don't know how or why but Der got back in touch with our Joey who led him astray,' she said. 'They was caught trying to rob Mappin & Webb jewellers in the City.'

Rose put a hand up to her mouth.

'He's alright, Rosie,' Marie said. 'Seems he was driving the getaway car. He's at Wood Street police station. He had no part in the raid itself. He's not hurt anybody and he ain't got hurt himself. I'm sorry, Rosie. I wish I knew why this happened.'

Rose squeezed Marie's hands. 'What about Joey?' she said.

Marie shook her head.

'Oh my God!' Rose said.

'He was carrying a gun,' Marie explained. 'You carry a gun ...'

'What about Auntie Kitty?' Rose said. 'Oh, God!'

Marie hugged her. 'Mammy's doing as she always does,' she said. 'She's coping and she's praying.'

She already knew it had gone wrong. At the very least Joey had hopped off with the jewellery on his tod and left her. At the worst the cops had arrived. But there was only so long that Sharon could look at her packed suitcase on the bed and so, close to midnight, she went out.

Soho was alive with music and neon light. Walking down Greek Street, she saw a load of dancing girls giggle their way out of one club and into a drinking dive. They disappeared down a metal staircase in a fug of fag smoke.

Sharon didn't have friends in Soho. Only Joey's mates and

174

they'd been on that job with him. Reg Kray was back in the army and so she was alone. But she knew a couple of people by sight, one of whom she saw as she walked onto Old Compton Street. A weird queer bloke with his hair dyed purple, he liked to hang out at that pub where all the rent boys gathered, the Salisbury.

As she passed him, the man looked at her and narrowed his eyes. 'Is your name Sharon?' he asked.

'Yeah.' For once she didn't also ask *who wants to know* because she felt in her bones that why he was asking. This was important.

'Friend of Joey Lynch?' he continued.

Her heart beat so fast she couldn't speak. The man, seeing her distress, took her elbow. 'Oh, my dear, I can see you don't know ...'

She said, 'Know what?'

He took her to some drinking den. Whether it was on Old Compton Street or not she couldn't later recall. What she did remember was the man's kindness; in fact, the kindness of everyone in the place when he told her that Joey had been shot dead and she screamed the place down.

Chapter 15

April 1953

It wasn't easy pretending to be in good spirits when you felt as if your world had ended. But Becky Shapiro was nothing if not a trouper. As they finished making her father's bed, she said to Rose, 'Do you fancy a bit of breakfast now?'

She knew what the answer would be and Rose said, 'No.'

She was never hungry now, not since her world had been turned upside-down by her husband's arrest back in December. Not only had Rose lost Dermot, she'd also lost his wages and their home in Hullbridge. Not that Becky's father had required her and little Maurice to move out, he'd always said they could stay on his land for as long as they liked. But it was way too far from Wandsworth Prison, where Dermot was being held on remand. Now they lived back with Nell in that tiny old flat next door to the Lynches. As before, Nell worked as maid to working girl Blessed while Rose was a part-time cleaner at the pub at the end of the road, the old Ten Bells.

For a change, Rose and Morry had stayed over at the Shapiros' the previous night, which was why she was helping Becky with the housework. All three girls' lives had been affected by Joey Lynch's failed Mappin & Webb job. Now it was common knowledge that Solly Adler's missus had been Joey Lynch's girlfriend, that family too had been dragged into the general misery. Back in January, Sharon Adler had returned to her husband. She'd had nowhere else to go. And Solly had taken her in.

Becky had been and still was devastated. Solly had cried when he'd told her and they'd clung together for hours, making love and then dissolving into tears in her bed. Becky knew that if Solly hadn't taken Sharon back, he wouldn't have been 'her' Solly anymore and so she had to respect him for his decision. But separated from her lover, she felt so sad.

'I've made some porridge,' Becky continued. 'Try and have a little bit.'

Rose shook her head.

Becky walked over to her and took hold of her friend's shoulders. 'You must, Rosie,' she said. 'You're so thin. It's not good for you.'

Rose looked up at her with black, sunken eyes. 'I don't care.'

'You must care, for Morry's sake,' Becky said. Then she took her by the hand. 'Come downstairs and just have a little bit.'

Rose allowed herself to be led down to the kitchen. Already at the table, Moritz Shapiro put his newspaper down when the women entered.

'Ah, Rose,' he said with a smile. 'Good morning to you.'

'Good morning, Uncle Moritz,' she said. 'Anything much in the newspaper today ...'

Dermot, the Craxi brothers, Ted Moore, Stuart McColl and Mick Hanrahan had been found guilty – the Italians, Ted and Stu to robbery with violence, Mick and Dermot charged as accessories – two days before. The papers were still full of it and, although she could neither read nor write, Rose knew about it.

'Nothing much,' Moritz said. He pulled a chair out for her. 'Now, come, sit. Morry ate a very hearty breakfast before he went to school. So should you.'

Rose sat while Becky made more tea.

'I can't help thinking about the sentencing,' Rose said.

'That's next week,' Moritz said. 'We can know nothing until then.'

'I keep on wondering how long he'll get . . . '

'Dermot has no previous offences,' the old man said. 'He did nothing but attempt to drive for his no-good brother . . . '

'Papa!' Becky said.

'May God rest his soul,' he conceded. 'God be merciful but the boy did shoot a police officer . . . '

Rose turned her face away. The officer Joey had shot had died three days after the attempted robbery. Had Joey lived he would have faced the death penalty.

Quite where the conversation would have gone after that, Becky didn't know because, mercifully, the telephone began to ring.

Living together again was hard on all of them. Only Natalie was glad to see Sharon back in the Adlers' flat and even she was in two minds about it. In the last few months the young girl had enjoyed going out with her dad and Nurse Shapiro. Now her mum was back all that had stopped. And although her mum showed her more affection than before, the atmosphere between Sharon and her mother-in-law Dolly was poisonous.

Wherever Sharon was, Dolly didn't want to be and vice versa. Now sitting in the living room, Dolly could hear Sharon doing the washing-up in the kitchen. It made her want to scream. Eventually she said to Solly, 'Can't you send her out to work or something? Sick to death of her always under me feet!'

'She's not under your feet, Mum,' he said.

'You know what I mean!'

Solly put his newspaper down. He leaned towards his mother so that his wife couldn't hear and said, 'We've talked about this. Her mother wouldn't have her ...'

'So she'd have to go on the streets! Where she's already been in all but name!'

'Mum!'

'Well ...'

Solly said, 'Dermot Lynch'll be sentenced next week, then it'll all be over. We can all move on, including you, Mum.'

'Me!'

'Whether you like it or not, Sharon is Nat's mum and so I have to give her a chance. If I don't ...' He flung his hands in the air. 'What does that say about me?'

'That you're no mug,' Dolly said. Then she dropped her voice. 'You had something with Nurse Shapiro. I know she was keen on you too ...'

'That's all done and dusted now,' Solly said. 'So leave it.'

'Yeah, but ...'

'Leave it!'

Dolly settled herself against the back of the chair, feeling aggrieved. When Solly had got together with Becky Shapiro she'd felt as if her son had finally been blessed. Then, unexpectedly, Sharon had slipped out of the woodwork again and everything had gone to the bad.

*

179

'A boy!'

In spite of the fact that she was an adult, Becky screamed.

'We're naming him Shimon.'

Bernie's voice at the other end of the line was faint and so Becky had to relay what was said to Rose and her father.

'Shimon,' she said. 'That's his name.'

Her father nodded. That, at least, was a good Jewish name.

'When was he born, Bernie?'

'Yesterday,' she said. 'Five o'clock, our time.'

'So three ...'

'There, yes,' she said. 'How is everyone? How's Mammy? And Rosie?'

'Rosie's here,' Becky said as she passed the phone over to Rose. 'Papa, can you go and get Auntie Kitty?'

Moritz left to go across the road and see whether Kitty Lynch was still at home.

'How you doing, kid?' Bernie asked when Rose took the receiver.

'Waiting on the sentencing now.'

Poor thing, she couldn't think about anything except Dermot.

'My bloody stupid brother,' Bernie said.

'He never grassed Joey, Bernie,' Rose said. 'Even though Joey's dead.'

'Because he's a bloody fool!' Bernie said. 'First thing Dermot should've done was tell them everything he knew about that waste of space.'

'Bernie, Joey was your brother too!'

'Yes, and I knew bad things about him, Rosie,' Bernie said. 'Anyway, how are you? How's Morry?'

'We're living back with Mum.'

'Becky told me. How's that going?'

Rose sighed. What was the point of telling Bernie how

180

horrible life had become for them? She was thousands of miles away and couldn't do anything about it.

'We're alright,' she said.

Moritz Shapiro returned shaking his head.

'I think your mum's gone to work,' Rose said as she handed the phone back to Becky.

Rose left the hall and went back into the kitchen.

'She sounds in a bit of a state,' Bernie said.

Becky looked around to see whether her father was still about, but he wasn't.

'Truth is that because Joey shot and killed a copper, there's not much chance of Dermot getting a light sentence even if he didn't do anything. The other blokes'll go down for life, almost certainly. And there's some as think Dermot's sentence won't be far behind.'

'Jesus!'

'You know how it is if you kill a copper. But we'll look after Rosie and Morry . . .'

'She's back with Nell!'

'I've got my eye on it, Bern. Although Nell's not so bad these days.'

'And what about you?'

Becky hadn't told her anything about Solly and now really wasn't the time to do so. Besides, all that was over now Sharon had returned.

'I'm alright,' Becky said. 'Working . . .'

'No one in the picture?'

'No.'

'You want to hurry up,' Bernie said, 'or you'll get left behind!'

She was only joking and Becky laughed, but deep inside she felt pain. She was not getting any younger and had begun to wonder whether Solly Adler had been her last chance at love.

*

181

How do you write to someone who can't read? You address your letter to someone who can and then you trust that person to read it aloud to them. Dermot had agonised over whether to send this letter to Becky or to his mother. Becky would be more understanding and would help Rose to get over it, but his mammy deserved to know the truth. He wrote a note at the top to Kitty, asking her to read what followed to Rose and begging his mother's forgiveness.

Dear Rosie

I can't say much as our letters are censored here in prison. So I'll get straight to the point. I agreed to drive for Joey because I was being leaned on for money. The young boy I worked with was going to tell our boss about how he and I were in an immoral relationship, unless I paid him money. I am so sorry I deceived you. I am a rotten man. But I fell in love. I've not brought any of this into my defence and I never will. But you deserve to know. I'm likely to get at least ten years for what I've done and so I'm asking you now to forget me. Find someone else and get yourself some happiness. You deserve it and Morry deserves a good man as his father.

Whether she'd take his advice or not, he didn't know, but he hoped so. In reality his marriage to Rose had always been a fantasy. They had loved each other, there was no doubt about that. But while he'd still had feelings for other men, it had been impossible for him to settle into a relationship with a woman. And Rosie had been jealous. Although she'd not wanted sex herself, she'd acutely felt the shame of her husband turning to other men.

He looked at the note he'd put at the top of the letter to his mother. She'd never speak to him again. Poor Mammy. Her eldest son dead, Dermot in prison, Bernie unmarried and pregnant . . . Little Paddy had done well for himself, true, but he rarely came home these days, and as for the girls, Aggie and Marie . . .

Although neither of them had exhibited any desire to leave home, Dermot knew they also felt pressure to stay and support their mother. Kitty was of course still working at Tate & Lyle's but, according to Aggie, she was getting worn out with it. Even if one or other of the girls did meet someone, Dermot knew that Kitty would always come first with them.

In a way he found he was looking forward to sentencing. He knew that the other blokes would probably get life. When a copper died, whoever did it hung, but Joey was dead and so society's revenge had to be taken out on other members of his gang. As the driver, Dermot would probably not get life, but as Joey's brother, he might. Not that it mattered. His life was over whichever way you looked at it. By the time he got out . . . No, it was best not even to think about getting out.

His cell smelled of damp stone and piss and when he looked at the toilet bucket in the corner he felt sick. Soon he'd be let out to go and get lunch, which would taste like cardboard, and then he'd be back here again, to look up at a window that was too high to see out of and think about death.

A suicide in the family would just about finish Kitty off. But thinking about it didn't mean he'd actually do it. Thinking about it was probably quite a sane thing to do given the circumstances.

Tilly de Mer put her wig on the block that stood on her dressing-room table and looked at herself in the mirror. Herbert had been going an iron shade of grey for some time, but now there was a bald patch too. It was horrible.

183

The figure was still good. Tilly didn't even have to work at that. Always been slim and trim she had. The face was quite another matter though. Drink, drugs and fags, not to mention late nights and anxious trysts with young men in dodgy places, had done Tilly's complexion no good at all. Underneath all the make-up, which highlighted more than it hid, her skin was grey.

As she smeared the thick lipstick away from her mouth and onto her cheeks, Tilly looked at the way her wrinkles rippled like waves in the sea. Carrying on in drag was becoming depressing. Alright, she knew that the whole point of Tilly de Mer was to laugh at herself and her ageing drag queen persona, but it was taking it out of her. The stiletto heels did her ankles in and she suspected the wigs harboured wildlife, which didn't help her male-pattern baldness. At least she still had the day job, shivering her life away in an office that hadn't changed since Charles Dickens created the character of Ebenezer Scrooge.

All the other queens she knew had either left London or were making small change in after-hours drinking dives, where the punters more often than not threw dog-ends at you or tried to grab your bum in the bogs. It wasn't any way to get old.

Tilly had said she'd be at the Old Bailey to support Rose when Dermot's sentence was read out. Poor little cow was falling apart. Upset about her husband, she didn't like living with her old brass of a mum and hated being back in London. It had all gone wrong for her. But then, Tilly had never thought seriously that it could go right. Dermot had been far too attractive to live on the shelf for the rest of his life. Not that sex had been spoken about at his trial; it was said he'd been led astray by his brother who had been a right wrong 'un. Dermot had wanted money, pure and simple. But Tilly had wondered for a while how and if his sexuality might be implicated.

Life was a bitch sometimes but she knew that you had to take your opportunities where you could. In a previous incarnation, she had run a small grocer's shop for an old widower she knew back in Norwood. That place where Rosie and Morry had lived didn't have any real shops to speak of and Tilly wondered whether she should use her meagre savings to do something about that. After all, Rosie and Dermot had grown quite a bit of veg in their garden and Tilly herself knew a baker out that way. It was worth thinking about at the very least.

Dermot was going to get banged away for a good long time. Rosie and Morry couldn't stay with her mother forever.

Chapter 16

Bernie looked down into the deep blue eyes of baby Shimon and smiled. He was so beautiful. At six pounds he'd been smaller than she'd hoped but he was absolutely perfect and that was all that mattered.

In a way it was a good thing mothers in Israel were supposed to go back to work soon after having children. They were treated as equals in the new republic. But in another way it did mean that she'd have to leave her baby while he was still nursing.

Heinrich had already organised a wet-nurse, a Christian Arab woman called Nasra. Bernie didn't know whether he'd chosen a Christian on purpose but of course it was apt, given who Shimon's real father was. Nasra, a matronly women in her early thirties, was not, as far as Bernie was aware, related to Gibrail but Bernie thought she probably knew of his family. Most of the Christians seemed to know of each other.

Her brother Dermot was due to be sentenced today. Her mammy had told her that as soon as she knew anything she'd call her from the Shapiros'. Dermot had always been Bernie's favourite sibling. Close in age, they'd played together along with Rose, Becky and Chrissy Dolan.

What she'd never imagined was that he would one day end up in prison. Joey, yes; Dermot and Little Paddy, no. But then it had been Joey who had led Dermot astray and she could easily see that happening. And now Joey was dead and unmourned by anyone except for his mother and the woman he'd apparently lived with in Soho.

Trust her mother to tell her who that had been, straight off.

'Solly Adler's wife, Sharon Begleiter,' Kitty had said when Bernie asked.

'How?'

'I don't know. But the woman was always out, carousing in pubs, making a show of herself.'

Sharon had always had a reputation, but actually to leave Solly for Joey ... The whole situation was more terrible than Bernie could ever have imagined. And yet despite it all she did find that she was comforted by the notion of Solly Adler carrying on regardless for the sake of his daughter. She had been so dazzled by him when he'd kissed her in the street all those years ago and still found it hard to forgive her mother for concealing his letters to her during the Spanish Civil War. If she'd let Bernie have them, who knew how different all their lives would have been?

Then she looked down at Shimon and was glad about the choices she had made.

Tilly hailed a cab and went back inside the Bailey to get the women. As she took Rose and her mother by the hand, she told them to pull their hats down over their faces.

'Bloody press are baying for blood outside,' she said as she rushed them out of the Old Bailey and across the pavement to the waiting taxi. All around them people shouted, flash-bulbs went off and a woman's voice rent the air.

'You shameless whores!' she shouted.

It was the wife of the policeman Joey had killed. She'd screamed out several times during the trial, accusing the Lynches of bringing a 'monster' into the world. The poor cow was beside herself. But then she had three kiddies to bring up without their father. When Dermot's sentence had been read out she'd loudly dissolved into tears. She'd hoped for life.

Rose sat in a corner of the cab while Tilly told the driver to head for Fournier Street. Kitty Lynch looked as if she'd seen a ghost.

'Twelve years,' she said as the cab began to move away, accompanied by raised voices and camera flashes. 'Jesus mighty!'

Rose was beyond tears and so Tilly just left her to sit and look at God knows what while they got out of the City.

All the other blokes in the gang had got life. That Dermot hadn't was lucky for him, but devastating for the copper's wife. If he'd been banged away forever she might well have seen it as some sort of justice for her grieving family. Then again, twelve years was a long time. And it was rumoured they were sending him to Dartmoor. Christ knew why! It was the prison for the most dangerous criminals in Britain and Dermot Lynch was hardly that. But Tilly reckoned, again, it was a sop to the copper's family.

The cab passed the Mansion House and the scene of the crime. Mappin & Webb looked serene in the knowledge that one of its employees had grassed up Joey Lynch and his gang. Tilly hadn't seen the boy Ernest in court. She hadn't been there that day, but Rose had told her he'd looked as if butter wouldn't melt in his mouth.

The things people did for gain! But then Tilly knew she was as susceptible to the lure of easy money as the next person. In fact, if she was going to get Rose back to her little cottage in the country and give young Morry a chance at a healthy life, she'd need more than just her own meagre savings. Not that she was going to broach that subject any time soon. Nell Larkin had come through her treatment for TB with flying colours but everyone could see she was drinking again. Good job that working girl she was maid to had been able to look after Morrie while Rose and Kitty had been in court.

Her mother-in-law had left Sharon a list of jobs to be done before Dolly got home. She was going out up West with some of the women she used to work with at Lyons Corner House. Sharon imagined them all in some pub, drinking port and lemons, all wearing their old black and white Nippy uniforms, ripping people to pieces.

She looked around the Adlers' kitchen and wondered why she'd come back here. Probably because there had been nowhere else that would take her. Not her parents, her siblings, no one. None of them had liked Solly. They'd thought Sharon was marrying way beneath her when she settled for him. And she had been. She'd married Solly for what he used to be, not what he was. God knew why he'd married her.

Sharon went into the parlour to switch the wireless on, then she stopped. They were sentencing Dermot Lynch and the others at the Old Bailey and she didn't want to hear it. This was her life now and so anything to do with Joey was consigned to the bin. She missed him so much! He'd made her life exciting, he'd made her feel like a woman. Until Reg Kray had come along ... but then he was stuck in prison too by now, civilian after the military had been unable to curb him and his twin brother. Maybe she should wait for him? Sharon felt her eyes fill with tears. What was it about wrong 'uns that she liked so much? She'd be led a dog's life by Reg just as she had been, if she were honest, by Joey.

She went into the kitchen and looked at the sink full of washing-up Dolly had left for her. Sharon didn't want to do it! She didn't want to do anything – so bloody boring! Before she could even think about what she was doing Sharon had thrown the kettle into the sink. All of the bowls broke and one of the big plates too and she was glad.

Then she lay down on the floor and cried until her husband came home.

Dermot could feel the Black Maria rock as the people outside kicked and threw things at it when it passed. People did that when those who'd committed murder were taken away. Not that he had killed anyone, but he might as well have done. Twelve years for not driving a getaway car! But then, what else had he expected?

He'd seen Rosie and his mammy in the gallery with Tilly. He'd never liked the old queen very much but now he was grateful to her as she appeared to be looking after the women. Had his mother read his letter to Rosie yet? he wondered. If she had then it hadn't made a lot of difference to the way his wife felt. She'd cried bitterly when the sentence had been read out. Probably even more than the wives of the men who had got life.

As soon as Dermot had thought of Rose he thought of Raymond too, and hated himself for it. Why had he given in to temptation with that boy? He'd known what he was right from the off. But he'd been bewitched – by Ray's body, his smart chat, his wonderful eyes ...

Now married to Viv, he'd do the nice little family thing until he got bored and went off into Southend to find a man. Or another girl. It didn't much matter to Ray. Like a lot of beautiful people, he was fickle and vain and felt as if whatever he wanted sexually was simply his due.

Dermot had had word from Marie just before his appearance in court that Bernie had given birth to a baby boy. Called Shimon apparently. He was glad for her and for Heinrich whom he had always liked. One day, with any luck, Heinrich's wife would give him a divorce and then the two of them could get married. Bernie had registered the kid as a British subject, which was good. Israel was holding its own against all the hostile countries that surrounded it, but would it last? If it didn't at least the kid would have somewhere to come back to, such as it was.

Letting his mind wander was good. He found if he fixated on anything that was when the panic set in. He'd spend the night back in Wandsworth and then he was going to be transferred to Dartmoor. Here his mind stopped its pleasant trains of thought.

Dartmoor was where they kept the hard cases. Men who'd killed and who would kill others in order to maintain their position in the prison hierarchy. That's what he'd heard the warders at Wandsworth say. Maybe they were simply winding him up, but maybe not. It made sense. If a bloke fetched up in a place like Dartmoor, he didn't have very much left to lose – except perhaps his life. But even then, was execution so very much worse than being buried alive with a load of criminal maniacs?

Joey's death had been easy, so old Ted had told him when they'd been taken away from Mappin & Webb in a van on the day of the Job. He'd just closed his eyes, some blood had come out of his mouth and then he'd snuffed it. Lucky Joey – if that was what really happened. But the circumstances of his death ...?

Dermot knew that as soon as his brother had shot Constable Eavis, all the other coppers had piled in to get the gun off him. But when it had gone off, who had pulled the trigger? And three times? That had hardly even come up at the trial, which had been all about Eavis and his untimely death. Nobody cared about Joey – and why should they? Dermot had always known what his brother was ever since Joey got that job with his dad in the docks.

Easily led was what Joey had been. In fact, the word 'easy' could be his epitaph because that was how he had always wanted life to be. Why work for things when you could nick them? Why work at a relationship when you could just fuck anyone you felt like? Although that was unfair. Whatever Joey's faults, Sharon Begleiter had loved him, in her way. And now she was back with her husband, she was probably paying a heavy price for it.

Kitty put the letter down once she'd finished reading it to Rose and said, 'Well?'

It had been waiting for them when they got back from court.

Rose wasn't crying anymore but her face looked crushed and she seemed to have aged in the space of the last few hours.

'Well, what?' she said. 'You want me to say I didn't know about him and other men?'

'I never,' Kitty said bitterly. 'Why'd you marry him if he's like that?'

Rosee shrugged. 'Because I love him.'

'Love him? How can you?' Kitty said. 'Him being like that, like ...'

She said no more. Tilly had gone out to give the women some space and they were glad of it.

192

'So ... Morry?' Kitty said.

'I was raped,' Rose said. 'By the doorman at the theatre where I worked. It was during the Blitz.'

Kitty shook her head. 'Who else knows?'

'Dermot ...'

'Well, I imagine he does, if he's ...'

'He wanted to take us on,' Rose said. 'He's a good man.'

'He's a fucking poof!'

Rose burst into tears.

Kitty shook her head. The little boy she'd doted on for years wasn't her grandson. It hurt.

'So did you ever ... Did you sleep with Dermot?'

Rose, realising that if she was to get through this she had to be calm, managed to stop crying. But she shook as she answered her mother-in-law.

'No,' she said. 'After what happened to me, with Morry's dad, I never wanted to.'

'Perfect for Dermot!'

'Maybe but he loved us too. I know he still does.'

There was a pause while Kitty lit a cigarette. Then she said, 'Who else knows? Apart from Dermot?'

Rose swallowed. 'Becky and Tilly.'

'Not your mother?'

'No, nor Mr Shapiro, nor Bernie. Only Becky and Tilly.'

'Who didn't see fit to tell me!'

'I told them not to. We decided, Dermot and me.'

'You decided to deceive me, make me love a child who isn't my grandson.'

'No!'

'Yes!' Kitty screamed. 'You made me believe that Morry was my blood! Was Pat's blood! Christ, child, where does that leave us now, eh?'

'You can still love him ...'

'Oh, can I? Can I really? Knowing what he is? What you've done?'

'It's not Morry's fault!'

'No, but it is your fault ... and Dermot's and Becky's and Tilly's!'

At that moment, Tilly returned carrying bottles of brown ale from the pub. She'd heard nothing except her name but she could see the fury on Kitty's face. She looked at Rose who said, 'She knows about Morry.'

'Yes, I do,' Kitty said to Tilly. 'And so you can fuck off right now!'

'Mrs Lynch ...'

'No! You fuck off and take this little slag with you!' Kitty roared as she dragged Rose to her feet and pushed her towards Tilly. 'I never want to see any of you lot again! Ever!'

She bundled them out into the street.

Becky, arriving home from work, ran up to Rose who was crying again.

'What's the matter?' she asked. 'Is it life?'

She was referring to Dermot's prison sentence. Rose curled into Becky's arms and howled. She looked to Tilly to explain what was going on

'Dermot got twelve years.'

'Oh, well, that's bad but ...'

'But Mrs Lynch knows about Morry's real father,' Tilly said. 'About what Dermot really is. The whole lot.'

'Oh, God!'

As Rose sank to the ground, Becky held her friend and sat on the pavement with her while she cried. She felt a cold breeze pass across her back. Nothing was ever going to be the same again.

Chapter 17

Nasra Aziz was a dependable women, but Bernie still felt strange handing her tiny baby over to a stranger.

'He will be well, you don't worry,' the woman said as she took Shimon from Bernie's arms. 'I have six babies, my own. I know what I do.'

'I know,' Bernie said. 'It's not about you, Nasra. I just feel...'

She put one large, sun-weathered hand on Bernie's shoulder. 'I know,' she said. 'When my daughter was born was 1948, we have to move quick. I have to give her to my mother for a time.'

The way that Nasra mentioned in passing the *Nakba*, which had been a catastrophe for her people, made Bernie feel both pain and guilt. She put her arms around Nasra and Shimon and kissed them both.

'Come on!' she heard Heinrich yell from the hallway. 'You don't want to be late on your first day back.'

And she didn't. Much as she loved her baby, Bernie was still the driven career girl she had always been and relished the thought of the assignment she had been given for her first day back post-maternity leave.

Once she was sitting beside Heinrich in the car, she smiled.

'I'm glad you feel secure with Nasra,' he said as he put the key in the ignition. 'She looked after Miriam Kohen's twins when she went back to work and Miriam was delighted.'

'I know.'

'So are you looking forward to being back at work?' he asked.

'I am,' Bernie said. Although she couldn't stop thinking about her brother Dermot who had been given twelve years in Dartmoor for his part in Joey's mad plan to rob Mappin & Webb. It made her feel anxious. Someone like Dermot would cope badly in any prison let alone a gaol full of hard-nuts like Dartmoor. And what of Rosie and Morry? Becky had told her that Rosie was living back with her mother and had some cleaning work but that was hardly ideal. And what of the little Plotlands cottage Rose and Dermot had put so much hard work into?

In many ways she wished she was back home. With her best friends and family around her, Bernie would know that Shimon would always be in safe hands. She wouldn't need some sort of recommendation in order to feel secure. But Nasra was a good woman, Bernie could feel it, and her first task back at work was to be photographing performers in a variety of new jazz clubs that were opening up in Tel Aviv. Life was good even if, sometimes, when she saw Heinrich look down at the baby, she felt sad that his face showed no emotion. But then it wouldn't.

Rose took Morry to school that morning and then went with Becky to the London Hospital. Now that Dermot's fate had finally been decided she needed to get more permanent work and so Becky had taken her to the hospital to enquire about working as a cleaner. Also because Becky had been obliged to tell her father about Morry's real parentage, things were tense in the Shapiro household.

The old man had been disappointed in Rose and his daughter. 'You should have told the truth to Mrs Lynch,' he had told Becky when she and Rose had finally come home after Kitty Lynch's outburst. 'You led her to believe that Morry is her grandson and that isn't right.'

To Morry, none of them had said a word. When he'd asked to go across the road to his Nanny Kitty's, Rose had told him she was busy. The child would have to be told the truth at some point but how she'd manage, she didn't know.

The housekeeping department of the London Hospital was run by a woman called Miss Lucas. A thin spinster in her sixties, she wore her hair in a severe bun, spoke in a thick cockney accent and chain-smoked.

'If we take you on, we allocate ya a ward, which you'll work on all the time and be responsible for,' Miss Lucas told Rose.

Her office, at the back of the old hospital, was little more than a cupboard and was stacked with brooms, buckets and piles of cleaning cloths and chamois leathers.

'We get our cleaning done early here and so you'll have to come in at five every morning. Can you do that?'

Rose nodded. She found this woman a bit frightening if she was honest.

'You'll have to do that hair of yours up in a scarf,' Miss Lucas continued. 'And we work clean and smart here, so no eating or drinking on the ward, you hear?'

'Yes.'

'You can smoke but don't go cadging the patients' fags, they're with us to get better not to have you taking their Woodbines off 'em.'

The job was full-time and the day started at five a.m. and finished at one, so it was perfect for going to pick Morry up from school. Rose would have to get her mum to take him in the morning.

'So why'd you wanna work here?' the woman asked her. 'Nurse Shapiro told me you're married.'

'My husband's in the sanatorium,' Rose said. This, according to Becky, had been the best thing to say in the circumstances. Miss Lucas looked at her with disbelieving eyes. But she said nothing.

'You'll need references before I can take you on,' Miss Lucas said. She pushed a piece of paper across the desk at Rose. 'Write down the names and addresses of two people who can give you a character.'

Rose froze. She should have anticipated this, or Becky should have done. She felt her face colour. She'd told people she couldn't read or write before but how did you do that to someone who wanted to give you a job?

But then Miss Lucas shook her head. 'Oh, scrub that,' she said as she took the paper away from Rose. 'Nurse Shapiro said she'd vouch for ya.'

Rose felt her heart-rate begin to slow. She'd known all along that at some point she'd have to sign something if she got a job but she could do that, just. Dermot had taught her.

'So does that mean . . .'

'We need young women like you,' Miss Lucas said. 'Too many old girls with bad backs. You work hard and you'll get no trouble from me. Mess me about and you're fucked.'

'Oh . . . Mr Adler.'

He was standing in the corridor, outside the door to the sluice. His sudden appearance made Becky's heart jump, but his smile made the day seem brighter if bittersweet.

'Nurse Shapiro,' he said.

'What are you . . .'

'Me cousin Simona's just had a little 'un,' he said. 'That's Mrs Berger.'

'Oh, yes, a little girl,' Becky said.

'I come along with her husband, Norris.'

'Oh. You won't be able to see Mrs Berger, you know, Mr Adler.'

'Yeah,' he said. 'Just come along with Norris, you know.'

A lot of new fathers' 'mates' came along with them to the maternity ward, but they usually stood outside, waiting for the happy man to join them down the pub. But Solly wasn't a big drinker and he was in the hospital. Before Becky could really wonder why, he'd pushed her back inside the sluice and shut the door behind him.

'I had to see you,' he said.

Becky didn't know where to look or what to say. She held the now, mercifully, clean bedpan up against her chest as a sort of protection.

Eventually she said, 'Your wife is home now. You should stay with her.'

Solly grimaced. 'I don't love her,' he said.

'That isn't my concern.'

'I love you!'

'Even if that's true, it's not possible for us to be anything to each other now.'

Becky looked away from him. But when she heard him begin to move closer to her she said, 'Don't come near me, Mr Adler, or I'll scream.'

His eyes blazed with hurt.

'I mean it!' Becky said. 'You and me, we're not together anymore.'

'Only because . . . '

'Of your wife, the mother of your daughter,' Becky said. 'Now please leave, Mr Adler. I have too much to do to be bothered by this.'

Solly looked as if someone had dropped a block of stone on him. He visibly crumpled. But he left and, once he had gone, Becky leaned back against the sluice table and rubbed her temples. She missed him so much! Every time she heard his name it hurt her! The last thing she needed was actually talking to him, hearing what the pain of their separation was doing to him.

Although Sharon had been unfaithful to him, which had culminated in her going off with Joey Lynch, she wasn't entirely to blame for the failure of their marriage. Solly, by his own admission, had never loved her. He'd married her because he had felt that Bernie had rejected him by not responding to his letters from Spain. That had been Auntie Kitty's work. Although apparently Bernie had forgiven her mother, Becky herself was beginning to feel that the Lynch matriarch's interfering was far from just benign concern.

She could understand why Kitty had been so angry with Rose. But, knowing her, she'd carry the grudge about Morry's real paternity forever, cutting herself off from Rosie and, more importantly, Morry himself because of it. She loved that little boy and he loved her. If she didn't bend her own stiff neck Kitty Lynch was going to damage the very people she should protect at all costs.

Moritz Shapiro sat at his drawing-room window waiting for Nell Larkin to come home. When, halfway through the afternoon, she appeared he went out into the street and invited her in. Never one to refuse a cup of tea, or something stronger, Nell accepted.

Once they were settled with their tea in the kitchen, Moritz said, 'I don't know whether you've been told about Rose and Dermot and . . .'

'Kitty Lynch has bent my ear'ole,' Nell said. 'I told her I knew nothing about her Dermot being a bum-boy.' Then, seeing the strained expression on Moritz's face, corrected herself. 'A homosexual.'

'Me either.'

'She talking to you, is she – Kitty Lynch?'

'I have yet to speak to her,' Moritz said. 'Rebekah tells me she was upset with her because she did know.'

'Them girls always had secrets among themselves,' Nell said. 'I'll be honest with you, Mr Shapiro, when Dermot got in trouble with the law, I was furious. Him and Rose, they had a good thing going down there in Essex. I wanted her back here, of course I did . . . ' She leaned in close to his ear. 'I put my curse on that boy.'

'Mrs Larkin . . . '

'I did!' Nell said. 'And I ain't ashamed. When my girl married him, I thought her troubles would be over. But he let her down. T'be honest, I hope he rots in there.'

'I think he was led astray by his brother.'

'Yes, but if he hadn't been mucking around with some other fella, none of this would have happened. Rose told me everything.'

'But that is in the past and we can't repair it, Mrs Larkin,' Moritz said. 'All we can do is make it right for the innocent child who finds himself caught in the middle of it.'

She sighed.

'My proposal is that we speak to Mrs Lynch,' Moritz said. 'Make her see what we all know.'

'What's that?'

'That she loves Morry and they will both be hurt if she

stops being in his life,' he said. 'And I believe she still has not acknowledged Bernadette's child.'

'Kitty's a stubborn one all right.'

'But it does nobody any good!' he said. 'It is most unlikely Morry will ever know who his real father is. He needs all the family he can get. Mrs Larkin, will you come with me now and speak to Mrs Lynch? I am not a man to interfere in the business of others, but I really feel that if I don't at least try in this case, I will never forgive myself.'

'Where have you been?'

Solly dropped his house keys into the fruit bowl on the sideboard and looked at his wife.

'Down the hospital,' he said. 'With Norris.'

'Oh.' Sharon knew that Solly's cousin Simona had just had a baby. She also knew that Rebekah Shapiro worked on the maternity ward. Her own cousin Fat Helen had told her about that situation. Not long after Sharon had left, Solly had been seen stepping out with Nurse Rebekah Shapiro. Sometimes he'd even had their Natalie with them. But Sharon also knew she couldn't mention that. The cruel fact was she was dependent upon Solly for somewhere to live.

Anyway as usual he was way ahead of her.

'And don't go whining on about how Nurse Shapiro works there,' he said.

'I wasn't . . . '

'I walked down there with Norris and then I took him down the pub. That's all.'

Sharon got to her feet. 'Do you want . . . '

'No. I don't want nothing,' Solly said. He took an ashtray off the dining table and went back out into the hall. 'Going to lie down for a bit.'

'OK, but if you need me ...'

'I won't.'

Sharon sat back down again. Fat Helen was of the opinion that Solly and Rebekah Shapiro had done more than just go out together. She reckoned you could see that they'd 'done it' from the expressions on their faces. Sharon knew that she shouldn't care, but she did because his happiness upset her. In fact, anyone's happiness did. Her own life lay in ruins around her feet and she couldn't see how or even if she could put it back together again.

Her family didn't want her and neither did her in-laws. Although she knew that what had happened was her own fault, she was so unhappy some days she just cried. Having Natalie should be enough for her, but Sharon knew that it wasn't. She was a woman who needed to be loved by a man, but that wasn't going to happen again. Her life might as well be over.

Against her better judgement, Kitty let them in. She even put the kettle on.

'So,' she said, once Moritz Shapiro and Nell Larkin had sat down, 'what do you want? As if I didn't know.'

'It's about little Maurice,' Moritz said.

'What about him?'

'He loves you and wants to see you,' Nell said.

'He ain't my blood, why should he?'

'Because he's a small child,' Moritz said. 'And he has grown up with you. A relationship has been forged.'

'Based on lies!'

She looked at Nell with fierce eyes and got a cold stare in return.

'You are a silly cow, Kitty Lynch,' Nell said.

'What!'

'You are,' she continued. 'Blimey, if there was a ha'penny given for every kid born the other side of the blanket, most families would be rich. I bet it ain't the first time there's been a cuckoo in the nest among your lot.'

The kettle began to boil and Kitty turned away to pour water into the teapot.

'And this is a very particular situation,' Moritz added. 'Poor Rose was attacked . . .'

'While flashing all she's got at men for money,' Kitty said. 'I bet that weren't the first time!'

Nell went to speak, but Moritz held her back.

He said, 'Mrs Lynch, whatever happened is in the past. What we know is that Dermot agreed to take on Rose and Morry in the full knowledge of what had happened. I believe he did this because he loved Rose . . .'

'Oh, don't talk soft!' Kitty said. 'The boy's a bleedin' poof! He took us all for a ride, especially you!'

'Me?'

'When you let them have that land down Essex,' she said. 'Right cushy number it was for Dermot. Think about it! He had a place to live and a woman who didn't want intimate relations, leaving him free to do his disgusting . . .'

'Dermot built the cottage on my land with his own hands and looked after it for me. He took no one for a ride, Mrs Lynch.'

'Have it your own way.'

Kitty got to her feet while her guests stayed sitting. She looked down on them, her eyes ice-cold. Then she said, 'I don't want nothing to do with Rose or Morry or any of yous. I know you didn't know either but I don't much care. My family's been made to look like a den of perverts and thieves . . .'

'We appreciate that your eldest son, God rest his soul, has died ...'

'Was shot,' Kitty said. 'With his own bloody gun. Always was a wrong 'un was our Joseph. My Pat chucked him out after that business with Fred Lamb, told him never to come back. I don't know if Dermot found him first or if it was the other way around, but Joey should have left him alone.'

'What's done ...'

'But would he? No. Got him involved in Joey's hare-brained schemes instead. And him, Dermot, he put hisself in a situation with another bloke ...' She shook her head. 'All I want to do is go to work, come home nights and get my girls married off to decent blokes. The only one made anything of theirself's our Paddy. I've got proper grand-kids off him.'

'And you have Bernadette ...'

'Oh, that's right!' she said. 'Bring her name up, why don't you? Another disappointment ... Off with a married man in a foreign country! A baby with no name!'

'He has, he's called Shimon,' Nell said.

'I don't mean like that, Nelly! I mean ... Well, you know. You know what our Bernadette's done!'

'She has a very successful career,' Moritz said.

'As a tart, yes!' Kitty shook her head. 'I don't know why you're here, trying to persuade me to change me mind, because I won't. They're all dead to me, do you hear me? Your Rosie, Dermot, Morry, Bernadette – the whole boiling lot of them!' She looked at Moritz. 'And you can tell your Becky to keep away from me too. Bloody little mare knew about Rosie and Dermot all along!'

'Kitty ...'

'No, I've heard enough. Get out, the pair of you!' she yelled.

'Coming here, trying to get me to change me mind ... well, I won't. Now get off out of it!'

It was the smell that woke Solly up. It wasn't strong, but it was definitely present and, at first, he couldn't make out what it was. But when he did, he got out of bed as fast as he could. Gas leaks in old flats like the one rented by the Adlers were common.

Getting painfully to his feet, Solly walked out into the hallway and turned his head to try and work out where the stink was coming from. He made his way towards the kitchen and turned the door handle. But it wouldn't budge.

There were no locks on any of the internal doors and so he called across the hall to Sharon whom he had left in the living room.

'What's wrong with the kitchen door?'

But there was no answer. Silly cow had probably gone out.

Solly pushed his shoulder against the door and felt it give slightly. The smell of gas was getting stronger. He pushed again and then, tiring of smacking his shoulder against hard wood, raised his one good leg and kicked the door in.

The smell was almost overpowering, of rotten eggs and something acrid that made his eyes water. He put a hand over his mouth. There was a loud hissing sound that must mean all the rings on the hob were turned on. He didn't realise that the oven, unlit, was on too until he'd pulled a load of tea towels away from around the window and opened it.

And it was then that he saw her, Sharon, collapsed on the floor, her head still just inside the oven. With a shaking hand, he felt her wrist for a pulse but found nothing.

Chapter 18

5 November 1956
St Catherine's Monastery, Sinai Desert

The road, such as it was, was dusty and bumpy. As the truck bounced across its surface, clouds of dirt and debris made seeing what lay up ahead very difficult. Paired with reporter Renate Heller, a Jewish refugee from Germany, Bernie was travelling in the wake of the Israeli troops invading the Egyptian-held Sinai Desert. Much against her instincts as a mother to stay with her three-year-old son back in Jerusalem, Bernie's current mission was to record the invasion in photographs.

Rumours had flitted around Jerusalem and Tel Aviv for months about the Israelis taking back still more of their ancestral lands, and the name Sinai had been whispered as a possible target. But when the invasion had started six days before, and been met with only limited resistance, no one could quite believe it.

The women's driver, a Christian Arab called Musa, pointed into the distance through the windscreen.

'The Monastery of St Catherine,' he said.

Bernie and Renate narrowed their eyes to see, but could make out little through the dust and fog that hung low over the desert. The ancient monastery lay beneath Mount Sinai, whose massive dark shape they could just make out.

Here, they were in true biblical territory. The mountain was where Moses had communed with God and been given the tablets recording the Ten Commandments. The monastery, it was said, housed the original burning bush through which God had again spoken to Moses. It was said the Greek Orthodox Monastery of St Catherine's housed documents from the first century AD and protected relics of St Catherine of Alexandria. The monks who lived there had existed in a state of sometimes uneasy peace with their Egyptian rulers for many centuries. Now that they were about to become Israeli citizens, how was that change going to affect them?

'What questions will you ask?' Bernie asked Renate as the vague outline of a building came into view.

Renate shrugged. 'How they feel about it largely, I suppose,' she said. 'Nasser hasn't given Christians an easy time since he became President of Egypt. Maybe their lives will be better under Israeli rule.'

'Do you think they will?' Bernie asked her.

'I don't know. In the past Christians have probably persecuted Jews more than Muslims, like Nasser, but it depends.'

'On what?'

'What other countries say,' her colleague answered. 'How will Britain respond? The United States? France?'

'I don't know.'

'Nor does anyone. Although for Israel to persecute a load of unarmed monks will not play well before the world's press.'

'The monks have invited us in, though?'

'Oh, yes,' Renate said. 'A very smart move on their part. They'll get their side of the story out there before anyone else does.'

Mr Arnold put his newspaper, the *Daily Sketch*, down on the bed in front of him and lit a cigarette.

'Makes me wonder when our boys'll go in,' he said as he pointed to a headline on the front page.

Rose, busy dusting his bedside cabinet, looked over his shoulder.

'Go in where?' she asked.

There was a picture of a tank on the front page of the paper, but of course she couldn't read what the headline referred to.

'Egypt,' Mr Arnold said. 'The Israelis have invaded the place. Don't you read the news, gel?'

'No, not really.' Then she remembered. 'My friend Bernie lives in Israel.'

'Well, you wanna tell him to get hisself home,' the old man said. 'Bleedin' dangerous it is out there at the moment.'

Bernie was of course a girl, but Rose couldn't be bothered to correct Mr Arnold. He was in hospital for a long time as he had a hernia and was in a lot of pain. The men's Surgical Ward wasn't her favourite but it was better than Casualty, which was all blood and people groaning.

'You have to hand it to 'em,' Mr Arnold continued.

'To who?'

'The Jews!' he said. 'Went over to that country with nothing but the clothes on their backs and created one of the best armies in the world. Not as good as ours, of course ... I reckon we'll join 'em soon. Have a go at Nasser ... '

'Why?'

'What? Why have a go at Nasser, do you mean? 'Cause he's been threatening to shut the Suez Canal,' said the patient. 'Cut off our ships, strand them in the Med. Can't have that! I mean, who does he think he is?'

Another elderly man, from the bed opposite Mr Arnold's, said, 'He's President of Egypt, you silly old sod! He *owns* the Suez Canal!'

'How'd'ya work that out?' Mr Arnold said. 'You some bleedin' Commie, are you? That's part of our British Empire that Suez Canal is!'

'No, it ain't,' the other man said. 'Don't have no British Empire no more, thank God. And, yes, mate, I *am* a bleedin' Commie – and proud of it.'

'Agh!' Mr Arnold waved his words away.

Rose began mopping underneath his bed. She took his slippers off the floor and put them on his chair.

'I used to be a Communist,' she said. 'Back in the nineteen thirties. And my friends were too.'

Mr Arnold said nothing.

Rose continued speaking. 'Everyone was a Commie back in them days,' she said. 'It was the best hope for the future.'

'Still is, love,' the man in the other bed said.

'Yes, but what about the Russians?' she said. 'They're Communists and everyone hates them.'

'Oh, you don't wanna believe everything you read in the papers about the Russians,' the other man said. 'Saved us during the war they did.'

Mr Arnold muttered, 'That was the Yanks.'

'No, it weren't.'

'Yes, it were!'

'Oh, shut up, will ya, the both of you?' another man said. 'What does a bloke have to do to get some kip around here?'

The ward became uncomfortably quiet. Rose wondered why she'd not heard about Israel being at war. Her mum listened to the radio sometimes but she'd not said anything. Rose resolved to ask Becky about it when she was on her break.

Moritz Shapiro looked out of his front window and saw Kitty Lynch going off to work with her youngest daughter, Aggie. He'd heard that the girl was going to be married just after Christmas, though Kitty herself hadn't spoken to him, Becky, Rose or Nell Larkin ever since they'd had that argument in her parlour three years ago. It was Morry who had suffered the most as a result of it. He'd carried on running up to his nana for months after all that and Kitty had just pushed him away without a word. And for what?

For a principle that didn't matter to anyone but her. Loads of girls had 'got into trouble' during the war and, although none of that had affected Moritz personally, he knew that to deny it was happening was wrong. Of course, it wasn't ideal, and if Rebekah had come home pregnant he would have been furious. But what was the point of falling out with loved ones over it?

So much had changed since the war, what with the coming of the National Health Service and lots of people being rehoused in homes that had proper bathrooms and electricity. He'd changed too. He was still a man of religion but with some caveats these days. So what if someone couldn't always keep kosher all the time? Much of that had had to go by the wayside during the days of rationing.

Nell Larkin came out of her flat and walked up the area

steps into the street. Rose and Morry were living with her permanently now, leaving the cottage in Essex as nothing more than a shabby, rundown bolthole to visit occasionally in the summer. Rose's mate Tilly had said she might move there and open some sort of shop when Dermot had first gone to jail, but that had all gone by the wayside now. Nell didn't know why. It was such a shame. Moritz still intended to leave the place to Rose, if not Dermot, in his Will. But while Nell Larkin lived, he suspected Rose and Morry would stay in London, which was also, marginally, closer to Dartmoor Prison. Rose only visited Dermot once a year but it was something she wanted to do for the duration of his sentence. Nell had told him that when Dermot got out her daughter was going to take him back. It was difficult for Moritz to know how he felt about that. He'd always liked Dermot, though what he'd done had been terrible and stupid. But at least Rebekah was happy.

After nearly two decades she had finally got her man. Although not 'serious' as yet, which meant engaged, Rebekah was walking out with Solly Adler and they both looked really happy. They'd started seeing each other again a year after his wife had died. A terrible thing, for Sharon to take her own life like that. But that had been nothing to do with Moritz's daughter. At the time, she and Solly had been barely on speaking terms, much less girlfriend and boyfriend. Sharon Adler, everyone agreed, had been the author of her own destruction when she'd chosen to live with Joey Lynch.

But that was all in the past now. The future beckoned and Moritz hoped maybe for a wedding for his daughter and peace in the world, although that didn't seem too likely now that Israeli troops had invaded Egypt.

*

212

Brother Spiridion was the youngest monk in St Catherine's Monastery; he was also one of the few who could speak English. Originally from the Greek island of Santorini, he was unnerved by the Israeli invasion.

'I was twelve when the Germans invaded my country,' he told Bernie. 'One day we were ruled by Athens, the next day by Berlin. Here we were administered from Cairo until days ago and now Tel Aviv says they are in charge. I think you maybe can understand my anxiety.'

'Yes.'

They stood in front of a tall metal grille behind which were what seemed like endless shelves containing scrolls.

'Some of our manuscripts date from the first century,' Spiridion said. 'They are in many languages including Hebrew, Greek, Persian and Aramaic. We keep them here behind lock and key because they are so valuable as well as being very delicate.'

Bernie stared into the gloom. The air smelled stale from the aroma of aged paper and parchment.

'May I see one?' she asked.

'Oh, no,' her host replied. 'They are far too fragile.'

'Do you know what they're about?'

'They are all holy scriptures,' he said. 'Some are early trans-lations of the Gospels into languages like Bulgarian. Some are commentaries on the life of Our Lord. Some may be the work of St John Climacus, one of the saints from the sixth century. He lived as a hermit here in the Sinai.'

Bernie said, 'This is a fascinating place.'

He smiled. 'Your reporter speaks to our Abbot, I know. He has asked me to find you some places to photograph. We have the original burning bush, you know.'

'Yes. Although I'd quite like to take some shots of you and maybe some of the other brothers too.'

'You may do that,' he said. 'You ...'

His words were cut short by the sound of gunfire coming from somewhere outside the monastery.

He said nervously, 'Egyptian troops are still in the area.'

'But the gates are closed.'

'Of course, but that doesn't mean that the fighting is over,' he said. 'In my experience, fighting can go on for years even after the war is lost.'

'Bernie's nowhere near the fighting,' Becky said to Rose.

The two of them sat in the hospital canteen together, drinking tea. Rose smoked a cigarette. It was something she had taken to doing ever since Dermot's trial.

'Isn't it Jerusalem they're fighting over?' she asked.

'No. The Israeli troops have invaded the Sinai Desert, which is a long way from Jerusalem and used to belong to Egypt,' Becky said. 'There's nothing for us to worry about.'

Rose chewed on a fingernail. 'I hope not. What's it all about anyway?'

'The Israelis say that Sinai is part of their ancestral homeland and so they've invaded Egyptian territory to take it back. I don't know, I don't like the idea of Jewish people doing aggressive things like this, but ...' She shrugged. 'What it's also about is access to the Suez Canal.'

'What's that?'

'It's the waterway that allows ships to cut through Egypt rather than having to go all around Africa to transport goods to and from Europe,' she said. 'I'm surprised British and French troops haven't been involved as yet. The canal is especially important to us.'

There was a pause and then Rose said, 'I'm going to see Dermot tomorrow.'

Becky knew it was hard for her friend to make the long journey to Devon, have an awkward half-hour with her husband and then drag herself all the way back.

She put her hand on Rose's shoulder. 'Send him my love, won't you?'

Rose smiled.

Then Becky said, 'Do you know whether Auntie Kitty ever goes to see him?'

'No,' Rose said. 'And I don't like to ask the girls.'

'Me neither.'

Although Kitty Lynch had nothing to do with Rose, Becky and their families, her daughters Marie and Aggie still kept up contact on the quiet.

'You know Aggie's getting married after Christmas?' Rose said.

'Yes. To a lad from Poplar, I heard.'

'In church, she says. Auntie Kitty must be so happy that's happening at last,' Rose said.

Becky smiled. 'Yes, a nice church wedding with the bride all in white.'

They both laughed then Rose said, 'Becky, do you think you'll ever marry Solly?'

'I don't know, Rosie.' She shrugged. 'I don't think about such things. So much has happened, I don't know where the years have gone to really. Young Natalie is thirteen now and, for all that Sharon wasn't the ideal mum, she still misses her. I've no doubt that if Solly and I married, she'd feel a bit resentful.'

'Do you think so?'

'Just between us, she's a little bit rebellious at the moment,' Becky said. 'Nothing bad but Solly has told me he's caught her hanging about with some of the Teddy Boys you see around.'

'Are they them ones what wear them old-fashioned suits?'

'And the greasy hairstyles, yes. Natalie's got interested in boys early ...'

'Like her mum.'

'Don't,' Becky said. 'God, if she turns out to be like Sharon it'll break Solly's heart.'

'What's he doing about it?'

'Dolly's fetching her from school every day, which she hates, and she's not allowed out unless her dad knows exactly where she's going and with whom. I think he's probably being a bit too strict with her, but I can't get involved.'

'Too strict? How do you mean?'

'Well, she provokes him,' Becky said. 'We can all remember being young – you know what I mean. Tells him about this boy and that boy and what he said and did and how all her mates have got boyfriends ... and Solly just loses his mind, shouting and screaming at her. It doesn't help, but as I say, I can't get involved.'

'Kids are a problem,' Rose said. 'I worry about how Morry'll be when he gets a bit older. I mean, what with all that's happened to him in his little life ...'

There was a strange man in the middle of the street holding a clipboard. He was looking up at the houses to both sides of Fournier Street and writing things down.

'Can I help you, mate?' Marie Lynch asked him.

She was on her way to the London Hospital to start her shift as an ambulance driver. Tall and slim, wearing trousers, apart from the short hair she looked not unlike her sister Bernadette.

The man, who wore thick, round glasses, looked at her over the top of them.

'Who wants to know?' he said.

216

'I live here,' Marie said. 'Who are you?'

'Council.'

'Oh. So, what you doing?'

'Having a look.'

'At what?'

He took his glasses off and scrutinised her closely. 'I've been given the job of looking at the condition of these houses.'

'What for?'

He put his glasses back on but didn't reply.

Marie repeated, 'What for?'

He sighed. He was probably in his late forties but looked older; most middle-aged men in London did. The smog here, as Aggie was wont to say when people's ages came up, was no good for the complexion.

'A lot of these buildings are a disgrace,' the man said.

'Hang on!'

'Well, you should know,' he said. 'If you live here. Rats, bomb damage, poor sanitation . . . '

'Tell that to the landlord, not me,' Marie said. 'My mammy's been trying to get something done for donkey's years. But what can you do if landlords won't spend money?'

'That's why I'm here,' the man said.

'What? To make the landlords do something?'

'Maybe.'

'Maybe?'

'Well, that's one option,' he said. 'Which I am sure the Council will explore.'

'And what else?' Marie asked.

He looked her in the eye and said, 'Demolition.'

Chapter 19

The news was enough to make you swear. Not that Moritz
Shapiro would do anything so sinful. But when he switched
on the radio that morning, his heart sank. Britain and France
were apparently at war with Egypt. Troops had landed in
Suez and were attempting to occupy the canal with a view
to keeping it open to their shipping. They'd also gone in in
support of Israel.

However, with regard to the canal, Egyptian President
Nasser had other ideas and had sunk numerous ships in
the waterway, making it unusable by anyone. The reality,
of course, was that the British and French were reluctant to
give up their imperial interests in the Middle East. It was
ridiculous.

Moritz put the kettle on for his early-morning tea and sat
down at the kitchen table. Becky was still asleep and so he'd
have his first cuppa on his own before he went up to wake her.
As usual she was working very hard. Ever since the end of the
war, the birth rate had escalated as people grew accustomed

to peace. Moritz hoped they weren't going to be set back by what was going on in Egypt.

Even though Spitalfields had gone down a lot in recent years, the country as a whole was finally beginning to flourish. People had immigrated here from India and the West Indies to do the jobs there were no longer enough British people to do. People now had houses with gas, electricity and water; if you were lucky, you could rent one from your local Council instead of a private landlord. It was even said that soon capital punishment would be banned. Now that the war was over, a lot of people found the idea of the State killing people repellent. Moritz didn't know what he felt about that. After all, if a person murdered someone shouldn't they sacrifice their own life?

More immediately, however, he was worried about a man Marie Lynch had seen the previous afternoon. From the Council apparently, he had talked about the poor state of the property in the area and the need for landlords to do something about it. But he had also talked about demolition. Moritz had always owned his house and had tried, inasmuch as he could, to keep it in good order. But he didn't work all the time now and so had very little income to make repairs. He knew the place was shabby, but what could he do? And if the Council did decide to demolish the street, would they include private property in their plans? How would that work?

Rose placed the small net bag containing apples and oranges on the table in front of her.

'I got these for you,' she told her husband.

Dermot put his hand on the bag. 'Thanks.'

One of the warders watched the handover and then came to the table to inspect the gift.

'The guards at the gate looked at it,' Rose explained.

The warder carried on looking until he was satisfied and then walked away.

'How was your journey?' Dermot asked.

'Not bad. Bus from Plymouth to Tavistock was packed but after that it was OK.'

Dermot, who though grave-faced looked rather more healthy then he usually did, said, 'You know you don't have to do this, don't you?'

'Yeah.'

'I mean, it's a long way. What time'll you get back home tonight?'

'About eleven,' she said.

Dermot shook his head.

Rose said, 'I want to see you. I know I can't come often but ... '

'You don't have to explain yourself to me.'

Other prisoners had their wives and/or their kids with them. It was obvious that some of the men could hardly keep their hands off their spouses. But not Dermot.

'When you come out ... '

'Don't talk about it, Rosie,' he said. 'Anything could happen between now and then. Maybe you'll meet someone ... '

'No!'

'Maybe you'll end up living with Tilly.'

'Why would I do that?' Rose asked. 'When I want to live with you.'

Dermot shook his head. 'I know Tilly'd have you and she'd look after you well,' he said. 'Better'n being with your mum anyway. Maybe you and Till and Morry could all go back down the cottage ... '

'No,' Rose said. 'Mr Shapiro keeps saying we can go back down there, but I don't want to, not without you.'

'You should go. We all worked hard on that place and you should make sure it don't fall into rack and ruin.'

'Mr Shapiro goes down there.'

'So maybe you should go with him one day?' Dermot said. 'Give him a hand. Think about it.'

She nodded.

'I mean it, Rosie,' he said. 'You go back down there; you'll feel all the better for it and so will Morry.'

'I'll see.' Then she said, 'You heard that British troops have landed in Egypt?'

'Yeah.' He shook his head. 'I thought about our Bernie.'

'Me too. But Becky said Jerusalem's nowhere near the fighting. Do you ever hear from Bernie?'

'She writes,' he said. 'Sometimes.'

'Becky says that Bernie's little boy's at nursery now. They have a lot of them over there.'

But Dermot didn't want to talk about his sister. He said, 'How's Morry?'

'Fine.'

Inasmuch as he could be, Rose thought to herself. It wasn't easy living next door to the Lynches with Kitty still giving them all the cold shoulder.

'Has Mammy . . .'

'No,' she said. 'No, you know how your mum is, Dermot. She won't change her mind even if little Morry's heart breaks.'

He shook his head. 'I'm sorry.'

'Not your fault,' she said. 'Well, it is, but . . . Don't she ever write or come to see you Dermot?'

'Never,' he said. 'Nor will she. I'll be honest with you, Rosie, I'd like to give her a piece of my mind over Morry. She can disown me but to take it out on that boy ain't fair. It ain't fair at all.'

*

Renate accompanied the Israeli commander to the monastery gates alongside the Abbot. Bernie kept her distance. The Israeli troops were reluctant to have their pictures taken and her Hebrew still wasn't good enough to allow her to converse with people easily. Instead she sat beside the large plant that the monks claimed was the burning bush of biblical fame. Somehow, she'd always imagined the plant through which God spoke to Moses would be smaller. But then there was no real reason for that. There was also, as far as she could see, no real reason why this should be the burning bush at all.

Bernie lit a cigarette and looked up into the cloudy winter sky. She'd finally managed to telephone Heinrich that morning and had actually got to speak to Shimon before he left for kindergarten. Clearly very happy, he'd just said, 'Hello, Mummy!' and then run off to play. Life in Israel, though far from perfect, was good. She had a lovely child, a devoted partner and a career that, while not earth-shatteringly successful, fulfilled her. All she'd ever wanted to do was take photographs and she was doing just that.

She would have liked to have made things right with her mother the last time she'd been back in England but Kitty was such a stubborn woman, that had proved impossible. If anything, these days Bernie missed her friends more than she did her family. She dreamed about Becky and Rose all the time. If she had them with her, life would be perfect even in a world that still kept on going to war.

In recent years both of her friends had changed a lot. Becky, while always smart, was now a stylish professional woman in her New Look skirts and little nipped-waist jackets. Bernie hoped that eventually she would get together with Solly Adler and realise her girlhood dreams. Rose had looked worn out when Bernie had last seen her, although she was still pretty.

She was a hospital cleaner now and, although Bernie knew that Becky always looked out for her, she feared for Rose: living with her drunken, if employed mother, and still pining for her no-good homosexual husband. At least she had Morry and her friend Tilly who, Bernie hoped, might one day take her friend in hand. Quite how, she didn't know.

Bernie knew she'd never go back to England for good, but she did hope that one day her friends might come and visit her in Israel. She was beginning to hear about some news photographs attracting huge sums of money, especially in the United States. If she could take one truly evocative shot, maybe she could pay for them all to come over.

But that was just a fantasy. Bernie laughed as she stood up and began to walk towards the monastery gate.

'Get that muck off your face– now!'

The silly kid looked like a prozzie!

'Where'd you get that anyway?' Solly continued.

Natalie, pouting to show off the colour on her lips, said, 'It's one of Mum's.'

'Which means you've been in my bedroom, going through the drawers in your mother's dressing table!'

'Well, you don't use anything in there.'

Against his better judgement, Solly grabbed the girl by the arm. 'Don't you dare go into my room again, you hear me!'

Natalie looked up into her father's face with an expression of complete defiance on her own. 'Don't you grab hold of me!'

'I'll . . . '

'No, you won't,' she said as her father let go of her arm. 'You'll never hit me because you never hit Mum.'

'Take that stuff off your mouth!' he roared.

'No!'

She ran from the room, out into the hall, down the stairs and into the street. She had her school bag with her but she also still had lips painted like a slapper's.

Furious, Solly punched the back of his chair and then threw himself into it.

Natalie was right, he had never hit Sharon. But maybe if he'd made her more scared ... But no, that wasn't him. For all the water that had flowed under the bridge he was still the same committed Communist he'd been in the 1930s. And Communists treated women as equal to men – except the ones who didn't. But Solly didn't care about them. He kept to his own beliefs irrespective of what others did, even though he often felt like part of a dying breed.

When he'd been coming home after his postal round, he'd heard blokes talking in excited voices about the British invasion of Suez. Supposedly sent in to guard the canal, British soldiers were fighting Egyptian soldiers in a conflict that, as far as Solly could see, was more about Britain's crumbling Empire than Egypt's canal. The country had only come out of a war ten years before and now, it seemed, some people were baying for blood yet again.

Although Jewish, Solly had no particular feelings about Israel. What had occurred to him when news of the Israeli invasion of Sinai had broken was that Bernie Lynch was out there with her fella and her kiddie. God, he'd been so sweet on her once! Maybe it had been the intensity of youth, but not even his feelings for Becky Shapiro now came close to the intensity of the way he'd once felt about Bernie. Then again, how would he ever have satisfied her need for adventure? Solly Adler, a man with a wooden leg? Anyway, that was then. He was a grown-up now and he was in love with a woman who made his soul sing.

Solly took a fag out of his packet and lit up. Dolly was pushing him to 'pop the question' to Becky Shapiro and he wanted to do it, but he had to consider Natalie. The kid was rebellious in part because she had no mother. And even when her mum had been around Sharon'd been next to useless. In spite of her occasional asthma attacks, Natalie was doing well at school and Solly didn't want her to mess it all up by getting involved with some bloody Teddy Boy.

Sometimes, a patient she knew personally came into the hospital and the unexpected sight of them made Becky start. It might be a friend, or a neighbour and their condition might be minor but was usually serious. On this particular occasion she was shocked to see someone she knew lying on a trolley in Casualty.

'Hyman?'

He didn't move; his eyes were glazed over with shock and pain. He was covered in blood. Hyman Salzedo had been a fixture in Becky's life for as far back as she could remember. The 'mad' brother of the local *mohel*, Hyman had ridden his old bicycle around every corner of Spitalfields for years.

As she moved her head close to his, Becky could smell disinfectant.

She had to get back to Maternity, but before she left Casualty she asked one of the nurses on duty about Hyman.

The girl took her to one side and whispered: 'Suicide.'

'Suicide? Is he . . . '

'Not yet,' the girl said. 'But he won't survive. He drank drain cleaner.'

Becky was speechless. Hyman? Kill himself? Why? She wanted to walk back over to him and ask him, but she knew this would achieve nothing. Hyman couldn't easily articulate what he felt at the best of times and now it was doubtful whether he could speak at all.

Becky went back up onto her ward feeling sad and anxious. Life changed a little every day but there were some days when it changed out of all recognition. Everyone was talking about the Council men who were going around Spitalfields noting, some said, buildings up for demolition. There was a lot of fear on the manor, fear of change. Someone like Hyman Salzedo wouldn't like that. And she could understand why. In Spitalfields he was known and accepted for what he was. Out in one of the so-called 'new towns', he'd be looked upon as an oddity. He'd not know where he was and he'd be alone.

The air was thick with dust kicked up in the wake of the Israeli troops' departure and with the strange fog that had settled over the monastery complex. It made the place look otherworldly, which of course it was.

Bernie had never been religious, but this place had a sense of permanence and importance that she couldn't ignore. The monks believed all this stuff – the efficacy of the poor martyred relics of St Catherine, the magical burning bush, the contents of those books and scrolls in their library. It meant something to them and so, even though it meant nothing to her on a religious level, it held a power that should be captured for the world to see.

Bernie positioned herself in front of the main building and put her camera to her eye. But that view didn't do it justice. She wanted to capture the mystery of the place and so she needed to interpret it in a certain way. She walked around the side of the complex just as the sun peeped through the clouds, illuminating the honey-coloured stone of the walls. No, that was far too safe. In fact, sunshine was not the effect she wanted at all.

She was about to go back inside when the clouds covered the sun yet again and a strange darkness enveloped the building. Combined with the thin, fibrous mist from the mountain top, this deep shade made the monastery look forbidding. Was this the image she wanted to portray?

Bernie looked through the lens and saw what looked like a magical palace of darkness. Eerie and yet somehow redeemed by the faintly illuminated cross on top of the bell-tower. She framed and took one picture and then four more shots in quick succession. That was it!

Excited by what she hoped she had captured, Bernie was replacing her lens-cover when she heard the crack behind her. She went to turn so that she could see where it had come from but found that she couldn't. In fact, even moving her arm behind her body was difficult and when she drew up her hand she was horrified to see that it was stained with blood. Bernie thought only of Shimon in that last moment before she fell to the desert ground, dead.

Chapter 20

Who the hell was that hammering on their door in the middle of the bloody night!

Kitty swung her legs over the side of her bed and called out, 'Alright! Alright! I'm coming!'

She lit the lamp on the dressing table and walked out into the living room, past the curtain that screened the nook where the two girls slept. Marie was out at work but she could hear Aggie snoring.

Whoever was outside the front door continued hammering.

'Alright ... for the love of God!' she shouted. Christ! What was happening, a fire?

Kitty shuffled towards the front door and opened it on a white face that she hadn't seen close up for many years.

'God Almighty!' she said as she stepped away from it.

Rebekah Shapiro in her bloody nightie! What the hell did she want?

'Auntie Kitty ...'

'Don't call me that,' she said. 'I'm Mrs Lynch to you!'

'Mrs Lynch, you …' She paused to gasp for breath and Kitty began to feel as if the world was shifting around her.

'What?'

'It's Bernie …'

And she knew. Rebekah was shaking and so it wasn't a giant leap of the imagination to realise …

Kitty felt the oil lamp shiver in her hands. She had an almost uncontrollable urge to shut the door. Shut this news out.

'What?' she repeated, knowing what the answer was going to be, begging God that it wasn't.

'She was shot.'

As she said the words Rebekah Shapiro's whole body shook and, in the light from the oil lamp, she looked like a black-eyed ghost.

'Shot?'

'Auntie Kitty, I must come in! Please let me in! I can't …'

Kitty moved out of her way. Holding herself painfully against her own trembling and the cold of a winter's night, Rebekah let tears burst from her like a fountain.

'They shot her and she's dead!'

'Who? Who shot …'

'I don't know!' Becky screamed. 'Heinrich called and said she'd been shot and …'

Aggie came in, her eyes bleary, and said, 'What's going on?'

It was then that it hit Kitty. Calmly at first, she said, 'Your sister Bernadette. She's dead.'

'Dead? How …'

And then Kitty began to howl. As the reality of what Rebekah had said felled her like a punch to the stomach, she sank to the ground while the two younger women watched. It was unbearable! If Bernadette was dead, why would her legs work to support her body any longer? Why would her mind want to function? Only her voice mattered and that was torn out of her as Kitty threw back her head and screamed.

How was he going to do it? How did you begin to tell a child its mother had died? Shimon was only three. Three!

Heinrich looked at the child as he slept peacefully in his bed and felt his own heart break. The poor boy didn't even know who his real father was and now he'd lost his mother. Of course, they'd never told Shimon that Heinrich wasn't his real father and now wasn't the time to do that. But one day he would have to know, one day Gibrail Khoury would have to be told that he had a son. If anyone could find him.

Bernie had been shot by a sniper. After the Israeli invasion of Sinai some of the Egyptian troops who hadn't been captured had been trapped behind the lines. It was likely to have been one of them. But why? Why shoot a lone woman?

Renate had told him that Bernie had been walking outside the monastery when it happened, taking photographs. Heinrich could understand why she'd been there, it was what she did. But surely she must have known she might be in danger. Renate had Bernie's camera, which she was going to give back when she returned from Sinai, with Bernie's body.

He walked out of the child's bedroom and into the lounge where he poured himself a large glass of neat whisky. He couldn't call Bernie's family because none of them had a phone and so he'd rung her friend Rebekah. She had said she'd tell Bernie's mother, although he could hear that she was falling apart at the other end of the line. Bernie had meant so much to so many people. She'd meant everything to him. Even when she'd been unfaithful with Gibrail. She'd loved Heinrich and he'd loved her, in spite of everything they had endured, and now she was gone he wished he could curl up and die. But he couldn't.

There was Shimon to consider, there was also Bernie's memory, which had to be honoured, and there was the issue of her body. Strictly speaking, as a British citizen she would have to be repatriated to England. When dawn broke and he had taken Shimon to kindergarten, he would have to go to the British Embassy in Tel Aviv to find out what needed to be done. Because Bernie had been a Christian there was no tearing hurry to inter her as there was in Judaism, but her body had to be put on a ship for London as soon as possible.

He'd decided that he'd wait until Shimon returned from kindergarten today before breaking the news to him. The child would be devastated. And what about his mother's body? Would he understand why she had to be taken thousands of miles away for burial?

Heinrich took a long slug from his whisky glass and lit himself a cigarette. To complicate things still further, Britain and France were now officially at war with Egypt and so the Mediterranean would be dangerous. How would they even get Bernie out and ... He didn't want her to go! He wanted her to walk back into the apartment smiling because she'd had a good trip to Sinai.

He cried, quietly so as not to wake the boy. The world was going mad and when that happened he lost things. In the Great War his Berlin-based family had lost much of their wealth, in WWII they had lost their home and almost their lives, and now he'd lost the love of his life. When was it going to end? And what had it all been for anyway? The British were saying that Nasser had blown up all the ships trapped in the Suez Canal, making it impassable. So even if the British and French wrested it away from the Egyptians it was useless. But then, that summed up war for Heinrich: death and destruction for nothing. Nothing at all.

*

Marie had come home and was sitting on the floor beside the range with tears in her eyes, one comforting arm around her sister. Moritz Shapiro had arrived just after Marie, bearing a bottle of brandy.

Sitting in Pat's old chair, Kitty Lynch nursed her glass against her chest, her eyes completely dry now that she had seemingly run out of tears. Becky sat with her father on the other side of the range. They'd all been quiet for over half an hour. In shock, no one able to believe what had happened. Eventually Becky spoke.

'Heinrich said he will arrange a phone call for four o'clock our time so that you can speak to him, Auntie Kitty.'

Kitty nodded. She'd never spoken civilly to Heinrich Simpson in her life. Now she had to. Now she wanted to because she knew, finally, that she owed him. For all the love he'd given her daughter, for standing by Bernie when she became pregnant by another man. And now she needed him too.

'I want our Bernie back home,' she said. 'I want her to have a proper burial.'

'I'm sure Heinrich will organise that,' Becky said.

Kitty nodded then said slowly, 'I have to thank you, Rebekah.'

'Me?'

'When that call come you must've almost near died of shock,' she said. 'You loved our Bernie. And then having me shout at you ...'

She got up out of her chair, went over to Becky and put her arms around her shoulders. Becky began to cry again.

Kitty said, 'I've been such a silly woman! Cutting everyone out of me life from pure pig-headedness. And now our Bernie's gone to her grave without hearing so much as a kind word from me in years!'

232

Moritz Shapiro put a hand on her shoulder. 'She knew you loved her, Mrs Lynch.'

Becky, who was less sure if she were honest, nodded her agreement.

Then suddenly Kitty put a hand up to her face.

'Oh, God help us!' she said. 'How are we going to tell Rosie?'

There wasn't so much as a peep from the building now receding into the distance behind him. Dermot pulled Father Delaney's coat close up around his neck and wondered how the priest was feeling. He probably had a sore head and Dermot was sorry for that but, when he'd decided to take an unlooked-for opportunity, he hadn't given too much thought to the consequences.

His cellmate old Dawkins had asked for Confession and so the priest had come to him. Dawkins had cancer and wasn't expected to live much longer, although he wasn't yet sick enough to be put in the hospital wing. Dermot had been brought up a Catholic himself and so he didn't really know what to do with himself while Dawkins was confessing his sins, which was meant to be a private matter. But he needn't have worried. When the priest bowed his head in prayer, the old man hit him with the slop bucket.

To say that Dermot was shocked was an understatement. He was even more taken aback when Dawkins began taking off the unconscious man's clothes.

'Here,' he said to Dermot. 'Get your togs off and put his on.'

'Why?'

'Because you look a bit like him, you daft bleeder,' Dawkins said.

Dermot had done as he was told.

'Now push him under my bunk,' Dawkins said. 'Now knock on the door.'

233

'What?'

'Knock on the door to be let out,' Dawkins said. 'You're always going on about how you want to get out of here and get back to your little boy. Here's your chance.'

Dermot looked at his cellmate in a new light. 'You've been planning this for a while, haven't you, Wilf?'

The old man laughed. 'I'm almost done with this world, son,' he said. 'Might as well give a youngster like you a hand while I still can. Now knock on that door – and be lucky!'

And he had and it had worked. Dermot left Dartmoor Prison in the guise of Father Milo Delaney, driving the car the good priest always used when he visited. However, unlike the priest, Dermot wasn't sure which way was his best route off the moor. The prison was notoriously isolated and he knew that if he took a wrong turning he could end up going still further into the wilderness.

Something big loomed out of the darkness in front of the car and then raced on its way. A Dartmoor pony – blokes inside said they were everywhere. The headlights of the priest's old car were weak but they did allow Dermot to see that the track in front of him forked in two directions. He stopped. Left or right?

That pause gave Dermot time to think. What was he doing? He'd already served four years of his twelve-year stretch and managed to keep his nose clean. When he came up for parole ... But, no, it didn't work that way when the death of a copper was involved. Old Dawkins knew that and so did Dermot. If anything, the screws would find a way to increase his sentence. When the opportunity had come, of course he'd taken it. He had to get out!

There was the sound of a click, then a rattling sound that Dermot knew well. It came from behind him and when it resolved itself into the wail of a siren from the prison, he put his foot on the car's accelerator and drove to the left.

Sleep didn't come easily to Nell Larkin these days. Being in that sanatorium had done for her, she always thought. Trying to get some kip around all those other sick women without a drop of brown ale to sustain her for months on end. Then when she'd come out life hadn't been the same for her. Blessed had only taken her back on condition she controlled her drinking, which she did, to some extent. But it was hard. Apart from the end of the Blitz life hadn't got much easier in the East End since the war, and with Rose and Morry constantly hanging around it was difficult for Nell to do as she pleased.

Rosie had finally got in around midnight after her prison visit. It took it out of her going to Dartmoor and Nell could hear her shifting restlessly in her sleep. What good it did her to go and visit Dermot, Nell didn't know. The boy was a strange one and she had always felt there was something amiss with him, though she hadn't known what exactly. That said, Rose claimed to love him, even if they'd never slept together. At first that didn't make a lot of sense to Nell, but when she thought about it some more, maybe it did.

She'd had sex with hundreds, maybe even thousands, of men in her time and it had never made her happy or ended well. Blokes always took advantage of women, one way or the other. If they could make a few bob out of a girl they would. But it was still sad that Rose's only experiences of physical love had been so bad. Neither of them would ever forget when Nell'd had to take her daughter to an abortionist. At least Dermot had never physically hurt either of them.

But if Rose meant to wait for her husband then she was probably on a fool's errand. When Dermot got out he'd want to find a man because that was what he liked. In prison blokes like him usually got held down and buggered or so she'd been told. Would that have put him off? Nell didn't know.

All she did know was that there had been screaming coming from the Lynches' flat earlier and she wondered what was up. Kitty, by the sound of it, howling her heart out.

Chapter 21

Three weeks later

A green copper serpent wound its way up St Patrick's staff as he looked down at it with motionless, stone eyes. It was said that when the saint arrived in Ireland he drove all the snakes from the land and into the sea. That was why there were none left in Ireland.

In London, on a cold winter's day in the Church of the English Martyrs on Prescot Street, the only snake visible was the one on the statue of the saint. However, those attending Mass that day were aware of the evil that existed elsewhere.

Although not a Requiem Mass, the service the Lynch family and their friends had just attended had been dedicated to Bernadette. Thousands of miles away in Israel their daughter, sister or best friend was being buried in a cemetery called Mount Zion in Jerusalem. Despite the best efforts of the man who had been Bernie's husband in all but name, repatriation of her body had been all but impossible. With both Britain and Israel on war footings the transportation of a corpse had very low priority. Heinrich had apologised to Kitty for this.

'I'm so sorry, Mrs Lynch,' he'd said when he'd called her. 'I did everything I could.'

And then he'd cried. And then she, the woman who had hated him for so long, had comforted him.

She'd said, 'It's not your fault, Mr Simpson. I know you loved our girl and I'm sure you did everything you could to send her home to us. I'm just so sorry that I treated you badly for so long.'

And then she had cried too. She cried again now as she left the church, her two daughters supporting her, her son Little Paddy walking behind. Behind him came two of Kitty's sisters, her husband's sister Mary from Devon, and then came the friends. Rose, weeping uncontrollably, held her young son's hand and leaned against her mother; Becky and her father were accompanied by Solly Adler, and finally came ancient Mr Katz who had given Bernie her first-ever camera.

As the party spilled out into the street and acquaintances gave their condolences to Kitty and her family, Becky took Solly's hand and leaned against him for support.

She said, 'I still can't believe it. I don't think I'll ever get over this.'

'She was my first love,' Solly said, sighed and lit himself a cigarette. He wasn't telling Becky anything she didn't already know.

She squeezed his arm. Then she looked over at Rose, sobbing in her mother's arms.

'It's her I'm most worried about,' Becky said. 'She's taking it so hard and what with this business with Dermot ...'

Dermot Lynch was still on the run from Dartmoor Prison and the police had already been round to Fournier Street as well as to the cottage in Essex, looking for him. Although not named as a police killer, because he had been implicated in a crime that resulted in a policeman's death he was being portrayed as a 'dangerous criminal'.

Becky let go of Solly's arm and went over to comfort Rose. Nell looked at Becky as she passed her daughter to her and said, 'I dunno what to do ...'

Becky took her friend in her arms and led her over to a low wall that surrounded the approaches to the church. She lowered her down on this and then sat next to her.

'Oh, Rosie,' she said. 'I'm so sorry. We're all going to miss Bernie so much ...'

Rose raised her red and tear-stained face and said, 'You and Bernie, you was like the sisters I never had.'

'And we always will be,' Becky said. 'I'll always be here for you, as long as I live. So will Bernie. She loved us and her love will always be with us. That will never die.'

'But we'll never see her again!'

Becky hugged her tightly.

'I can't bear it, Becky,' Rose said. 'I can't! Three of us always! Us girls together against the world!'

'We still are, Rosie,' Becky said. 'Nothing can or will change that. Bernie will live in our hearts as long as we are alive. Then there's little Shimon. Heinrich has promised Auntie Kitty that as soon as he can, he'll bring him here. That will be like getting a little bit of Bernie back.'

'You think?'

'I do,' Becky said. 'And there's also her work. You know the last photograph she took, of the monastery in Sinai is up for a prize in Israel as the best press photograph of the year?

Heinrich is going to send me a copy so we can all see it. Bernie would have loved that and we should all be so proud to have known such a wonderful, talented person.'

'But she's dead . . . '

Becky kissed the side of Rose's face. 'I know there are no good things about this, Rosie,' she said. 'But Bernie did die doing what she loved. I can't imagine her old and sick, can you?'

Rose stopped crying. 'She was so young.'

'And now she'll be forever young,' Becky said. 'Maybe that's how it is with those of us who are really brave.'

Nell, who had been swigging something from a hip flask, poked it in Rose's face and said, 'Want some whisky?'

Rose shook her head. Nell offered her booze to Moritz Shapiro who also declined.

Kitty Lynch, still being supported by her daughters, cleared her throat to get everyone's attention and said, 'We're having a few drinks for our Bernie round at ours now. You're all invited to help us toast our girl.'

Her daughters took her to a waiting taxi and beckoned to Moritz Shapiro to join them.

He kissed his daughter and said, 'I will not refuse a lift. My legs really don't want to walk all the way home.'

Becky smiled. 'That's fine, Papa. We'll see you at Auntie Kitty's.'

Once the cab had moved away, Becky helped Rose to her feet.

'Come on,' she said. 'Let's get moving. The walk will do us good.'

Rose, her eyes still full of tears, said, 'Yes, nurse.'

And in spite of everything the two of them laughed.

*

'Oi! Phil!'

The man at the bar knew Tilly was there and had chosen not to acknowledge her. But once hailed, she knew he'd turn around, which he did.

'Oh, hello, Till!' the man said. 'What you up to?'

'What does it look like?' Tilly said as she held up her empty beer glass. 'Mine's a pint.'

'Oh, right.'

Phil Zammit owned several properties in Soho including the flat where Tilly lived. An easy-going man with a casual attitude towards the draconian laws against homosexuality, in spite of himself being a very happily married man from a vast Maltese family, Phil Zammit's grimy bedsits were a blessing to local drag queens and rent boys.

After buying a drink for himself and a pint for Tilly, Phil came over and sat down next to her.

'Busy in here today,' he said as he looked around the ornate Victorian bar of London's foremost queer pub, the Salisbury. 'Something going on is there?'

'No. Just boys being boys,' Tilly said. Then she touched his arm. 'Been meaning to ask you what's happening with Daisy Summer's old room?'

Daisy was an ancient drag queen who had died back in the autumn.

'Why?'

'Why'd you think? I know someone as wants a billet.'

'Oh, well, it's a bit of a mess down there ...'

'Your places are always a bit of a mess, Phil,' Tilly said. 'The person I've got in mind ain't too fussy.'

'Oh, well ...'

'Give you a month up front and I guarantee no trouble,' Tilly said.

Phil frowned. 'Who's it for?'

'Nice quiet gentleman.'

'What?'

Tilly leaned closer to Phil. 'A good friend of mine. Just left his wife, if you know what I mean.'

'Oh.'

Phil had heard about this, blokes leaving their wives to pursue a life of what he called 'queerness'.

'So, you're . . .'

'Oh, we're not having an affair! Heavens, no!' Tilly said. 'He's just a mate and I want to help him out.'

'Alright,' Phil said. 'When's he want to move in?'

'Yesterday.'

'Oh. Well, I'll need to get Daisy's stuff outta there. I s'pose I could do it today . . .'

The downside of Phil's easy-going nature was that he was very lazy. Tilly knew that even if he did clean the room up a bit it would still be far from perfect or even habitable.

She put her hand in her pocket and pulled out a roll of banknotes. 'Here's your month in advance, to give you a bit more strength for all that scrubbing and polishing,' she said. 'I've given you the same rent I pay.'

Phil didn't even bother to count it. 'Thanks, Till,' he said. 'How long's your mate gonna want the room for?'

'Just the month, I reckon,' Tilly said. 'He travels.'

Most of the male mourners stood out in the back yard. The exception was Moritz Shapiro who sat opposite Kitty Lynch beside the range.

'My bones can no longer take the cold,' he said as Marie handed him a glass of sherry.

Now cried out, a calmer, white-faced Kitty smiled at him.

'I know what you mean,' she said. 'This business of getting old is not for softies.'

'My father always used to say that getting old was a privilege,' Moritz said. 'But then for Jews in the Russian Empire like him, it was. He had to come to this country in order to be sure of surviving.'

Kitty smiled. 'My family come here to find work,' she said. 'But my Pat's lot come over during the potato famine to save their lives.'

'The things people have done to each other and continue to do ... It beggars belief,' Moritz said.

Kitty leaned forward. 'Mr S,' she said, 'do you understand why my Bernadette died?'

'No,' he said.

'I mean, this war they've been having out there ...'

'About the Suez Canal,' he said.

'I know.'

'But not only that,' he continued. 'My own belief is that Israel invaded Sinai just before the British and the French went into Suez in order to soften up the Egyptian forces. All sorts of patriotic talk comes out of Israel ... taking back ancestral lands ... but the harsh truth is that economics plays its part too, a big one. Britain and France support Israel because they do not like the way Nasser is so close to the Russians.'

'So my daughter died to ensure a trading alliance?'

'No. She died because whoever shot her had lost touch with his humanity,' Moritz said. 'She was there in front of him, an obviously European woman, and he shot her just for that. He probably thought she was a Jewish settler.' He touched Kitty's hand. 'My dear, you must not dwell on how Bernadette died. Mr Simpson has told us that, according to the doctor who examined her body, it must have been immediate. That is a mercy.

And remember that in the New Year you have Agnes's wedding and Mr Simpson and Shimon visiting for the first time. I'm sure Bernadette would want you to be happy about these things.'

'I know she would.'

Becky, who had been listening to their conversation, came and sat down next to her father.

'Heinrich will send us pictures of Bernie's headstone once it's set,' she said. 'One day we should all go there to see it.'

Her father nodded.

But Kitty shook her head. 'I couldn't,' she said. 'I think maybe I'd go mad if I went there. I know it's silly to think that a place can kill a person, but however stupid it might sound, I don't think I'll ever be able to shift the idea that if Bernadette hadn't gone to Israel she'd be alive today.'

'Maybe … maybe not,' Becky said. 'Bernie was always adventurous. She always wanted to take risks. I don't believe, wherever she went, she would have been what you'd call safe. I remember her sitting on top of the barricade during the Battle of Cable Street. Defiant as hell, fending off missiles thrown by the fascists. Rose and me just went along for the ride but Bernie was one of those who actively kept the Blackshirts out of the East End.'

'And I tried so hard to stop her!' Kitty smiled. 'Of course, Pat knew what she was up to. Bernie and her dad were as thick as thieves.'

'Ah, she'll be with her daddy now,' Kitty's sister Assumpta joined in.

'Way before her time,' Kitty said. 'Pat'll be having a go at her, asking her what she's doing there!'

They all laughed. And then Kitty cried again.

Becky put a hand on her shoulder and then, looking around, said, 'Where's Rosie?'

*

The last time she'd seen him had been down in Essex. He'd just turned up one day, carrying an armful of willow branches out of which he'd made a big basket for her washing.

'What you doing here?' Rose asked her father when she saw him walking into the graveyard surrounding Christ Church.

'I heard you'd had a death,' said Nelson Lee. 'Mate of yours.'

'How?'

He shrugged. 'Word gets around.'

Rose said, 'Yes. My best friend, Bernie.'

'Sounds like she was a fine young woman.'

'She was brave and I loved her.'

Her father looked up at the sky. 'I heard your man got out of Dartmoor,' he said. 'He must be a brave one.'

'He is. But they'll catch him.'

'You think?'

Rose didn't reply.

Nelson said, 'I brung you some money, chavvy.' He thrust a pile of banknotes towards her. 'Here.'

Rose shied away from him.

'What for?' she asked.

'To make your life easier,' he said. 'For you, Nell and the boy.'

'I don't want it.'

He pressed the notes into her hand.

'I got it honest,' he said. 'I've been off the horses for a time now, selling cars. Take it for your mum, if not for you.'

Rose tightened her fingers on the money.

'Mum's still drinking, you know.'

'She always will.'

'It'll go on booze.'

'So you keep it for yourself and for the boy.'

Rose looked up at him. 'Why do you do this?' she asked.

'Why do you give us things? Mum told me you've got a woman ...'

'Died in August,' he said. 'Never could have no chavvies so it's just me now. Not that I'll try and come back into Nelly's life. She don't want that, I know.'

'So what do you want?' Rose said.

'Nothing.' He shrugged.

'Nothing?'

'Wanna make sure I do right by you,' he said. 'That's all. You never asked to come into this world. That was down to me and Nelly. I know it's too late now, but I want to help.'

Rose nodded. Nell had always remained bitter at the young man who had got her pregnant all those years ago in Epping Forest. It was because of what they'd done that she'd had to leave her people and seek her fortune in London. To survive she'd turned to prostitution and to endure that she'd turned to drink. She'd always blamed Nelson Lee and had refused to take anything from him ever since. But Rose understood that they'd both been very young at the time and that he wasn't a bad man.

She pocketed the banknotes.

'Alright, I'll take this,' she said. 'But I won't tell Mum.'

'As you wish.'

'Morry'll need new school uniform soon,' she said. 'He's doing really well with his lessons. Can read and write and do his sums. Don't have no trouble off him.'

'That's good.'

'His teacher told me one day he might work in an office.'

Nelson nodded. 'Be good if one of ours don't have to labour in the mud.'

'Yes, it will be.'

*

'Oh, bloody Phil!'

The room was still a tip, completely untouched in spite of what the landlord had told her.

Tilly ushered in the heavily dressed man beside her into what had once been Daisy Summer's room and said, 'I'm sorry about this. Phil Zammit's such a lazy bleeder!'

'He won't come in to clear up unexpected, will he?'

'He gave me the key, darling, he don't mean to do nothing,' Tilly said.

Daisy's clothes were still laid on her bed. The sheets hadn't been changed since the old girl had died back in August. The sink was still full of pots and the whole place stank. In spite of the fact that it was cold outside, Tilly opened the window.

'Smells like a fucking morgue in here!'

Her visitor sat in the only chair and put his head down on his chest.

Tilly, spotting this, said, 'It's alright, I'll clean up. You nod off if you like. I do understand.'

Tilly herself had been on the streets for a while when she'd first come to London. What it must've been like, doing that for months, she could hardly imagine. She gathered up the clothing off the bed and put it into a big suitcase she'd found on the top of the wardrobe. While the new tenant slept, Tilly did the washing-up and made them both a cup of tea.

She nudged him to get his attention. 'Oi, bugger-lugs! Cup of char.'

Dermot Lynch raised his head and smiled at her. His face was much thinner and his hair greyer than before but his eyes had a glint in them, just a little, because he was still free.

He took the cup from Tilly and said, 'Ta.'

He'd hung about the West End for months before he'd met up with her in Embankment Park. He'd been sleeping there for about a week and had been sipping from the water fountain when she'd found him. At first he'd worried that she might be about to call the police, but instead she'd invited him to stay at her place for the night. He'd been holed up there ever since.

But Tilly still had to work and her little flat had long been a place where drag queens and rent boys met up after work. When Tilly started telling people she wanted more time to herself, it had looked suspicious and, because the coppers were always watching what the queer girls and boys did, she knew she had to off-load her guest somehow. Hence the conversation with Phil Zammit and a large slice of her savings given over to paying one month's rent in advance.

'I've put some tea, sugar and milk in your larder,' Tilly said. 'And there's fags beside the bed. I'll get you some chips when I go out later.'

'Tilly, I . . .'

'Don't thank me!' she said. 'I'm doing this for Rosie, not you!'

'Yeah, but we never got along . . .'

'I don't wanna talk about it,' she said. 'I've paid your rent and I'll feed you until you can get yourself together to move on. You've got a month – unless of course the coppers nab you. Then it's nothing to do with me, you hear?'

'Yes, Tilly.'

Then she left. Alone in the small, still untidy room, Dermot was too tired to consider his options. After he'd had a sleep without being disturbed by Tilly every five minutes, he'd think about it. When he'd kipped in the park he'd met a bloke, also on the run, who claimed he knew a bloke who knew another bloke who took people illegally across the Channel to France.

But he'd need money for that and Dermot didn't know of any way to obtain it that didn't involve taking a huge risk.

248

Chapter 22

12 January 1957

Kitty's smile was not as wide as it would have been had her Bernie been outside the Church of the English Martyrs to greet her sister Aggie and her new husband Ron, but it was wide enough. All in white, just like a proper bride, Aggie looked radiant, holding the hand of the man who had taken her on for better or worse. Ron O'Hara was a gas fitter by trade and so he made good money. Once they left the Wedding Breakfast at the Shapiros' house, the two of them were going to get themselves settled in the small flat in Manor Park that Ron had rented. At last Kitty had her white wedding.

When all the guests got back to Fournier Street, Moritz Shapiro was there to welcome them together with the vast troop of women from Ron's family who had organised the food. The Lynches paid for the drink, which had been made easier by a really big contribution from Rose. Kitty didn't know where she'd got that from and nor did she care. Rose had wanted to contribute and Kitty had been touched by that.

Ushered into the Shapiros' large drawing room, all the guests were given glasses of sherry or whisky to warm them up after being outside in the cold. There were over a hundred people there and Kitty, for a while, found herself pushed into a corner beside Heinrich Simpson and her grandson, Shimon.

Although able to speak some English, the little boy was overwhelmed by the sheer number of people around him and clung to his father for reassurance.

Kitty said, 'I'm really grateful you could both come in time for Aggie's wedding.'

'My pleasure,' Heinrich said. 'It's important that Shimon knows his mother's family.'

But where was his father? All Kitty knew about him was that he was an Arab. And she didn't dare ask Heinrich even though she knew he was fully aware he was not Shimon's blood father.

'You are always welcome to come and visit us in Israel,' Heinrich continued. 'I hope that you will some day.'

Kitty just smiled. Did he, she wondered, realise how poor they were? Had he noticed that all the sandwiches on the buffet had already gone and people were filling up on pickled onions and jellied eels?

Shimon said something to Heinrich in Hebrew. He replied in English, 'No, Mama's best friend lives here. Mama was born across the road.'

They'd only arrived the previous day and, so far, Kitty had managed to get out of hosting them at the flat. But she knew it couldn't last.

'I'll take you over there later, Shimon,' she said to the little boy. 'Would you like that?'

He nodded solemnly. Blond like Bernie, he had dark eyes and skin the colour of ash-wood, very lightly brown. When Kitty had first met him she had thought he was the most beautiful child she had ever seen.

'I want him to know all about Bernie,' Heinrich said. 'She was an extraordinary woman. You should be proud to be her mother.'

'I am.'

He smiled. 'And of Agnes too,' he said. 'What a beautiful bride!'

Kitty smiled. Everyone she cared about had come today. Even Marie had consented to put on a dress so that she could be her sister's bridesmaid. That was a massive concession as she only ever wore trousers and had her hair cut so short that some people thought she was a man.

'Auntie Kitty?'

She turned and saw Becky standing at her elbow.

'Yes, love?'

'Papa is asking whether you'd like the cake left in the kitchen or brought in here?'

'Well, it's a bit crowded ...'

'So, shall we leave it?'

'Ah, no, bring it in,' Kitty said. 'It's too beautiful to be hiding in the kitchen.'

Becky left. When she returned she held one side of a board, with Rose holding the other, on which stood a cake three tiers high. Pure white and covered in delicate pink sugar roses, the cake was a celebration of everything opulent and pretty and definitely off ration. People gasped when they saw it.

Kitty stepped forward to help the girls put the cake on the dining table, then she called for silence.

'Just want to say a few words about this lovely cake before

we go any further,' she said. 'This was made for our Aggie and Ron by Lyons Corner House up West. I think they've done a smashing job and so I'd like to thank the person what arranged it – Mrs Dolly Adler. Come on, Doll! Come and take a bow!'

Blushing, but looking so smart and pretty in her royal blue fitted suit, Dolly Adler came out of the crowd and gave Kitty a peck on the cheek.

'It was my pleasure, gel,' she said. 'Those of us still living in these old streets of ours have to stick together.'

There was a slight pause before they all cheered because everyone knew what she was saying was true. With a lot of the local flats and houses being condemned and the Council talking about demolition, nobody knew where they'd be in six months' time, let alone a year.

'Penny for 'em?'

Rose sat down beside Tilly on the seat at the bottom of the Shapiros' garden. There weren't that many green spaces in Spitalfields, which made this tiny patch of grass precious.

Tilly – or rather Herbert today – had come to the wedding as Rose's companion. There was a reason for this and it was largely to do with the money that her father Nelson had given her the previous November.

'Still thinking about the cottage,' Tilly said. 'Even with that money from your dad to help out, there'll be a lot to do. Anyway it don't belong to you.'

'No, but Mr Shapiro's happy for us to do it up and live in it and we won't have to pay no rent.'

'Yeah, but what am I gonna do in the country?'

'I thought you wanted to get out of London,' Rose said.

Tilly shrugged. 'In a way, yeah,' she said. 'But ... what about Morry?'

252

'There's a grammar school in Southend,' she said. 'He can get the bus every day.'

'Yeah, but ...'

'He wants to leave London,' Rose said.

'What about your mum?'

'Oh, she'll stay here. Although I'm hoping she'll come down to Essex too some time.'

Tilly couldn't see that ever happening but she didn't say anything.

'Some places round here've already been emptied out,' Rose said. 'The worst places. So our flat can't be far behind. We've still not got running water let alone electricity.'

Tilly, who had been thinking, said, 'You and the boy could come and live with me, like we planned all them years ago.'

Before Rose had married Dermot, she'd accepted Tilly's offer to go and live with her once the baby was born so they could bring it up together. But, of course, then she'd met Dermot again and it had never happened.

'Your place is far too small, Till,' Rose said. 'We'd never all fit in just the one room.'

'We could rent more,' Tilly said. 'I could speak to Phil. You could work up West ...'

'Yeah? What am I going to do there?' Rose said. 'Can't go back to the Windmill. They'd pay me to keep me clothes on these days.'

Tilly laughed. 'Oh, you're still a looker, Rosie Red,' she said. 'Which is why I can't understand why you want to bury yourself away in the country with a teenager, a drag queen and your alcoholic mum.'

She shrugged. 'Because you're my family.'

'Yeah, but don't you want a bloke? I mean, it's years since you had that terrible experience with Morry's father. Don't you never want to have you-know-what again?'

'No,' Rose said. 'At least, I don't think so. I don't know as I ever have. When we was kids, me and Becky and Bernie, we was very different about all that. Bernie was the boldest one of all of us, kissing Solly Adler in the street, but then men always went after her because she was so beautiful and clever. Becky too. She was in love with Solly years ago but he never looked at her because he wanted Bernie. Then she went off to Israel and Solly married that slapper Sharon. Then she left him, then she killed herself . . . '

'You don't half have some dramas down here, girl!'

Rose smiled. 'But I weren't like Becky and Bernie,' she said. 'My mum's fella was interfering with me for years. Then I got pregnant – I've told you this. But you know, Till, I think that even if I hadn't been interfered with, I don't know as I would ever have wanted to go with a bloke.'

'What about a woman?'

Rose laughed. 'No!' she said. 'I knew girls as did that back in the war, but it never appealed to me.' Then she whispered, 'You know that Aggie's sister Marie's one of them?'

'What? A les—'

'Shhh! Auntie Kitty can't know,' Rose said. 'Becky reckons Marie's got some woman friend up Highgate somewhere.'

'Oh, like a girlfriend?'

'I s'pose so,' Rose said. ''Course, Marie's never been what you'd call girly, has she? I mean, each to their own. Or in my case, each to herself . . . '

'Oh, well . . . But look, Rosie Red, we're talking about what happens to you from now on and I want to make sure you ain't making a mistake with this Essex business. I mean, when you lived there last time, you did get bored as I remember.'

*

Becky found Solly on his own in the kitchen.

'What are you doing in here all on your tod?' she asked.

'Thinking about you,' he said. 'And how beautiful you are.'

'You're not supposed to say that!' Becky said. 'The bride is the one who is beautiful today!'

And Aggie did look beautiful. Wearing a pale teal-coloured sheath dress, her deep mahogany hair piled up in a neat chignon, she looked like one of the fashion plates from a magazine. Solly knew who had really caught his eye, though.

He held out his arms and Becky walked into them.

'I'm so lucky to have you in my life,' he said.

She heard his heart beat and it made her hold him even more tightly.

'We're both lucky,' she said.

'I look at poor Heinrich and I think how sad his eyes are.'

'He told Papa he's not been feeling so well lately,' Becky said. 'I expect it's because of everything he's been through.'

'And he's not young.'

'None of us are,' Solly said. 'Such a lot of water's passed underneath the bridge since we was kids back in the thirties.'

'I know.'

Gently, he pushed her away and then held her at arm's length.

'Gets a person to thinking ...'

'It does,' she said. 'I know Papa's worried about what might happen to the area.'

Solly swallowed hard and then he said, 'Mum's had an offer from the Council of a flat in Essex.'

'Oh?'

'Place called Harlow,' he said. 'They're building loads of new housing out there. New bathrooms, kitchens, the lot.'

Becky felt her face drain of colour.

'Nice for Nat,' he said. 'Now she's almost grown up, be good for her to have a bedroom to herself with no damp running down the walls.'

'Yes.'

'Not that Mum's said yes or nothing. I mean, I've got me job here and me brother only lives around the corner. But it's something we'll have to think about. You . . .'

'Oh, Papa owns this house,' Becky said. 'So if the Council wanted to demolish it, they'd have to pay him. But we'd fight that. The people who built this house were Huguenots, refugees from France. Like us, they came here to be safe. They did well and built these houses to show the world that they could make their lives beautiful again after years of persecution. Papa has always said we need to keep these places as memorials to their bravery. There's no way we'd leave here.'

'But this house is old,' he said. 'Your dad's told me it's got problems . . .'

'Problems, yes, but we won't leave it,' Becky said. 'I don't blame anyone else who doesn't feel the same way. I mean, if you want to go . . .'

'I do and I don't,' he said.

'Oh, well . . .'

Music floated in towards them from the drawing room. It was strange to hear something as modern as skiffle in the Shapiros' house.

'I think people are going to dance,' Becky said.

'Yes, I suppose they are.'

He didn't move. Solly, with his artificial leg, didn't like dancing.

'But I'll stay here,' Becky said as she took his hand.

She felt him squeeze her fingers and then he said, 'Becky, I want us to get married.'

She couldn't breathe. Ever since they'd got together she'd wondered whether this moment would come. She'd never sought it. She had a career for which she had fought and to which she had dedicated herself many years before. Neither of them was love's young dream anymore, but . . .

'Oh, Solly.'

'And if you don't want to go to Harlow, I won't go either,' he said. 'We'll get a flat of our own.'

'What about your mum? And Natalie?'

He sighed. 'Mum'll cope, she always has,' he said. 'About time she had somewhere easy to look after. And Nat's a young lady now. Those new flats won't be built for another year. She'll be leaving school then. Wants to work in the West End doing something, don't know what. She's been doing shorthand and typing at school. But, look, it'll be alright. Will you . . . Will you think about it?'

Becky had wanted to marry this man since she was sixteen. Nothing had changed – except life. She said, 'I want to.'

'So . . .'

'But these days, I must think about Papa. All his relatives have died in the last few years and so I'm all he's got,' she said. 'I have to do the right thing for him as well as for me. I'd have to remain near him. Unlike your mother, I know he won't move.'

'I understand.'

She leaned towards Solly and kissed him. 'It's not like when we were kids anymore, Solly. Now we have others we must take care of too. You as well as me,' she said. 'Let's talk again later when we've both had a chance to think. Weddings can make people emotional, you know?'

Digging out roads. It's what his ancestors from Ireland had done. It wasn't something Dermot Lynch had ever thought he'd do.

A month earlier he'd landed in France at a place called Boulogne. He'd slept rough there for a few nights, eating discarded food from the street or stealing from bakeries. Now he was in a place just outside Calais where he'd managed to get work as a navvy, helping to build a new road that would eventually lead to Paris.

But it was hard knowing so little of the language. Only one other workman could speak English, an Algerian who had also entered the country illegally. Not that the foreman cared. As long as he had a full complement of men to build his road, he was alright. And Dermot was alright provided he was paid regularly, which he was.

It had been rough leaving England. But he'd been too afraid to stay. Going back to Dartmoor was beyond him. Even living in the terrible dosshouse the Algerian had taken him to that first night on the roads, was better than that. He had a problem with the language but would have to try and teach himself as much as he could and pick up what was going on around him by watching closely.

The worst thing about his situation was the realisation that he could never go home. Never again being able to see Rose, Morry, his mammy and his siblings broke his heart. Maybe one day they'd be able to come to him. But then maybe one day he'd have to leave France too. And then where would he go?

Mainland Europe was still scarred by the battles fought over it during the war. It still needed rebuilding and so there was a lot of work available. But there were also police, just like there were in England, and he was wanted as a dangerous criminal implicated in the murder of a policeman. But with no passport, he could call himself anything he wanted. He chose the name Cliff Prior for no reason other than that it bore absolutely no relation to any of his family surnames and there was a popular singer called Cliff.

The foreman shouted something at them and all the men stopped drinking coffee or eating bread, picked up their shovels and began to dig. This was it for the time being, this was Dermot's life.

Chapter 23

Two days later

The day hadn't started well. First of all the water had mysteriously been off, then she'd cut her hand on the bread knife, then some bloke from the Council had come round the street door wanting to talk to her about her flat. Kitty had told him to sod off.

For the first time in what had to be years, she'd spent a whole night on her own in the flat. Now that Aggie had gone and Marie worked mainly night shifts that was how it was going to be. But Kitty didn't like it. She'd never been by herself before. Back with her parents in Wapping, she'd shared a room with all three of her sisters; her brothers' room had been next door. The lack of noise got her down.

She put the wireless on and began to get ready to give the flat a scrub. Now that the water was back on she could have a right good go at the floors and blackstone the range before Mr Simpson and Shimon came for tea. They were staying with

Heinrich's sister in Highgate. In a few days' time they'd move on to visit friends in West Sussex and then it would be back home to Israel for them.

Kitty hadn't had much time with her grandson so far and this visit was important to her. She hoped she'd get to know Shimon a little better. At the wedding the boy had been like a little frightened rabbit surrounded by so many unfamiliar adults and noisy cockney children running about. It wasn't surprising, especially since he'd just lost his mum. Kitty paused for a second, bucket in hand, and thought about the three children she had lost, Joey, Bernie and Dermot. Of course, Dermot could still be alive somewhere but how would she ever know?

She began scrubbing the floor. It was best to keep busy when you had sad thoughts and she must get the place halfway decent for her guests. From what she could gather, Heinrich had a nice flat in Jerusalem and so she wouldn't want Shimon to think that his mother's family lived in a slum. Even though they did.

The Council bloke had already been round to Nell's flat that morning. Kitty had heard her neighbour yell at him to 'fuck off' but it was obvious all their homes were at risk. Dolly Adler had been offered a new flat out in Essex with a proper bathroom and electricity. She'd told Kitty she intended to take it. Would she be offered something similar? Would Nell?

In spite of the cold and the damp in her flat, Kitty knew she didn't want to leave. She'd brought her children up in it; she'd lived with and loved her Pat here. And how would she get to work if they moved her out to Essex? She was due back at Tate & Lyle's the following day and actually looking forward to it. She liked the other women in the Blue Room and she'd be hard pressed to earn what she did there anywhere else. No, she wasn't leaving this flat without a fight. Kitty had always liked a scrap and at the thought of another to come she smiled.

Mrs Khan looked as if she was about fourteen, but according to her eight-year-old son, Qasim, she was twenty-eight.

'She is twenty-eight and my father is forty,' the little boy told Becky gravely.

As well as being his mother's translator, Qasim was also the only person to accompany her to the maternity ward. His father, he said, was at work while his two siblings were at school.

'So what language does your mum speak?' Becky asked the boy.

'Urdu. Mother and Father come from Pakistan.'

Which meant that they were likely Muslims. When India had been partitioned after Independence back in 1947, most of the subcontinent's Muslims had moved to the newly formed state of Pakistan.

Mrs Khan was not in heavy labour yet, but she soon would be and, because she hadn't seen a doctor during the entire course of this pregnancy, Becky had no idea how she was doing.

'Mother says she feel ill this time,' Qasim informed the nurse.

'In what way?'

The boy asked his mother and she replied, then he relayed, 'Feel very sick ... bad, bad pain.'

Becky asked whether she could take the woman's blood pressure and the boy said that she could. It was high.

'Do you know how many months pregnant your mum thinks she is?' Becky asked.

Her belly was huge even though the rest of her body was tiny, possibly malnourished.

'It is time,' the boy said.

'Full term?'

'Yes.'

'I will need to get a hospital bed ready for your mum so that a doctor can examine her,' Becky said. 'I think it would be safest if she stayed here to have her baby.'

Qasim translated and Mrs Khan nodded.

'I will go and tell the nurses to make up a bed,' Becky said. 'You stay here with your mum, Qasim.'

He nodded.

Becky left her office and made her way back onto the ward. The way Qasim was translating for his mother reminded her of stories her father had told her about his own youth. Neither of his parents had been able to speak English when they'd arrived in the country. The first family member to speak the language had been his elder sister Hodel, who had translated for her parents all the time until other children, including Moritz, had been born in London. Her father said it had been tough for his parents, especially his mother whose command of the language never really got beyond the most basic greetings. She'd not even been able to speak what should have been her native Russian well either. Becky's grandmother had communicated almost exclusively in Yiddish.

Thinking about her father brought to mind what it meant to her to be Jewish. Becky told two nurses to make up a bed and then began filling out a chart for Mrs Khan. Like this patient, her own grandmother had been a strange woman in a strange land. All her grandmother Yentl ever really had was her religion. But what did that mean to Becky? And if she did take up Solly Adler's offer of marriage, would the ceremony be religious or secular? Did it matter?

Nell looked at her daughter and frowned.

'Ain't you supposed to be at work?' she said.

'I got the day off,' Rose answered.

'Why?'

'I'm going up West.'

'What for?'

'To see Tilly.'

'You just seen her at Aggie's wedding.'

Rose sighed. 'Well, I want to see her again, Mum,' she said. 'Anyway what was all that I heard you shouting your head off about this morning?'

'Bloody Council man,' Nell said. 'Coming round here wanting to know things. I sent him away with a flea in his ear.'

'I know. But if he come to talk about demolition you should've listened.'

Nell turned away. 'I ain't going nowhere.'

'You might not be given a choice,' Rose said. 'This place has no electric, a toilet out the back ... '

'Alright by me.'

'Is it?' Rose said.

Ever since her father had given her money, Rose had been thinking about Ten Bells Cottage down in Essex. Maybe since Bernie's death she wanted a new start? She'd spoken to Becky and Mr Shapiro about it and they were all for it. But first she'd have to get a proper water supply put in, including a toilet and electricity. The Shapiros would help but Rose would use her dad's money too. Not that Nell knew about any of this.

'Mum, I'm thinking I might move back down to the cottage in Essex,' Rose said.

'Why? That ain't got no proper toilet or nothing,' Nell said.

'You can get them things put in.'

'How?'

'Mr Shapiro said he'd pay for it,' Rose said. 'So as I could look after the place like before. Get a job somewhere, Morry could go to the local grammar school ...'

Her mum narrowed her eyes. 'You're serious about this, ain't you?'

Rose nodded. 'It's why I'm going to see Tilly,' she said. 'If we all went, you an' all, we could make it work.'

'Don't know about that,' Nell said. 'I got me job.'

'Well, think about it,' Rose said. 'If the Council are going to knock these places down, wouldn't it be better to be with me and Morry than stuck in some new place all on your own?'

Solly hadn't been able to sleep since Aggie Lynch's wedding. Towards the end of the day he'd asked Becky Shapiro to be his wife. She still hadn't said yes or no and he was becoming anxious. He'd never felt like this about anyone before except for Bernie.

He and Becky had both declared their love for each other and he had no doubt that at least part of her wanted to say yes to his proposal. But she was also a career girl and so the thought of giving up her job when she got married was not something that was easy for her. Then there was the problem of where they would live. Dolly wanted to move out of their flat and go to Harlow. Natalie would almost certainly want to go with her grandma who had probably been the most consistent person in her life. And she still didn't like Becky. Becky herself didn't want to leave Spitalfields. But if the Council were looking to demolish the area then where could they go?

Even if Mr Shapiro did somehow manage to keep hold of

his house on Fournier Street, could Solly really live alongside him? He was a nice old bloke and had got a little less stiff and starchy in recent years but he was still, basically, a religious man. He'd want to keep kosher, which Solly didn't, and he'd probably want them to get married in synagogue.

For Solly who had married Sharon in synagogue, that was something he would do only if Becky insisted. If a person didn't believe in God, what was the point? At heart Solly was still a Communist and places of worship made him nervous.

'Did Mama sleep here?' the little boy asked, pointing to Kitty's bed.

'No, darling, she slept over there.'

Kitty pointed to the curtain that sectioned off the 'girls' room' from the parlour.

The little boy looked sad.

'They used to have a lot of fun in there,' Kitty said. 'Your mum and your aunties.'

She took him back to the table and poured tea for them all. She'd made a sponge cake which, now she saw it on the table, looked a bit flat. But it would have to do.

'Do you have a garden, Grandma?' Shimon asked.

'No, love,' Kitty said. 'Just a back yard.'

'What is that?'

'Well, it's a sort of a bit of ground with the privvy in it.'

'The toilet,' Heinrich translated.

'Oh.'

'Would you like a piece of cake?' Kitty asked.

'No.' Then Shimon said something to Heinrich in Hebrew. He took a book and some pencils out of a bag and put them in front of the boy.

'He wants to do colouring,' he explained.

'Oh.'

Shimon quickly opened the book and began colouring.

Heinrich sipped his tea then said, 'Agnes's wedding was lovely. Thank you so much for inviting us.'

'I'm glad you came,' Kitty said. 'After everything as happened it was only right.'

'You must be so happy for her.'

'I am,' she said. 'I expect Bernie told you I always wanted a daughter of mine to have a white wedding in church.'

'Yes, she did.'

They sat in silence for a few minutes and then Heinrich said, 'I am sorry.'

Kitty said, 'What for?'

'That I took Bernie away from you.'

'She wanted to go. She loved you,' Kitty said. 'Only I didn't want to see it. She was always an adventurous girl. Her dad knew she'd make something of herself and she did. If she'd stayed here with me, she would have been unhappy. I know that now.'

'And yet . . . she's . . .'

Kitty looked at the boy and shook her head. There were just so many times the child could hear about his mother's death.

Heinrich ate some cake.

'And how are you?' Kitty said. 'I didn't get a chance to ask while we were at the wedding.'

He shrugged. 'I love Shimon, he is my consolation. Even though . . .'

'No word of this Arab?' Kitty asked.

'No. It's difficult. I think he is in Egypt and of course Israel is still on a war footing with that country. He never knew.'

'I didn't think so.'

267

Heinrich leaned across the table, so that the boy couldn't hear and said, 'Kitty, I have not been well lately.'

'Oh, I'm sorry to hear that,' she said. 'What's wrong?'

He shrugged. 'I don't know. I had some tests back home before I left to come here. I will find out when we return. I've been feeling tired and just not well for a long time. It's probably nothing.'

'I hope so. More tea?'

She poured out second cups for both of them and watched as Heinrich appeared to wrestle with something he wanted to say, but couldn't.

Eventually she took his hand. 'What is it, love?' she asked. 'Anything I can help with?'

'It's, well . . . ' He shook his head. 'Look, I will be honest with you. I have had some tests for cancer and if . . . '

Kitty reined herself in. She wanted to gasp in horror. Cancer was a death sentence and they both knew it.

'If I have . . . cancer,' he said, 'I want to make sure that this little man is taken care of. Although I'm his guardian, I am not his blood and so my family, well . . . there's nothing I can do. I left my wife and children here and so he is none of their concern. But Shimon . . . '

Kitty sat back in her chair and breathed out. Then she nodded. 'You want me to take him?'

'Yes,' said Heinrich. 'You are his blood. You and your family. '

Kitty considered what she had just been asked, but only for a moment. She squeezed Heinrich's hand and said, 'Of course I will. But let's hope I don't have to, eh? Although he's my blood and I love him with all my heart, you are his dad, Heinrich, and I can see how much you love each other.'

He smiled.

'I'm just sorry it's taken the death of our Bernie to make me come to my senses,' Kitty said. 'But now I have, I want to do everything I can for both of you.'

The sound of the huge metal coffee machine nearly made Rose jump out of her skin. As it fired up under the talented hand of its Italian owner, she gave a little squeak.

Tilly laughed. 'Thought you'd be amused by this place, Rosie Red.'

'What is that?' Rose asked.

'Called a Gaggia machine. Makes a frothy coffee what you have in a glass.'

When Rose had first walked into the Moka Coffee Bar on Frith Street, the smell of what she later learned were coffee beans had nearly knocked her flat. A waiter brought them both frothy coffees.

'See what you think.'

Rose sipped. God, it was strong! She'd never had coffee like it.

'What is that?' she said.

'It's real coffee, love,' Tilly said, 'as it's supposed to be.'

'Mum always gets Camp Coffee.'

'Which is why you've never had real coffee before. You like it?'

'Yeah.'

Rose looked around. The Gaggia machine was a huge thing, a bit like a great metal robot. The cafe itself was clean and bright and was full of young people wearing some really mad-looking clothes. There were young men wearing brightly coloured suits and ties, girls in pointy cats-eyes glasses, dresses with loads of petticoats underneath and ballet pumps. A lot of them seemed to be reading books.

'What kinda place is this, Til?'

'It's where the Bohemian set meet,' she said. 'Art students, writers, actors, that sort. And, of course, yours truly. I love it here and I'll miss it.'

Rose looked down at the table.

'You don't have to come down Essex, Til,' she said. 'I do understand.'

She touched her friend's hand. 'I know you do, girl, and I ain't saying no. I just want you to know that it won't be easy. Out in the country people aren't so happy about being around people like me. I can be meself here.'

'You can be yourself with me.'

'Yeah. But as soon as I leave Ten Bells Cottage, I'd have to be someone else. I mean, look what happened to your Dermot when he tried it.'

Tilly was right. Maybe Dermot would have had affairs with men even if they'd stayed in London but that thing he'd had with Raymond had been the desperate act of a man who was not happy with the life he was expected to lead. And Rose knew it.

'I could move out of my place and we could all rent somewhere together,' Tilly said. 'There are some good schools round here. Think about it.'

She nodded. What Tilly was saying made sense. Staying in London had a lot to be said for it. Rose would still be near her mum and Becky, she wouldn't have to change her job and Morry could carry on at his school. Did she really want to get out of London for good or was she just running away in the wake of Bernie's death? And if she did run away, then what? Rose realised she'd better sit down and do some serious thinking because this decision would not be easily reversed. Where would she and Morry be best off living until he was old enough to take care of himself?

Chapter 24

Mrs Khan's baby was born at just before five o'clock that afternoon, a healthy girl she called Shamima. When her husband finally turned up after his shift driving tube trains he thanked Becky for acting so quickly.

'She hides things from me,' he said when they spoke out in the hospital corridor. 'She doesn't want me to worry. I tell her that's wrong but she still does it. Thank you so much for helping her, Sister.'

It was a good way to end her shift and Becky left the hospital with a smile on her face and a spring in her step. When the emergence of new life went well there was nothing better in the world and, although she rarely thought about having a baby herself, the sight of little Shamima in her mother's arms had touched her. The woman was younger than she was, the family lived in what Becky knew was a terribly dilapidated block of flats in Stepney and Mrs Khan already had three other children. But she was happy because she was surrounded by the love of her kids, a unique and fierce love Becky had witnessed so many times before – and envied.

'Walk you home, lady?'

Deep in thought, she hadn't noticed Solly, walking along beside her.

'Oh!'

He laughed. 'Lost to the world!' he said. 'What you thinking about?'

She kissed him on the cheek.

'Oh, just that sometimes my job is so good,' she said. 'It's a real honour to be able to help women at the most exciting and emotional time of their lives.'

He smiled. 'You love it, don't you?'

'I always have. Even in the war when we spent a lot of our time in the basement hiding from the bombing, it was a privilege to be there. You know, Solly, we're so lucky to have this Health Service now. The woman who came to us today, Mrs Khan, her and her husband live in a right rat-trap in Stepney, but they could come to the hospital and she could have her little girl safely and with no charge. I don't often think about it these days, but it's a miracle really.'

Was she trying to tell him she didn't want to marry him because of her dedication to nursing? Solly could not bring himself to ask.

'And I suppose the only thing better than doing my job would be to have a baby of my own,' Becky said slowly.

It had just come out and now it had, did she want to take it back? Solly still said nothing, but he did grasp her hand.

No, she didn't want to take it back. Any of it. 'Let's get married – and soon,' she suggested.

That stopped him in his tracks and made Becky laugh.

'Well?'

'Christ, girl, you don't half have a way of taking a fella unawares!' Solly said.

And then he kissed her. They kissed for such a long time, there on the street, that people began to cheer and whistle.

Coming up for air eventually, Solly said, 'You know I'll do anything you want, don't you, Becky? If you want a big white wedding in synagogue, that's what we'll have. If I have to live with your father I will . . .'

She put a finger onto his lips and said, 'Shhh. All that's for later. Let's just tell people what we're going to do first. Let's tell everyone now!'

Moritz Shapiro had got the measure of dealing with Nell Larkin many years ago, back in the war. She could often be abusive when she was drunk. Or maudlin. Or both. Rarely was she happy, unless she had a man to flirt with or the prospect of more booze on the horizon.

When he saw her totter along Fournier Street, chattering to herself, Moritz invited her in 'for a glass of wine'.

As she sat down stiffly in one of the Shapiros' drawing-room chairs, she said, 'Really kind of you to ask me in, Mr S. Really kind.'

He poured her a glass of claret and himself another cup of tea.

'Lovely do you put on for Aggie Lynch,' Nell said as she raised her glass and then tossed the contents down her throat in one go. There'd be the best part of a bottle got through before she was done. But as Moritz knew only too well, it was the only way to get to the bottom of whatever was troubling Nell. And talking to herself meant that she was really upset.

He refilled her glass while she lit herself a cigarette.

'It's a blessing to help a newly-wed couple,' he said.

273

'Oh, she's set for life is Aggie,' Nell said. 'Her Ron's got a good job and they've already got their own flat. Good luck to 'em.'

'Indeed.'

At least she wasn't drinking more for the moment, which was a good sign.

Moritz said, 'I saw Mr Simpson and little Shimon came to visit Mrs Lynch earlier.'

'That's good. I'm glad of it,' Nell said. 'I said to Kitty on Sunday, I said, "You could go out to Israel if you play your cards right." But she said she weren't interested in going abroad. Not like poor Bernadette. Cor blimey, I remember her when she was a kid going on about going to Egypt – I thought she was off her nut! But she did it. People can do all sorts of things . . . '

'Bernadette was always very determined,' Moritz said. 'But also my Rebekah and your Rose too.'

'Oh, Rosie ain't done a lot,' Nell said. 'When you can't read nor write, not much you can do.'

Moritz had always wondered why Rose was illiterate. He knew that Nell couldn't read or write but the girl had been to school and so surely she'd had some sort of help?

'Me mum and dad could read,' Nell continued. 'And me brothers. But I couldn't never make sense of it. Rose is the same. Them letters just don't make nothing I can recognise, don't matter how much teaching I get. And we was always on the drom – the road.'

She finished her second glass of wine and he poured her another. Now she was sitting down she didn't seem as upset as she'd been in the street. But then Nell liked talking to him these days, it seemed to calm her.

'I think that Rose has done a wonderful job with young Morry,' Moritz said. 'That boy is really bright and works hard at his lessons.'

'Oh, yeah. Teacher told her that he could even work in an

office one day if he keeps that up,' Nell said. 'Mind you, how he'll get on if she takes him away back down Essex, I don't know. She spoke about that to you, Mr S?'

Of course Rose had and so he said, 'Yes. I think she wants a quieter life and, to be truthful with you, Mrs Larkin, I do need to repair that cottage and either sell it or see it put into regular use. I'm happy whatever happens. But I can't leave the place to fall into ruins.'

She nodded. Then tears filled her eyes and he knew that this was what had been making her sad.

'I don't wanna go down there,' she said. 'Rosie says she'll get a job and I can come and live with her, but I don't want to. Then again, the Council's coming round talking about demolishing me flat . . . '

'Well, we're going to fight that,' Moritz said. 'I certainly won't let them take my house and we must all make sure that your flats are made better rather then pulled down. I get rats here, everyone does, but for you and Mrs Lynch to live in such damp, with no electricity . . . it's an outrage.'

'Old man Brown won't do nothing,' Nell said, mentioning the name of her landlord with a sneer.

'Then he must be forced,' Moritz said. 'It isn't like before the war now. There are rules for landlords. But . . . Mrs Larkin, if Rose wants to live on my land, I will not say no.'

'But what about me?'

'You and I must do what is best for our children,' he said. 'This is their world now.'

Nell wept. 'But I don't want to be on my own! I hate being on me own!'

'You won't be,' Moritz said. 'Not while you have friends. And you do have them, Mrs Larkin. And we will not let you down.'

*

275

'Mum?'

Dolly had been sleeping in her chair. Solly's voice woke her up.

'Oh, Gawd blimey!' she said. 'Where'd you spring from?'

He had Becky with him.

'Hello, Dolly.'

'Oh, hello, love,' she said as she sat up and pulled her fingers through her hair. 'How are you?'

'I'm fine, thanks.'

'Mum, we're getting married,' Solly blurted.

She'd always hoped for this. Ever since they'd first started seeing each other. But knowing how career-minded Becky was, Dolly had never let herself get too excited until now. She jumped out of her chair.

'Really?'

Her son smiled. It was one of those moments when he looked young again, like the old Solly, ready to take on the world.

'Really,' he said.

Dolly took them both in her arms and said, '*Mazeltov*!'

'Thanks. Mum.'

When she finally managed to disengage herself from the couple, Dolly said, 'Now let's have a drop of sherry to celebrate and you can tell me all about it.'

She went over to the sideboard and took out a very dusty bottle and three glasses.

Solly, who had sat down next to Becky on the sofa, said, 'Well, there's not much to tell yet, Mum. Becky's only just said yes.'

'Then you'll have to get a wiggle on if you want to get good caterers,' Dolly said. 'And I'll have to speak to the girls up Lyons to get busy on some cake designs ...'

'If we have any of that, Dolly,' Becky said. 'Because neither of us is sure we want a big wedding.'

'No,' Solly said. 'No, might just go down the register office and ...'

'This is because of what happened with Sharon, ain't it?' his mother said. She shook her head. 'I should never have agreed ...'

'No, Mum,' Solly said. 'It's nothing to do with that, not really. Remember, last time I didn't want none of that big wedding stuff either? I told Sharon that it was against what I believed in, but she ignored me.'

'That family of hers took over,' Dolly said, frowning.

'I don't want a big wedding either,' Becky said. 'A register office do with a few drinks afterwards is all we want. Just as long as it's soon, that's all that matters. We want to be together soon.'

Dolly knocked her sherry back, calmer now that other things were beginning to occur to her.

'So where you gonna live?' she said. 'You know I've been offered a new place by the Council?'

'We don't know what we're doing yet,' Solly said. 'But we both understand that you must do what is best for you.'

'I mean, you're welcome to come too ...'

'Thanks, Mum, but we're not sure yet. Natalie, I know, is dead keen to go to Harlow.'

'She can come with me whatever,' Dolly said. 'But she might want to be with you too. She don't know yet, do she?'

'No. Nobody else does,' Becky said. 'I still have to tell Papa.'

'Do you think your dad'll be pleased?'

'In one way,' Becky said. 'Papa likes Solly and will be relieved that I am finally to be married. But ever since Mama died I have been his world ...'

She looked down at the floor.

Dolly didn't know Moritz Shapiro well, but she was aware of how devoted he was to his daughter. She remembered how broken he had been when his wife had been murdered all those years ago. How shocked the whole community had been that whoever had burgled the Shapiros' house had also killed Chani. If Rebekah didn't feel she could leave her father even after she got married, Dolly could understand. Although how her son would manage his life around the old man, even in such a vast house, was a concern.

But she watched Solly and his fiancée drink their sherry with a smile on her face. Her son's first marriage had been so unhappy she was thrilled to see him and Becky look at each other with love in their eyes. Details about the wedding and where they might live would have to wait.

When Heinrich and Shimon had left the flat, Kitty had wondered whether she should tell anyone else what she had just been told. But by the time Marie came home from a day off out with a friend, she'd decided against it. All she told her daughter was that they'd all had a nice tea together and that Shimon and Heinrich were going on a visit to Sussex.

Kitty had made a lamb stew with dumplings for their dinner. As they both sat at the kitchen table eating, Marie said, 'You know there's blokes from the Council all over the place now, looking at all the houses and the bomb sites. What you gonna do if they say we've got to move?'

'I dunno,' Kitty said. 'I s'pose I'm hoping it won't happen.'

'But it might.'

'I know.'

'How'd you feel about it?'

'I don't want to go,' Kitty said. 'What about you?'

Marie put down her spoon and fork. 'Well, actually, Mammy, I wanted to talk to you about that.'

'Oh?'

'Yeah. You know I've been working with Rene for a number of years now ...'

'She your friend who lives up Highgate?'

'Yes. Well ... Mammy, me and Rene didn't go up West shopping today. We went to look at rooms to rent.'

Kitty stopped eating.

'Rooms to rent together,' Marie said.

'Why?'

'Why? Well, it's because it's a laugh,' Marie said. 'Living with a mate. We go almost everywhere together ... And, well, you know I told you I was going to do the Knowledge years ago? Rene wants to do it too. We'll do it together ...'

'But what'll any young men think of you?' Kitty said. 'If you meet men, they'll wonder why you're not still living at home with your family. And they'll take advantage!'

'I'm not gonna go out and meet men, Mammy,' Marie said. 'When me and Rene go out, we go to the pictures or we see a show up West. We don't go to dance halls or nothing.'

'No ...' Kitty knew they didn't and not for the first time wondered why. But then she knew why really. Just like she knew why Marie wanted to move out to live with this Rene. But she said nothing and neither did her daughter.

That evening Rose came over to the Shapiros' house with Morry. Her mum was blind drunk at home apparently and so Becky invited them both to dinner. She'd told her father about her engagement to Solly by that time and at dinner she told Rose and Morry who were both very happy for her.

Because Nell would probably range around for much of

the night, feeling sick and going to the privvy outside, Becky asked Rose and Morry to stay over. They'd done it many times before and Morry liked the fact that he was allowed to sleep in a room lined with books – even though they were mostly in Hebrew and so he couldn't read them. Rose always shared a bed with Becky.

'We won't be able to do this anymore when you're married to Solly,' she said as she got into her friend's bed.

Becky laughed. 'We'll still have good times,' she said. 'Rosie, did you think that Papa looked alright about everything this evening?'

'What – about you getting married? Yes,' Rose said. 'I think he looked happy. I mean, he's been wanting you to get married for years and now you are. And Solly's Jewish too.'

'Yes, but we're not getting married in synagogue.'

'I thought you said you hadn't made up your mind about that yet?'

'I have really.' Becky got into bed. 'Solly's against it.'

'But he'd do it if you wanted.'

'I know, but I don't want to force him,' she said. 'A big wedding isn't important to me.'

'Don't you want to wear your mum's dress?'

That came as a shock. It had been a long time since Becky had thought about her dead mother's wedding dress. Rose had worn it when she had married Dermot but, after her papa had cleaned it and put it away, Becky had not thought about it since.

Eventually she said, 'Yes. Yes, I do want that . . . '

And then she began to cry.

Rose put her arms around her.

'What's the matter, Becky?' she asked. 'Getting married is a good thing and you've always loved Solly.'

Becky took a handkerchief from underneath her pillow and wiped her eyes. 'Oh, it's not about that, Rosie,' she said. 'I was just thinking about Papa and my job.'

'What about them?'

'Well, when I get married, I'll have to stop working,' she said. 'You know how it is.'

Women rarely carried on working after marriage in the 1950s. It was thought to reflect badly on a man if his wife worked.

'Yeah,' Rose said. 'But you're a Ward Sister, you're highly trained. I know you won't be able to work once you're a mum but why don't you ask if you can stay until you have a baby?'

Becky nodded. It wasn't likely the hospital would agree but, as Rose had said, she could ask.

'You know Bernie'd go with you and make them keep you on if she was here,' Rose said. 'She wouldn't take no for an answer off no one.'

Becky laughed. 'No, she wouldn't!' she said. 'Maybe I should take a leaf out of Bernie's book?'

'That's the ticket!'

'God, she'd be annoyed with me if she knew I was being so soft!'

'She'd still love you though ...'

Becky hugged Rose. 'What would I do without you?' she said.

'As for your dad, he'll be alright,' Rose said as she cuddled into Becky's arms. 'He's still working, he owns this house and I can see he's happy for you. You need to live your own life now, Becky. You've spent so much time looking after everyone else. And anyway, we both have to live a bit more now, for Bernie.'

And she was right.

Chapter 25

Heinrich placed the telegram down on the table in front of Kitty. Bleary-eyed from lack of sleep, she could nevertheless see that she wouldn't be able to read it.

'It's in Hebrew,' Kitty said.

Heinrich shook his head. 'I'm sorry,' he said. 'Of course it is. This is from the hospital in Jerusalem. It seems I have something called leukaemia.'

Kitty, in spite of herself, gasped. Her cousin Minnie had died from leukaemia back in the war.

'I'm so sorry,' she said. 'I couldn't sleep all night for thinking about it.'

They were alone in Kitty's parlour. Shimon was playing in the Shapiros' garden.

'So I must go back,' Heinrich said. 'Immediately. Which is why I have come to you. About the thing we spoke of yesterday … My treatment will be brutal and I … Well, I may not survive. It's is more than likely I won't, in fact.'

Kitty put her hand on his and said, 'Of course I'll take him.'

'I can't let him see me die.'

'He loves you and it'll be hard for the poor little soul when you go,' Kitty said. 'But, God love you, I can see why you're doing it.'

'It's breaking my heart. On top of Bernie and ...'

He began to cry. Kitty had rarely seen men cry, but she knew that sometimes they needed to. She stood up and put her arms around him.

'All I can tell you is that I'll do me very best,' she said.

He clung to her as if he was one of her children and not her almost son-in-law.

'You don't worry about Shimon, you just get better,' Kitty told him.

'I can give you money! Money isn't ...'

'Ssshh!' She smoothed his thick grey hair. 'Don't you worry about that. Between me and our Marie and the Shapiros, we'll look after Shimon. You just go and get your treatment.'

But he didn't stop crying. To Kitty it seemed as if months, if not years, of unhappiness and grief were pouring out of him and so she just held him and let him weep until he could weep no more. Then, once he was exhausted, she put him in her bed and told him to rest until he felt able to face life again.

Heinrich Simpson did as he was told while Kitty woke her daughter. Marie was, as usual, on nights, but this news about Heinrich was too important to wait.

In hushed tones, in case she woke him, she told Marie what he'd told her. Kitty didn't ask for help because she knew that Marie would offer.

'I can take Shimon to school when I get off my shift,' she said, 'and pick him up after. And you'll be here at night.'

But then Kitty had a thought. 'Oh, blimey, but you're moving out with your mate ...'

Marie ran her fingers through her thick, short hair. 'I can't now,' she said. 'You can't manage him on your own, Mammy.'

Kitty knew she couldn't. And yet, much as the idea of Marie moving out had upset her, she knew that the girl needed her freedom. Lynch girls did.

'Well, we'll find a way for you to move out and still have Shimon properly looked after,' Kitty said. 'I can do a different shift at work. Maybe go part-time . . . No, you take that flat with your friend, Marie. I'll take your help with Shimon when you can give it, but you have to live your life too.'

He was called Mr Jackson and he wore little round spectacles that covered his little round eyes that were an unexpectedly attractive shade of green.

Once Moritz Shapiro had come in with the cup of tea the man had accepted, Mr Jackson opened the file that was on his lap.

'Because you own the freehold you will be offered a cash sum in compensation for this house,' he said.

'But I don't want to move,' Moritz told him.

'I'm afraid it looks as if this property may well be made subject to a compulsory purchase order,' the man from the Council replied.

'What does that mean?'

'It means, Mr Shapiro, that the Council will be able to buy this house from you whether or not you wish to sell. To be frank, sir, we've been surveying these houses for some time and most of them have suffered some degree of bomb damage.'

'I've had my house repaired! I got compensation money for bomb damage.'

'Yes, but most of your neighbours didn't,' Mr Jackson said. 'Most of the property on Fournier Street is owned by private landlords and most of it is in a terrible state of repair. A lot of these flats don't have electricity or even running water and most of the toilets are out of doors. The tenants will be resettled in convenient flats with access to all mod cons including indoor bathrooms. You can, if you wish, Mr Shapiro, apply for one of these yourself. We're building some beautiful new blocks out in Essex . . . '

'Harlow, I know,' he said.

'Light, bright and clean. Your old neighbourhood but in the sky. Think about it, Mr Shapiro! You could have the money from the sale of this house and a brand new flat in the country!'

He had a point and with Rebekah's forthcoming wedding, it would in some ways make a lot of sense. But then Moritz also knew it would be Rebekah who would object to this the most. Although nothing had as yet been decided, he knew that what she really wanted after her marriage was for them all to live together in what would one day become her house.

Moritz let Mr Jackson ramble on about how many rats had been counted on the street in the last month, about broken sewers and rusted stand-pipes, and then he said, 'That is all very well, sir.'

'Good.'

'But what you are failing to take into account is the emotional attachment people feel to this area. My father bought this house in eighteen eighty. He and my mother came here as immigrants in the eighteen seventies. I was born here and so was my daughter. Before us this house was home to people from Ireland and before that to the ones who built it, the French Huguenots. This house is in my blood and is a monument to what home means to people who have been persecuted. I will not let you take it, Mr Jackson.'

The Council official pursed his lips. 'Well ... Well, you'll have to, Mr Shapiro. We intend to demolish ...'

'Then I will have to be knocked down along with my house,' Moritz said. 'I won't leave and nor, I think, will many of my neighbours.'

'But they're only tenants ...'

Moritz raised a warning finger. 'They are also East Enders,' he said. 'Never underestimate them, Mr Jackson. If they don't want to move then they will not.'

Mr Jackson looked down at his file. 'The offer I am authorised to make is a considerable amount of money ...'

'I don't care,' Moritz said.

'Well, if I tell you, you ...'

'I will not change my mind,' Moritz said. Then he smiled. 'Please do finish your tea, but then I would really like you to go. I will not change my mind. The answer is no.'

It hadn't taken long for word to get out around Spitalfields that Rebekah Shapiro and Solly Adler were going to be married. When she went to buy beigels from Sarah the 'beigel lady' who sat on a box outside the vapour baths, dispensing her baked goods to a grateful public, Natalie Adler heard everyone talking about it.

Only old Sarah herself was critical of the match, describing Natalie's father as a '*shlemiel* who only wants to get married so he can *shtup* old Shapiro's daughter'.

But most people were kinder than that. Even Mrs Rabinowicz the matchmaker who declared, 'Of course I knew that Mr Adler and Miss Shapiro were in love many years ago. I told the girl's father he should make the match a year after Sharon Adler – God rest her – died. I said that was a decent amount of time to have passed. But he didn't listen. What can you do?'

Natalie felt similarly helpless. She'd liked Nurse Shapiro when she was little, but she wasn't so sure about her now. Life was changing really fast and Natalie felt as if she was living in a whirl.

Her nana was moving to Essex in the next year and her dad had put it to Natalie that maybe he and Becky were going to move into her old man's house on Fournier Street. Natalie definitely didn't want to go there. That house was creepy. But she wasn't sure she wanted to go to Harlow either.

Ken and all the other Teds and their girls she knew hung about round Limehouse and how would she see them if she went to Essex? She could still work up West, as she'd always wanted to, if she moved to Harlow as there was a train that came into Liverpool Street, then she could get the Tube. But Natalie felt as if she was between a rock and a hard place. She didn't want to leave her mates and yet she didn't want to live with old man Shapiro either.

People were talking about how the Council wanted to knock the whole area down and build new flats. Natalie liked that idea but wondered why they couldn't just resettle everyone locally. But her nana told her that wasn't possible. Too many of the old houses had too many people living in them to make that possible. If everyone was going to have their own bathroom and modern kitchen there wouldn't be room.

When he'd finished work for the day, a buoyant Solly Adler went round to the Shapiros' house. Becky wasn't yet home from work and her father was toiling away in his workshop in the back yard. But Rose answered the door. Apparently she was looking after Bernie's little boy Shimon who was playing outside. Solly was surprised as he thought Heinrich and the boy had gone down to Sussex.

When Rose explained, he shook his head.

'Poor geezer,' he said. 'Christ, how's Kitty Lynch gonna manage with the boy and her job?'

'We're all going to help out,' Rose said. 'Me, Mr Shapiro, Becky, even me mum. We have to, for Bernie.'

Solly lit a fag. 'Count me in then,' he said. 'Anything I can do.'

'Thanks, Solly.'

Rose put the kettle on to make tea. She said, 'So do you think you'll move in here when you get married?'

He shrugged. 'I dunno,' he said. 'I know Becky wants to but there's talk this whole area's coming down.'

'Oh, I shouldn't listen to any of that,' Rose said.

'Yeah, but there's Council workers all over the place!'

'There may be,' Rose said, 'but Mr Shapiro sent one of them away this morning with a flea in his ear. He said he'd never move, no matter what. And me mum put a curse on the Council man.'

'Oh, so that's a done deal, is it?' Solly said.

'Is to me.' Then she smiled at him. 'So when's this wedding of yours and Becky's then, Solly?'

Chapter 26

April 1957
Essex

Becky looked so beautiful. As she got out of Tilly's old car and stood in front of the newly painted Ten Bells Cottage, everyone gasped. Although she and Solly had been married back in London, the idea of coming down to the cottage in Hullbridge for the reception had been a good one – even if everyone was a bit tired after a long journey by train or car. The spring weather was lovely, just warm enough to be comfortable for all the guests who now flocked in search of the sandwiches, cakes and drinks laid out on tables in the garden. In the distance was the River Crouch upon which the sun was shining, making its surface look as if it was scattered with stars.

As many people as wanted to were going to stay at the cottage that night while the happy couple were to be transported to a hotel in Southend. Some people said they were going to camp in the garden. Ten Bells Cottage was not, even after some of the improvements Moritz Shapiro had made to it, large enough to accommodate everyone.

As the bride got out of the car with the help of her new husband, Moritz had to wipe away a tear. Although Becky and Solly were going to come and live with him now they were married, it wouldn't be the same and with the house on Fournier Street still under threat from the Council who knew how long they would be able to stay there? But in the meantime here was his beautiful daughter, the image of her late mother, in swathes of antique silk, her veil held in place by a coronet of fresh flowers.

He was so proud. So many people had taken the time to come all the way out to Essex to celebrate with the Shapiros and the Adlers, when the couple stepped out of the car they were almost lost in a blizzard of confetti. And everyone had brought their children. Rose's Morry, who was very tall and very grown-up now, Solly's beautiful if rather sullen Natalie and dear little Shimon, the image of his beautiful mother. Everything Moritz felt was a *mitzvah*, a blessing.

Rose took the bottle of brown ale out of her mother's hand and put it back down on the table.

'You promised me you wouldn't get pie-eyed,' she said.

'I won't.'

'Well, you make sure you don't,' Rose said. 'I saw you have two of these and some of that punch already.'

'It's a wedding!' Nell said. 'God's teeth, Rosie, I behave meself whenever I'm helping to look after the little 'un. Let me have some fun when I ain't!'

In order to allow Marie Lynch to move out to Holloway, Nell Larkin took little Shimon to school every day, delivering him back to Kitty's flat in the evening. Of course, the boy missed his dad, and his mum, but he was becoming happier all the time as he made friends at school and enjoyed sleeping and playing in the alcove that his grandma had lovingly decorated for him.

Heinrich had given Kitty more money than she'd ever had before. In truth it was enough for her to move to somewhere much better, but she didn't want to leave Fournier Street. For the moment the Council seemed to have backed off. No one had seen any of their people round and about the area for weeks. But nothing was certain.

Rose went into the cottage that had once been her home and looked around. Mr Shapiro had made sure that it was done up lovely. He was going to use it as a place that everyone could visit for holidays in the summer and at weekends. Rose hadn't spent a penny of her dad's money on it; instead she'd used that to rent a big flat in Soho that she shared with Morry and Tilly. Much as she loved this place, she hadn't been able to see Tilly living anywhere else but London and Rose couldn't imagine her life without Tilly in it. And although the drag queen would never replace Becky and Bernie in the 'best friend' place in her heart, she was far more precious to Rose than a cottage in the country, however pretty it might be.

On this occasion it was very pretty indeed. Kitty, Nell, Marie, Aggie and Dolly Adler had all come down a few days before the wedding to clean and decorate the place with streamers and silver paper roses. Then Rose, Morry and Tilly had driven down with all the booze, and Solly's sister-in-law and her daughters had made the sandwiches that morning. Everyone had worked really hard. But then everyone loved Becky and Solly. People had come from all over the place to attend this wedding including many of Solly's old mates from the British Communist Party. And Rose was really glad that Stella Silverman had come. She was the mother of the man who had been Solly's best friend back in the thirties, Wolfie Silverman. Sadly, he'd died in an air-raid during the war, but it was good to see his mum and Rose knew that Solly appreciated her coming.

Rose and Dermot's old bedroom still looked much the same as it had done when they'd lived at the cottage. There were new bed-clothes, put on 'specially for the wedding guests, and there were new covers on the chairs, but there was still that same old view out over the river that Rose had loved so much when they'd first moved in. It was the only part of the building that directly faced the river and Dermot had fitted an old glass-panelled door so that they could go straight out into the garden in the mornings. She did that again now.

Dolly helped Solly bring the cake in from the car. Becky still hadn't seen it but when she did she was delighted.

'Oh, Dolly, that's wonderful!' she said.

'Yes, the girls at Lyons really done us proud.'

It was only one tier, square and covered in pure white royal icing. But what made it so beautiful was the mass of delicate sugar flowers that crowded every inch of it. Sugar roses, lilies and even freesias, all painted with blue, green, orange and pink food colouring.

'What a smasher!' Kitty said. 'Cor blimey, Dolly, do you remember them things we had during the war! All cobbled together, made of turnips and any old bits of dried fruit people could find?'

'Half of them cakes was made of cardboard,' Dolly said.

People laughed. The war and its privations seemed like they'd happened a million years ago. With a new flat in the offing for Dolly and people beginning to earn more money and have more time to themselves, it seemed as if a new world, a much better world, was finally being created.

Becky and Solly, hand in hand, walked down to the river while Dolly and the other women got the plates and knives ready for the cutting of the cake.

As they stood on the shore, the flatlands of Essex in front of them, Becky said, 'I still can't quite believe we've done this.'

Solly kissed her.

'When you married Sharon and then had Natalie, I thought I'd die an old maid,' she said.

'You were that set on me?'

'Right from the first time I saw you,' she said. 'But I knew then that you loved Bernie ...'

'Who wouldn't've back then?' he said. 'It was her courage, I think, that made me take to her so much. I didn't notice at the time that you were brave too. In a different way.'

'Bernie was so beautiful,' Becky said.

'And so are you.' He kissed her again.

Then they both looked out across the river and Becky said, 'I wish Bernie was here. Even if you were marrying her and not me, I'd do anything to have her back. You know, the three of us, Bernie, Rose and me, we've always been like sisters. During the war I dreaded anything happening to them. I think I was more frightened for them than I was for myself. You know Bernie came to see you in hospital when you fell off Christ Church roof?'

Solly had been a fire-watcher during the war and had almost died during a raid.

'But you were with Sharon by then,' she said. 'Bernie was frantic. I tried my best to calm her down. She still held a torch for you then. I wonder what would have happened if Auntie Kitty hadn't destroyed that letter you sent to Bernie from Spain?'

'Probably the same as did happen,' Solly said. 'And I

wouldn't wish our Natalie away, I'm proud of her even if she is a bit of a rebel.'

'Wonder where she gets that from?'

Solly laughed. Then he said, 'I'd love to have Bernie back with us too, especially today, but I wouldn't swap her for you. I'd still marry you. I can't believe how lucky I am.'

Rose waited until Becky and Solly walked back up towards the cottage before she wandered down to the river. There was a small copse of trees to the right. She walked into it and took one of her shoes off so she could dip her toes in the water. In spite of the warm sun, the water was cold.

'Rosie?'

She knew the voice immediately. It came from somewhere behind her.

'Dermot?'

She turned and there he was, half-concealed by the trees. Dermot Lynch was much thinner and far more weathered-looking than he had been the last time she'd seen him.

'What are you doing here?' she asked. 'How . . .'

Dermot put a finger to his lips. 'Keep it down, Rosie,' he said. 'Don't want no one else to know I'm here.'

'Yes, but your mum . . .'

'I come to see you. Just you,' he said firmly.

'How did you manage it?'

'I work on the fishing boats now,' he said.

'Where?'

'Best you don't know.'

But he had an accent that sounded a little bit foreign. Had he somehow made it abroad?

'I see Morry walking around reading a book,' Dermot said. 'He's a clever lad. I'm so proud.'

'So you living here again or ...'

'No,' she said. 'We're all here for Becky's wedding to Solly. You're lucky to have caught us.'

He smiled. 'I saw them walk down to the river, her all in white. I'm happy for them. But what about you? What are you doing, Rosie?'

Would he approve or not? And did it matter if he didn't? Rose said, 'Me and Morry could've carried on living here but we went back to London to be with Mum, as you know. I needed a job after you ... left ...'

She saw him lower his head.

'But now we live with Tilly in Soho,' she said. 'And we're very happy there.'

'Is Nell with you?'

'No, she's still in the old place,' Rose said. 'She helps your mum look after Bernie's little lad.'

'Bernie's little lad?'

And then Rose realised that Dermot didn't know about Shimon. Nor did he know about his sister's death. When she told him, he cried and she cradled him in her arms.

'I'm so sorry you had to find out like this,' she said. 'You know everyone still cares about you, including me.'

He kissed her on the cheek.

'You're such a good person, Rosie,' Dermot said. 'I was never good enough for you.'

'You were.'

'No.'

'I'll always love you, Der,' she said as she gently let go of him and began to back away. 'But I'll have to go now. Becky and Solly are about to cut their cake. And ... and I know that if I stay with you, I'll never want to leave and I can't do that, 'cause of Morry.'

He reached out to her and kissed her hand.

'One day,' he said. 'Probably when we're old and grey, I'll come back here and meet you and then we'll never leave each other's side ever again.'

Rose said, 'You have a deal for yourself, Dermot Lynch.'

'Where's Rosie? I can't cut my wedding cake without Rosie!' Becky said. Then she saw her friend running up the garden from the river. 'Come on!'

When Rose arrived, flushed and perspiring, Becky took her hand and placed it on the knife she was going to use to cut the wedding cake. Then she put her own hand on top, followed by Solly's.

People looked a bit confused, including Rose, who said, 'What you doing?'

Surrounded by family, friends and well-wishers, Becky called for silence and then she said, 'Today I am so pleased and proud finally to be able to call myself Mrs Adler. I have loved Solly all my adult life and I am happy to be his wife. I'm also very happy to see all of you here today, my loving family and treasured friends. We've all been through so much together and I want to thank you all for being so good to me. But I also want especially to thank my two best friends in all the world.

'One, I am happy to say, is about to cut this cake with me and Solly. Thank you, Rosie. The other, Bernie Lynch, sadly can't be with us. Bernie, as most of you know, died doing what she did best, which was being brave and bold and fearless. I would give anything to have her here with us today, but because she can't be, I'd like you to imagine that she is cutting this cake here with me and Solly and Rosie. And I'd like you all to raise your glasses to Bernadette Lynch – our very best friend!'